**Two brand-new stories in every volume...
twice a month!**

### Duets Vol. #53

Popular Ruth Jean Dale takes the spotlight with a
special Double Duets book on the theme of "animal
passion." This writer has a "talent for combining
comedy with romance...and creating memorable
characters," says *Romance Communications*. Ruth
also writes for Temptation and Superromance.

### Duets Vol. #54

Quirky Tina Wainscott is back with another delightful
Duets novel about a gorgeous hero determined to
land his ex—hook, line and sinker! Ms. Wainscott
tells "a charming story full of love and laughter,"
notes *Rendezvous*. Completing the month is Golden
Heart winner Barbara Dunlop, who makes her debut
with a funny tale in the spirit of *Due South*. Enjoy!

**Be sure to pick up both Duets volumes today!**

## Something About Eve

# *"Shacking up is not my thing,"*
# *Thalia insisted.*

"When I move in with a guy," she continued implacably, "it'll be after I get a ring on this finger." She pointed to the third finger of her left hand. "I'm in no hurry, you understand."

Luke winced. "Shacking up, huh." That one stopped him even colder than the reference to marriage. "That means living together. Does it also cover a little messing around?"

Thalia drew in a deep, forceful breath. "If it did... would I be here, Mr. Dalton?"

It took an instant for that to sink in. "Does that mean what I think it means—damn, what I *hope* it means?"

Her mysterious smile rocked him. "What do you think...hope...it means?"

"You and me...happily horizontal and all that."

She laughed. "Oh, Luke," she murmured, "just shut up and kiss me."

*For more, turn to page 9*

# The Purrfect Man

## *Michael stared at her, horrified.*

"You can't keep him!" he said. "He's mine."

"Isn't possession nine-tenths of the law?" Emily demanded.

He stared at her incredulously. "Have you been watching TV again?"

"Don't make fun of me. I'm serious." She leaned forward. "I...just realized I'm kind of used to having Dog around."

"What are you saying, exactly? Are we in a custody battle?"

"If that's what it takes."

"I'm a very good lawyer," he warned, "and I'm sick of being a long-distance pet almost-owner."

"Then we're at an impasse," she declared.

That's when it hit him: the answer to this predicament. "Emily," he said, "I don't want to put Dog through the trauma of a custody battle. There's only one fair way out of this mess."

"And that would be...?"

"You'll have to marry me."

*For more, turn to page 197*

HARLEQUIN DUETS

ISBN 0-373-44119-3

SOMETHING ABOUT EWE
Copyright © 2001 by Betty Duran

THE PURRFECT MAN
Copyright © 2001 by Betty Duran

Visit us at www.eHarlequin.com

Printed in U.S.A.

# Something About Ewe

## Ruth Jean Dale

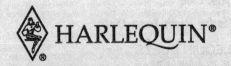

# HARLEQUIN®

TORONTO • NEW YORK • LONDON
AMSTERDAM • PARIS • SYDNEY • HAMBURG
STOCKHOLM • ATHENS • TOKYO • MILAN • MADRID
PRAGUE • WARSAW • BUDAPEST • AUCKLAND

Dear Reader,

I was having a great time writing my first Double Duets, but about halfway through I suddenly realized I was making life very hard for myself. I had named my fictitious animals all wrong! The Border collie was Jack, the calico was Missy and the black cat was Jet.

As it happens, I *have* a Border collie, but the name is Reckless. Not too surprisingly, I also have a calico named Patches and a black cat named Rosie. It was tough keeping the names straight.

So I went back to my computer and now the animals you'll be reading about are all my own, right up to and including their names and their adventures. Sure made my life easier!

There's another dog in here that I don't own in real life and that's Dog. I have had my share of strays, but the newest member of the family is a tiny Maltese named Spike. She weighs something like five pounds and has the heart of a lion. In the future I think there'll probably be a story that includes Spike....

Anyway, here's hoping you enjoy my Animal Passions. Old animal lover me sure had fun in the writing.

Best wishes!

*Ruth Jean Dale*

## Books by Ruth Jean Dale

My Animal Passions books are for Aunt Patty the Cat Lady, who likes *anything* if it has enough dogs and cats in it. Put one on the cover and she's in hog heaven. Love ya!

# 1

"DOCTOR, PLEASE DON'T keep anything from me. Will Gertrude live?"

Dr. Luke Dalton, D.V.M., smiled reassuringly at the little silver-haired lady bravely confronting him in the sparkling clean waiting room of the Shepherd's Pass Animal Clinic and Hospital. The hand she laid on his arm trembled and he covered it with his own.

"Take it easy, Miss Pauline," he said, gently leading her to a chair. "It's just a simple ear infection. Gertrude will be fine."

"What?" Miss Pauline looked indignant and not quite ready to give up her fears so quickly. "But she was yowling something awful and throwing herself around. When I picked her up she tried to bite me! She's never done such a thing before."

Luke knelt before her, still holding her cold hand. "Gertrude was in pain or she'd never have turned on you that way," he assured her. "Believe me, it's nothing life-threatening." He added as an afterthought, "And Dr. Miller agrees."

He knew that bit of news would reassure her. The elderly lady might give the thirty-ish Luke his

proper title, but she obviously considered him a kid.
And why shouldn't she? She'd known him since he
was a baby and his mother before him, had taught
him in third grade, had watched him leave Colorado
after college and go on to study veterinary medicine. She'd even attended the welcome-home party
when he returned six months ago to join the practice of longtime Shepherd's Pass veterinarian Dr.
Gene Miller, more commonly called Doc.

She *knew* Luke was a real animal doctor, but this
was *her* beloved cat. He didn't blame her for not
wanting to take chances. He understood that. He
even respected it.

"May I see my Gertrude now?" She leaned forward with a pleading expression.

"Better than that." He smiled. "You can take
her home. You'll have to put drops in her ears for
a few days, but she won't give you any trouble now
that she's not hurting."

Relief and gratitude suffused her lined face.
"Thank you, Doctor," she said as formally as if
she'd never kept him in at recess for launching spit-
balls. "You've been very kind. Please don't feel
obliged to wait with me. I know you're busy,
and—"

"Not at all." He was, but she'd done so much
for him in his misspent youth that he wanted to
show her every consideration. He slid into the chair
next to hers. "Cindy will bring Gertrude out just as
soon as she fills the prescription. In the meantime,

I'd enjoy keeping you company, if that's okay with you."

She looked pleased. "Quite okay," she said. "So how have you been, Lucas?"

"Fine. And you? I haven't seen much of you lately."

"I've been quite busy, actually. I'm working part-time at Lorraine's Pretty Posies. Did you know that?"

"I hadn't heard."

"Oh, yes. I answer the phone from time to time, and take orders when Lorraine gets really busy or the regular girls don't come in."

"That's great," he said, firmly believing that a busy mind was a healthy mind. "How is Lorraine? I haven't seen her around lately."

"Actually, she's quite excited. Her daughter arrived yesterday for an extended vacation. You remember Thalia, no doubt?"

*Thalia!* The name galvanized Luke and he shot to his feet.

"My goodness." Miss Pauline frowned. "I didn't expect quite that reaction."

He sat back down. "I just remembered something I have to do later," he apologized lamely. "Of course, I remember Thalia. Is she still living in California?"

"Yes, indeed. Apparently she has some free time—something about her company merging with another company. I'm not real clear on the details, but she'll be home for a month or so, I understand."

Her tone dropped lower. "Lorraine's been quite concerned about her since the divorce."

"Was it nasty?"

"Good heavens, no. Quite the opposite, apparently, but you know how mothers are. They worry when their children are far away and—" She let out a little gasp of pleasure and rose to her feet with surprising spryness. "Gertrude! You poor little thing, let me take you home and nurse you back to health."

A smiling Cindy passed over the huge white cat. Gertrude purred loudly and pressed her head against Miss Pauline's neck above the lacy collar of her navy-blue dress. The cat looked none the worse for her experience.

Cindy offered a small brown paper bag stapled closed, a white prescription label pasted on the outside. "Here's her medicine, Miss Pauline. You put drops in her ear every—"

Satisfied that another crisis had been averted, Luke turned away with a farewell wave. Miss Pauline and Gertrude would be just fine.

So would he, especially now that he knew Thalia was back. Thalia, serious little Thalia, the girl who never left anything to chance. Just thinking about her made him smile.

He entered the gleaming examining room and paused, his thoughts tumbling. He hadn't seen her in years. Would she be changed? Would she look different, act different...want different things?

He hoped not, he surely did, because once upon a time she'd wanted *him*.

"HEY, YOU, WAKE UP!"

Luke snapped upright over his desk and blinked. Turning in his chair, he gave his mentor a sheepish grin. "Sorry, Gene," he said. "I was thinking." He was supposed to be doing paperwork but was having trouble concentrating, with Thalia very much on his mind.

"Obviously." Gene Miller pushed back the extra chair and sat. "If it wasn't September, I'd think you had spring fever."

"Yeah, well..." Luke couldn't argue with that.

"Obviously I'm going to have to keep an eye on you." Gene chuckled. "I wouldn't be young again for all the tea in China—but I digress. I just wanted to let you know I'm leaving now. Doris is waiting for me to go to Denver with her to pick out the new carpeting." He made a face. "Like I care what shade of blue it is, but you know women."

"Not as well as I'd like to." Suppressing a smile, Luke opened the top folder on the stack. "You go ahead and take off. I'll hold the fort and see you in the morning."

"Thanks, kid." Gene rose. "I knew there was a reason I hustled you into coming back here to work with me after you got your license. What I don't know is why you agreed—but I'm not asking!" He held up his hands, grinning and backing toward the door. He looked, as always, rumpled and friendly.

The door closed behind him. Luke looked back down at the files without enthusiasm. He hadn't become an animal doctor to deal with paperwork. He'd done it because he liked animals, all animals, and truly believed that people who owned animals were superior to those who didn't.

But lately he'd become increasingly aware of one tiny little hole in a life filled with professional satisfaction and hometown approval. That lack came under the heading of feminine companionship.

He hadn't given more than a passing thought to romance since his return, although he had known a lot of women when he got here and had met more since. None had attracted him the way he wanted to be attracted, so he hadn't bothered to pursue any of them beyond a casual date or two.

But he was plenty bothered now. Thinking about Thalia Myers Mitchell brought back memories eleven long years old—memories of "doing the right thing," or more precisely, not doing the wrong thing.

Yes, she'd been a mere sixteen to his almost twenty-one. On the other hand, she'd picked *him* to relieve her of her virginity, a rational decision made with her usual thoroughness. He should have been flattered—hell, he *had* been flattered. And attracted. And confused. And at the last minute, responsible.

He knew he'd hurt her feelings when he turned her down, as he finally had to do out of deference to her youth and inexperience—and a little bit of deference to her brother, John. John and Luke had been best buds all through school and Luke didn't want their friendship to come to blows. Hell, he wasn't sure he could lick the guy.

So he'd done what he knew was the right thing, although it hadn't been easy. Nor did it get easier with time. He and Thalia were never comfortable around each other again; the encounter had left them with unfinished business, as far as he was concerned. She probably felt the same, he mused, doodling all over the manila folder. Now that age was no longer an issue between them, why shouldn't he think about making up for lost time?

The door flew open and Cindy entered, a concerned frown on her face. "Are you okay?" she asked bluntly. "I've been knocking on that door for five minutes—okay, two minutes, but it seemed longer. I was beginning to think you'd sneaked out the back way with Doc."

"I might as well. I can't seem to concentrate on this stuff." He pushed the files away and glanced at his wristwatch. "Maybe if I had something to eat—"

"You mean you haven't had lunch yet?" Cindy, a motherly type with several grown kids, tsked-tsked. "Honestly, Luke, you and Doc are cut from the same cloth. Why don't I go next door to the Paper Sack and grab you a sandwich, okay? I was coming to tell you that Mrs. Bushmiller just canceled Trixi's appointment, so unless something else comes up, you should be able to get out of here by five today."

"Okay, but—"

"No buts. It's almost three o'clock and Jimmy Morton's dog needs shots at three-fifteen, remember? I'll be back in a flash with a ham and cheese on rye. Don't argue!"

He didn't.

AT A LITTLE AFTER FIVE that day, Thalia Mitchell paused in front of the large glass windows of the Sew Bee It Craft and Fabric Shoppe, next door to the Paper Sack on the main drag of Shepherd's Pass, Colorado. Just inside, where he'd have a view of passersby, a big striped cat basked in the sun on a carpeted shelf attached to the window ledge. Behind him was a sewing machine always set up and at the ready. Pins and fabric scraps covered a cutting table littered with mats and rotary cutters, and brightly flowered fabrics draped a dressmaker's dummy.

Some things never changed, she thought. Tapping her fingertips lightly against the glass, she managed to attract the cat's attention. He looked up with an annoyed scowl, then closed insolent amber eyes.

Thalia couldn't help smiling. It was wonderful to be home in the Colorado mountains on this gorgeous September day—and a little strange, too. She'd been gone such a long time, since high school, actually. Once she'd departed for college she'd never really come back for more than a few weeks at a time.

She'd spent the past several years in Southern California, which was a far cry from Colorado any way you sliced it. With a sigh, she pushed open the heavy glass door and entered the cozy shop, a tinkling bell announcing her arrival.

Several browsing customers glanced at her with brief curiosity. The young woman rearranging items on the back wall looked around with a smile and promptly dropped several bolts of fabric.

"Thalia!"

"Emily!"

The two met in the middle of the store, between the buttons and the cash register. They hugged, they squealed, they hugged again. Finally Thalia drew back.

"What a welcome!"

"I've missed you," Emily said. "I'm so glad you're here. I saw your mom a day or two ago and she told me—"

"Emily, dear." One of the shopping ladies had made her choice. "Can you ring these notions up for me?"

"Sure, Mrs. Adams." Emily walked behind the counter and began tapping at the cash register keys. "You remember Thalia Myers, don't you?"

"Mitchell now." Thalia smiled at the woman. "Nice to see you, Mrs. Adams."

"Nice to see you, dear. I'll tell Angeline you're back."

Emily made change and thanked the woman with a smile before turning eagerly to Thalia. "You've got to tell me everything! It's been years since we had a good—''

"Bye-bye, Emily." Another woman waved from the front of the store. "I don't see what I'm after so I'll drop by again next week."

"Fine, Mrs. Weller. See you then. Remember, I can special-order anything you want." Emily came out from behind the counter, grabbed Thalia's hand and drew her over to the small sitting area near the coffee service. "Gosh, Thalia, you look wonderful."

Thalia didn't feel wonderful. Next to Emily with her long black hair and sparkling blue eyes, her lace-frosted denim dress with all its hand-crafted details, Thalia felt brittle and…and *foreign*.

But she just said, "Thank you. So do you. And in answer to your question, I'm fine." Bored with life, but fine.

Emily's smooth face creased in a frown. "I hate to ask but…the divorce…?"

"Wasn't as bad as it might have been." Thalia accepted the foam cup of coffee Emily offered. "Don and I parted amicably. Even so…"

"Yes, even so." Emily sat down on the wicker footstool. "Poor Thalia."

Thalia frowned. "Why poor me?"

"I know you, Thalia. I'm sure you take the divorce as a personal failure."

"It *is* a personal failure."

Emily pursed her lips. "Of course, it *isn't*. The marriage was obviously a mistake. Everybody makes mistakes, but that doesn't mean they've failed.''

Thalia had to smile at that one. ''Em, you've always had the most convoluted reasoning. You should have been a lawyer.''

''God forbid!'' Emily looked honestly appalled. ''I can't abide lawyers. The thing is, I *know* you, Thalia Myers Mitchell. You *do* take everything too seriously.''

''Few things are more serious than a marriage.''

''Oh, piffle!'' Emily wrinkled her nose. ''Don't forget, I knew you when.''

''That's for sure.'' Thalia had to grin. ''But I was just a kid then.''

''Are you saying you've changed?''

''Well...'' After serious consideration, Thalia added, ''No.''

''Last I heard, you wanted a serious husband, two serious children and a serious career. At least, that's what you kept saying.''

''I got the career,'' Thalia said a bit lamely, thinking that was the least important item on her wish list. ''Considering how the marriage ended, I'm grateful we didn't have children.'' She gritted her teeth, then burst out, ''I really hate failure! Now it's start-over time and I'm not looking forward to it.''

''But you're home,'' Emily reasoned. ''It'll be easy, much easier than starting over in California. It'll be like old times.'' She frowned. ''And you're nodding your head *no* because...?''

"I'm only here temporarily, or didn't Mother mention that? My company has merged with a larger company and—"

Emily interrupted with a dismissive groan. "Insurance, I understand?" She wrinkled her nose with distaste.

"An honorable endeavor," Thalia pointed out.

"And certainly serious." Emily's blue eyes gleamed with mischief.

Thalia made a face. "Can I finish what I started to say? The two companies are merging. As a result, I've taken leave during the transition. When Mother heard, she insisted I come home. Otherwise, I would have stayed out there and…and…"

"And what? Doesn't sound as if all those *ands* would have been much fun."

"I have friends," Thalia said defensively, "and fun is not the point of life. I could certainly have kept busy. But since I hadn't been home in so long, I decided to come to make Mother happy." She grinned. "And if you won't tell anyone, I'll even admit that I wanted to renew acquaintances with old friends."

"Who've you seen so far?"

"You. You were my best friend, after all."

Emily looked smug. "What a nice thing to say." A dimple appeared at the corner of her mouth. "Flattering, too. I thought you might have gone to see *Lucas* first." She dragged it out. "Lu-cas."

Thalia hoped her cheeks weren't too red. "Certainly not. Why would I go see Luke Dalton?"

"Because you're on the rebound and interested in old flames as well as old friends?"

"I am not on the rebound and Lucas is not an old flame."

"You wanted him to be your *first* flame," Emily teased. "Aren't you the least bit curious about him?" Her eyes widened. "You did know he's back in Shepherd's Pass and in practice with Doc Miller?"

"Mother...might have mentioned it."

"Oh, really. Did she also mention that he's even better looking than he was before?"

"You've got to be kidding. I didn't think that was possible."

"There!" Emily sounded delighted. "That's my old pal, Thalia. I'm glad you're home! We're going to have so much fun that you'll never leave."

The bell above the front door tinkled and Emily frowned. "Drat. I'll have to see who that is." She rose. "Maybe whoever it is will leave without buying anything—and come back later, of course."

Thalia relaxed back against the cushions to wait. It was wonderful seeing Emily again, but she felt as out of place here as she had in California. Emily belonged because she had never left. Her grandmother had owned this store for decades. When she'd retired two or three years ago and moved to warmer climes, she'd left her favorite granddaughter in charge.

It was no surprise that Emily had taken hold with such enthusiasm. A whiz with a sewing machine since childhood, she was doing what she loved. Thalia, by contrast, was doing something valuable, but she didn't love it.

Sighing, she looked down at her conservative brown skirt and beige silk blouse. She should have worn jeans and mountain boots. In her California clothes, she even *looked* like a foreigner, no matter how nicely everyone treated her. All she wanted to do was blend in, make her mother happy, and flee back to the coast at the earliest opportunity.

She heard footsteps but didn't turn. "That didn't take long," she said. "Was it anyone I know?"

Hands covered her eyes and a deeply masculine voice said in her ear, "That all depends on the meaning of the word *know*."

She caught her breath, then covered his hands with hers and tried without success to drag them away from her eyes. "Luke! Turn me loose!"

"Shoot," he said, promptly releasing her. "You guessed. How's it goin', Thalia?"

Leaning her head back, she looked up into his smiling face. Even upside down, he looked wonderful, especially with that lock of sun-bleached hair spilling over his forehead.

"It's going fine," she said. Looking at him this way made her dizzy. She straightened self-consciously. "I see you haven't changed one bit, Lucas Dalton."

"Why would I want to change?" He rounded the settee and took a seat across from her in the wicker chair.

"I don't know." Emily was right. He *was* better looking than before: more mature, his rangy frame nicely filled out. Thalia cleared her throat. "I just thought that now you're all grown-up and a doggy doctor, you might be more...serious." She'd also expected that sexy gleam in his eyes would be gone, which it wasn't.

He laughed incredulously. "Boy, that hurts. I *am* serious. I always *was* serious. I just never saw the point of wearing it like a hair shirt."

"Meaning I did?" She bolted upright.

"If the hair shirt fits—"

Emily's voice sailed into the middle of the blossoming fray. "Thalia, isn't it great that Luke dropped by? He said he saw us through the window and wanted to say hi. Don't beat up on him, okay?"

"I certainly wouldn't do that," Thalia said, as cool as if she hadn't once, many years ago, wrapped herself in a plastic shower curtain and sprung out from behind a door to seduce him.

Emily offered him a cup of coffee, which he accepted with a smile of thanks. But his attention was clearly on Thalia. "How long will you be here?"

"A month, maybe two."

"We'll have to get together." He gave her a coaxing smile that melted her like a birthday candle.

"Whatever," she said noncommittally.

"That's a great idea," Emily said eagerly. "There's a bunch of us who get together now and again at the Watering Hole. Next time I'll give you both a call."

"Sounds great," Luke said.

"I don't think so," Thalia said.

Emily frowned. "Why not? You know most everyone already, so what's your problem?"

"I'm not too crazy about bars," Thalia admitted. "For one thing, I don't drink all that much."

Emily's eyes widened. "Like I do? Look, it's just a friendly little happy-hour get-together."

Thalia cast an oblique glance at Luke. "Do you go to these friendly little happy hours?"

He shrugged. "Once in a while." That roguish gleam was back. "But if you're going, I'll make a point of being there."

His response startled her and she looked quickly away. Why was he coming on so strong? He hadn't been interested in her when she was interested in him; now that she wanted nothing more than to avoid all emotional entanglements, he wanted to hit on her?

Not in this lifetime. With lips pressed tightly together, she listened idly to the comfortable banter between Em and Luke. How were her cats? Fine. How was the Benson dog that had been stomped by a horse last week? Also fine, or would be soon. How was business? Fine—

Thalia stood abruptly. "I think I'd better be going," she said. "Mom's expecting me and it's going on six now."

"Don't go yet." Emily looked genuinely disappointed. "We really haven't had a chance to talk."

No, because Luke had horned in. "There'll be time."

"Hey, I'm sorry." Luke rose, too. "I barged right in here, I was so happy to see Thalia again." But he didn't offer to leave, just looked expectantly at Thalia.

"I close at six," Emily said. "If you'll just hang around, we could have dinner or something. Call your mom. She'll understand."

Luke added hopefully, "That sounds good."

Thalia wasn't falling into that trap. Let the two of *them* go to dinner together. "I hate to beg off, but can we do it another night? Mom's really expecting me."

Emily pouted. "Oh, all right. But I don't like it."

"I'll call tomorrow." Thalia squeezed her friend's hand and turned for the door. "Nice seeing you, Luke."

"Really? Then you'll be happy to learn I'm going home with you."

She stopped so suddenly that he stepped on her heels. "What?"

"I'm going to follow you home in my car." He looked quite pleased with himself.

She frowned. "I don't recall inviting you."

"Like I need an invitation?" he scoffed. "Your mom's always glad to see me. Besides, her Border collie is under the weather. You can just consider it a house call."

"Darn it, Luke." She glared at him. "You're crowding me."

"Really?" His amber eyes widened with disbelief. "I'm just doing my job, Thalia. The health of your mom's dog is important to me. But if you don't want me following you…"

"I don't." Feeling guilty but refusing to yield, she met his gaze.

"Okay, then I'll meet you there." He dipped his chin to Emily. "Have a nice evening." Turning, he walked away whistling.

Thalia stood there, listening to Emily's giggle and feeling dumb as a rock.

# 2

SHEPHERD'S PASS HAD GROWN in the years Thalia
had been away. Her mother's home and property
used to be at the edge of town, with nothing between it and the mountains. Now it was necessary
to drive through an upscale planned community of
new homes—Shangri-la, according to the signs—to
even get there.

Nice homes, she thought, navigating slowly
along curving landscaped streets. Decent-sized lots,
too, at least by California standards, where a post-
age-stamp-sized property was often labeled an "estate." Where were all these people coming from?
Would life in this formerly slow paced community
be forever altered?

Speaking of altered—

A car stood at the curb next to her mother's
driveway. Luke leaned out an open window of the
red Jeep Cherokee to wave. Surely he didn't intend
to hang around and taunt her while she was home.
If he did, she just might have to alter her plans and
go back to California early, even if it meant ignor-
ing her mother's pleas.

She no longer wanted a thing from Luke Dalton,

and most definitely not what she'd wanted before. She'd been young and foolish then. Now, she was...well, not old at twenty-seven but certainly *seasoned*. There was nothing left for him to teach her.

She shivered at the possibility she might be wrong.

Parking her mother's old pickup truck in the driveway, she climbed out and waited for him to join her. No complications, she reminded herself. She was a serious person with a serious life and a serious plan for leading it. She was not interested in a quick tumble with every good-looking man she met—check that.

She might be *interested;* what woman in her right mind wouldn't be? But she wouldn't act on that interest, no way, no how. She was not a woman who'd consider a cheap affair, no matter how attractive—

Oh, my. Luke gave new meaning to the word *attractive.* Tall and lean and lithe, he strode toward her, the lowering sun striking blond sparks off his brown hair. When he grinned, even white teeth flashed.

"You waited for me," he said.

She shook herself free of her imagination. "I didn't. I—"

I—nothing; she *had* waited and he hadn't even had to ask. Spinning around, she led the way up the steps of the big old Victorian house. Flinging open the door, she indicated with a wave that he should enter first.

You'd think a serious person like Thalia would have a serious mother. Instead, she had Lorraine, who now looked up from the free weights she was swinging with abandon, a broad smile of welcome on her crimson lips.

"YOU BROUGHT LUKE HOME with you," Lorraine exclaimed with pleasure. "That's wonderful!"

Luke didn't think Thalia considered it all that wonderful. He looked from mother to daughter, trying to suppress the smile that tugged at his lips. Lorraine must have been a trial to Thalia her entire life, but he'd have given anything to have a mother with hair like Lucille Ball's and a bawdy humor that made him grin just thinking about it.

At the moment, Lorraine was working with barbells. A black headband held back a tumble of red-gold curls and her ample figure was barely constrained by a black leotard and tights. Her cheeks glowed; she looked healthy and happy.

Thalia kissed her mother's proffered cheek. "I didn't bring Luke home, Mother, he brought himself."

Lorraine put the barbells on the floor. "Regardless of how he got here, I'm glad to see him. I've got a cookie jar just stuffed full of those chocolate chip cookies he and John used to gobble up." She turned toward the kitchen, waving them to follow.

"Come along, kids. Mother Lorraine will spoil your suppers for you."

As she'd been doing as long as Luke could remember. It used to piss his own mother off something awful when he'd pick at his food after a visit to the Myers house. Still would.

Thalia was dragging her feet. "I think I'll pass on the cookies and go on upstairs," she said. "It's awfully close to dinnertime and—"

"Thalia Renee, you get yourself in this kitchen," Lorraine said without slowing her pace. "This may *be* your supper, young lady."

Trying not to grin too broadly, Luke pulled out a chair at the table in the middle of the big old-fashioned kitchen. Thalia and Lorraine couldn't be more different and yet he liked them both. His mother had told him once that Thalia was more like her father, who had died young. Best buddy John, on the other hand, was a lot like his mother: funny and daring and ready for anything.

Lorraine plunked a dinner plate piled high with cookies on the table and went to get glasses, talking a mile a minute about everything from the weather to the stock market.

When she paused for breath, Luke said, "So what's new with John?"

"He's still in Chicago working for that Internet start-up company, still has the same wife and kid, still likes it. He's going to try to get home while Thalia's here but it's iffy with his workload."

Luke picked up a chocolate-studded round. "I'd sure like to see him one of these days."

Thalia said, "Me, too. Fortunately, his company sends him to California now and then, so we get together there."

"You like California, do you?" Luke pulled one of the three tall glasses of milk close enough so he could dunk his cookie. Biting into it, he closed his eyes in ecstasy. Lorraine was probably the best cookie baker in Shepherd's Pass, with the possible exception of Emily. He couldn't think of anything else Lorraine could cook worth diddly, but her cookies were first-rate.

He chewed blissfully for a moment, only belatedly realizing Thalia hadn't answered his question. Opening his eyes, he saw her looking down at the cookie in her hands, her expression closed.

Before he could repeat his query, Lorraine spoke up.

"Of *course,* she doesn't like California. What's to like? All those people, all those cars, all those freeways, all that smog? She's only living there because she's stubborn."

"Oh, Mother." Thalia put down her cookie. "My life is there. I have an apartment, friends—"

"An ex-husband," Lorraine informed Luke. "Sometimes I think she's still carrying the torch for Don."

"No way." Thalia's denial sounded heartfelt. "We tried and now it's over. We've both moved on."

"Better you should move back—back home to Colorado," Lorraine said. "Like Luke did." She swung her attention his way. "You're glad to be back, right?"

"Of course, but I'm not glad to be living at home." He grimaced. "Mom was dead set on it, and since Dad had only been gone a few months when I got here…" He shrugged. "It seemed like a good idea at the time, but boy, have I lived to regret it. I'm planning to get my own place as soon as I have time to look."

Thalia's tight expression relaxed into sympathy. "I was sorry to hear about your dad's death."

"Thank you," he said. "It was quite a shock to all of us, but we're getting along." Not that it had been easy. Just digging through his father's far-flung business interests had been a chore in and of itself. Then there was the shock of realizing just how big the estate was. If money could buy happiness, his mother would be a very happy woman, indeed.

Instead of what she was: miserable.

Lorraine reached for a cookie. "You haven't seen his mother's new house, have you," she said to her daughter.

"No."

"It's at the end of this road," Lorraine said darkly. "It's a darned mansion, is what it is. Of course, it was the Daltons who sold all that land to the developer for Shangri-la. They tried to buy my measly little five acres, and when I wouldn't sell, they just built around me like I was a tree stump in the middle of a road.''

Thalia glanced questioningly at Luke, who nodded.

''That's pretty much how it happened,'' he agreed. ''But it's not like your mom's stubborn or anything, or like they didn't offer her ten times what this land is worth.''

Lorraine burst out laughing. ''Oh, you!'' she said affectionately. ''Thalia's on my side no matter what you say.''

''I certainly am,'' Thalia agreed.

''As a matter of fact,'' he said, ''so am I. You've got a great place here, Mrs. Myers. It's eccentric, like its owner. I like that in my houses and in my women.'' He winked broadly.

Lorraine looked pleased; Thalia merely looked annoyed.

''Really, Luke,'' she said, ''aren't you ever serious?''

''Of course. I'm serious now.'' And he was. He did like eccentric people, people who did the unexpected and did it with flair. Like Thalia herself on that long-ago day, when she'd done her much-too-young best to seduce him. What he wouldn't give to have her try that again!

Damn, she needed something to loosen her up. If he didn't know what she was capable of, he wouldn't give a second thought to the buttoned-up woman with the disapproving air. Even if she was beautiful. Even if she did occasionally slip and let genuine emotion show on her face.

Ah, hell, maybe he would.

A banging on the front door defused the increasingly taut moment. Lorraine frowned.

"Who the heck could that be?" Rising, she left the room.

Luke waited until she was gone and then said, "You've got a heck of a mother there."

"Don't I know it." That could be the first genuine smile he'd seen so far on Thalia's smooth face.

"Didn't you ever want to be like her?"

She looked astonished. "Good heavens, no. I love her, but she's so out of control."

"And you don't like that."

"You know I don't. I like things neat and tidy."

"And predictable."

"That, too." Her chin lifted. "There's nothing wrong with predictable."

"There's everything wrong with it, Thalia. It's…it's limiting."

"It's reliable."

"It's boring."

"I could take that personally," she snapped.

"Everything I've said to you is personal," he agreed. "I—"

Raised voices from the living room intruded. Both of them knew immediately that his mother, Sylvia Dalton, had arrived.

SYLVIA AND LORRAINE MIXED like oil and water, always had and probably always would. Thalia could imagine them as wizened little old ladies— one silver-haired, one orange-haired—sitting side by side in their wheelchairs at some senior citizens home sniping at each other night and day.

Nevertheless, Sylvia had always been nice to Thalia, who jumped up to greet the newcomer. She couldn't imagine why Luke's mother was here, but it couldn't possibly be good.

"Thalia! Darling." Silvery-blond Sylvia gave Thalia a big hug. Whoever said a woman couldn't be too blond or too thin or too rich was probably thinking of Sylvia.

"Hello, Mrs. Dalton. It's good to see you."

Sylvia straightened and turned. "There you are, Lucas. I saw your car outside and wondered if something was wrong."

Luke looked as if he considered this a pretty feeble attempt at an explanation. "Nothing's wrong that I know of." He looked at Lorraine and daughter. "Anything wrong?"

"Not a thing." Lorraine glowered. She didn't look as if she liked having her archenemy invading her turf. The next words seemed dragged out of her. "We're having cookies and milk if you'd care to join us, Syl."

Sylvia's nostrils flared at the casual use of a nickname no one else had uttered in decades. She got revenge by saying, "Don't mind if I do, *Rainy*."

Lorraine rolled her eyes but said nothing, just led

the way back to the kitchen. Sylvia fell in behind her while Thalia and Luke exchanged dubious glances before following.

Sylvia sat down and looked at the plate of cookies with disapproval. "I cannot *tell* you how many of my son's meals were ruined in this house by cookies and milk," she announced. "I held you personally responsible, Lorraine."

"Good reasoning." Luke picked up another cookie, his third or fourth. "She used to tie me to a kitchen chair and jam cookies down my throat. It was hell."

Lorraine let out that raucous laughter. "Yes, and everyone can see how it stunted his growth. I think you should call the nutrition police, Sylvia."

"I would, if I thought it would do any good."

Luke pushed the plate toward his mother. "If you can't beat 'em, join 'em, Ma."

She picked up a cookie, pointedly using her thumb and one exaggerated finger. "I don't believe I can eat this without something to wash it down."

"Milk?" Thalia jumped up, eager to avoid further dissension.

"I don't suppose there's coffee made." Sylvia said it as if it were a test for gracious living.

"Darn it, Syl!" Lorraine grimaced. "I am not going to make a whole pot of coffee just for you and end up tossing most of it away. There might be a little left over from breakfast in the carafe, but—"

"Never mind." Sylvia gave a condescending sigh. "A glass of water will be sufficient." She tore off a crumb and lifted it to her mouth as if suspecting it of containing hemlock.

Thalia pulled a small bottle of water from the refrigerator and offered it hopefully. Lorraine watched impatiently for about thirty seconds before she burst out, "Okay, out with it, Syl. What are you doing here?"

"I can't drop by to visit a neighbor?" Sylvia countered.

"You ask me that after forty years' worth of cold shoulders?"

"It isn't forty. More like thirty-five."

Lorraine appealed to the gallery. "She's quibbling."

"No, seriously." Sylvia leaned forward. "Lorraine, I must speak to you about Shangri-la number two."

Lorraine caught her breath sharply. "There is no Shangri-la number two."

"But there will be, if you'll stop trying to rouse the populace against it."

"Don't count on it."

"But Rainy, you know it'll benefit the community, and the land will eventually be developed anyway. In fact—" Sylvia's voice dropped, became confidential "—the developer has agreed to raise his offer for this little ol' plot of land of yours. I'm sure you'll be pleased with what he—"

"Out!" Lorraine rose in all her leotard-and-tights-clad dignity. Her red-gold curls quivered with indignation. "Out of my house! If you have intruded into the sanctity of my home to insult me with another pathetic offer when I've already made my feelings perfectly clear—''

"Mother!" Thalia tugged at Lorraine's elbow. "You're going overboard. Mrs. Dalton didn't insult you."

"But I will now." Sylvia also rose, regal in her classic designer suit. "I don't know why I waste my breath. There's no reasoning with an unreasonable person."

"Out!" Lorraine's pointing arm quivered.

"I'm going. Lucas, come along."

"Not yet, Mother."

"You'd side against your own flesh and blood?" She looked horrified.

"I'm not siding with anyone. I came to check out Lorraine's dog and that's what I intend to do."

"Fine." She lifted her chin still higher. "I'll expect you for dinner at seven."

"I may not be hungry after all these cookies."

"*Lucas!* I will expect you for dinner at seven."

"Yeah, right, whatever."

Sylvia marched to the kitchen door, then spun around to glare at Lorraine. "I am assuming this altercation will not affect Saturday."

Thalia frowned. "What's Saturday?"

"Lucas's birthday party," Sylvia said grandly. "Lorraine's Pretty Posies is providing flowers and decorating for a pool party. Or was." She gave her nemesis an accusing look. "Are you still?"

Lorraine's jaw tightened. "Certainly, I am. That's business. This is personal."

"Then I expect you to have everything there at noon and *don't screw this up!*" Sylvia turned and marched out of the room and the house.

Lorraine stood as stiff as a poker until the front door slammed. Then she closed her eyes, clenched her hands into fists and said, "*Ohh!* That woman makes me crazy."

"It's mutual, Mother," Thalia assured her. "You two go at each other like junior high kids."

"Maybe because that's when it started," Lorraine snapped. "Well, *my* supper's ruined. Excuse me. I've got to go change."

Alone, Luke and Thalia looked at each other in mutual puzzlement.

"What do you suppose started this feud?" she wondered aloud. "It seems to grow worse with time, not better."

"They may not even remember themselves."

"That's certainly possible. Your mother's always been really nice to me."

"Your mother's been nice to me, too. In fact, she's one of my favorite people."

The corners of her mouth curved down. "I suppose you think I should be more like her," she accused.

He surprised her.

"Nope, I'd like you to be more like *yourself,* Thalia. I don't believe you're the uptight pulled-together person you're trying so hard to convince yourself you are. In fact—" he leaned across the table, his gaze locking with hers "—I think the real you is the person who conceived what is probably the only wild and crazy thing you've ever done in your life.''

Her eyes narrowed. "I hope you don't mean what I think you mean.''

"I certainly do." Thrusting his hand around her neck, he yanked her forward and planted a quick, hard kiss on her unprepared lips. "I saw the real you—literally—for about two seconds. Because I didn't lose my head and ravish you on the spot, you seem to think it was a disgraceful episode best forgotten. I don't happen to agree. I think it was a glorious episode I'd like to repeat at the first possible moment—and this time, no backing away.''

Releasing her, he straightened. She stared at him, stunned, her lips tingling. She wanted to press her fingertips to her mouth but didn't want him to guess how much he'd affected her—annoyed her!

"So where's Reckless?" he asked.

"R-Reckless who?''

He laughed. "Reckless, the dog.''

"The dog?" She had to shake this off—without shaking, of course.

His smile teased her. "Reckless...the...dog," he said with slow emphasis. "Remember? I am making a house call.''

"Oh, good grief." Flustered and on the defensive, she jumped up. "He must be out back. I'll call him in.''

"I can go where he is. Come along.''

"Me?" She backed away.

"What if he tried to bite me?''

"Reckless doesn't bite.''

"What if I need help?"

"You can always call for—"

"What if I just like your company?"

She had no answer to that. Rising, she followed him out the back door.

"THAT'S A GOOD BOY. You've been real patient with me." Luke ruffled the dog's silky black hair and got a mournful look in return. He glanced at Thalia and frowned. "I don't like this," he said.

"You don't like what?"

"I saw Reckless last week for a sore paw. The paw's cleared up just fine and I can't see anything else obviously wrong with him. Beyond the fact that he's too thin and just not real perky."

She knelt in the grass beside Luke, her expression concerned. "Is he sick?"

"I don't think so. But just to be on the safe side, you or Lorraine might like to bring him by the clinic next week for some lab work. Maybe I missed something." Or misinterpreted something, he thought, because something was bothering this dog.

She pulled back visibly. "I'll tell Mother."

"Tell Mother what?" Lorraine walked down the steps to join them. She'd changed into jeans and a sweatshirt with lettering across the chest that read Shangri-la It Ain't!

"I'm a little worried about your dog," Luke explained. He stood, Thalia rising with him. Reckless didn't move, just sat there looking, brown eyebrows on his black face giving him a sad expression.

Lorraine frowned. "What's wrong with him?"

"I'm not sure."

"He has been a little peaked lately." She cocked her head and frowned at the dog sternly. "Reckless, what's your problem?"

The old dog pulled himself up and walked over to her, his feathery tail moving slowly and without enthusiasm. She leaned down to stroke his head.

"How long have you had this dog?" Luke asked.

"A couple of years. I had a friend—a rancher—who sold out and was moving to Denver. I'd just lost Geezer—you remember him, Luke."

He nodded. That mutt must have been at least fifteen years old.

"Anyway, I had the room here." She gestured to the rolling, pine-studded land beyond the open gate. "I also like Border collies, although I've never had one before. I was happy to take Reckless in, and he seemed to settle in just fine. But lately—" she frowned "—it seems like Reckless is aging right before my eyes."

"We'll figure it out," he reassured her. He looked at Thalia, who'd been listening quietly. "I've got to hit the road." Which he regretted, since she was loosening up at least a little bit.

"Okay."

She didn't seem to care, but that didn't deter him. "Walk me to my car?"

"Why? Did you forget where you parked it?"

He saw her stifle a faint smile. "I'm willing to say so to get my way," he countered.

"Oh, all right." She was trying to sound annoyed,

but he didn't buy it. "I'll be right back, Mother, and then there's something I want to talk to you about."

He wondered what that might be.

They started for the gate, but Lorraine said his name.

When he turned, she said through tight lips, "I'm sorry about the way I spoke to your mother. Will you tell her that I—"

"Nope."

"What do you mean, nope?" She looked offended. "You don't even know what I'm about to say."

"It doesn't matter. I'm not getting in the middle of that."

Thalia looked at him with approval. "Good for you!" she said.

Lorraine said, "Well, I never!"

"Oh, Mother!" Thalia laughed. "I'll be back in a minute."

And they walked away from the seething woman.

AT THE CHEROKEE, he turned to her. "I expect both you and your mother to stay at the party Saturday as guests. I'm spelling it out just in case you didn't understand."

Her eyebrows shot up. Was he kidding? "We're the hired help," she reminded him. "No way."

"Hey, it's my birthday." His golden-brown eyes smiled at her. "Shouldn't I get what I want?"

The thought of what he might want took her breath away. She barely managed to say, "You got a pony when you were seven."

"And a Porsche when I was sixteen. Uh-uh, what I want at thirty-one is you...at my party, of course."

Her mouth was so dry she could barely speak. "We don't always get what we want, even on our birthdays."

"I remember *your* sixteenth birthday."

He reached out to brush her hair away from her cheek and she flinched. "Don't," she said.

"Don't what?"

"Don't p-play with my hair and don't remind me of my sixteenth birthday."

"Why not? It's not a bad memory, Thalia."

"Maybe not to you, but it's humiliating to me. Besides, that's in the past." She lifted her chin and looked him in the eye. "Thank you for checking on Reckless. We'll bring him in next week."

He seemed about to say something but changed his mind. "Okay. I'll see you soon, Thalia."

She stood there while he climbed into his car and drove away with a final wave. And then she stood there some more.

She hadn't counted on being so discombobulated by Luke Dalton. She hadn't expected him to come on so strong, and she certainly hadn't expected his attention to fluster her so.

Turning, she walked slowly back to the house to have a little talk with her mother. But she was thinking about Luke Dalton....

# 3

"OKAY, MOTHER, LET'S HAVE IT."

Lorraine looked up from the stove where she was stirring something red in a skillet. "Have what?"

"Chapter and verse about this latest problem with Luke's mom."

Lorraine wrinkled her nose. "Oh, her. You know how Syl is."

"I also know how you are." Thalia peeked into the skillet. It looked like sloppy joes for dinner. "It's this Shangri-la thing, isn't it?"

Lorraine sighed. "I suppose so, but if it wasn't this it would be something else. The thing is, the Daltons sold off that big chunk of land and construction was underway before anyone around here really knew what was happening."

"I'm sure the plans went through the city process just like everything else."

"Yes, but who was paying attention? And you know what else?"

"What else?"

"I think Sylvia did it deliberately to bug me. I mean, my property is already surrounded on three sides. And now they come along with Shangri-la number two, and if it goes through, that'll block me off on the fourth side.''

"You don't even have a road over there," Thalia pointed out. "You won't be any worse off than you are now."

Bad tactic. Lorraine nodded enthusiastically. "Exactly—I'm *already* worse off and I resent it. That's why I've vowed to stop the next phase of development." She pointed to the Shangri-la It Ain't lettering on her sweatshirt. "That's why I've organized the opposition. This time they won't sneak their sleazy plans through city hall, at least not without a fight."

Thalia groaned. "Are you sure you want to do this, Mother? I didn't think the new houses were all that bad." Not by California standards, anyway. The lots were a tad shy of personal space by Colorado standards, however.

"Not bad!" Lorraine glared. "They're awful."

"What's the worst thing about them?"

"Why, they're—they're *new!* I hate new things." Which was obvious, since she lived in an old Victorian stuffed with antiques.

"What about new people?"

"Oh, the people are fine, but I want the town to stay the way it's always been. Instead, it's spreading out like a…like a malignant growth. That's why I've made it my business to call a halt to this horror."

Thalia knew that tone. She'd seen her mother this way before. Like the time she led a protest against construction of a new elementary school in a location she deemed unacceptable, or the time she picketed city hall to halt a plan to sell off city land previously designated for a park.

In each case, she'd won. But in neither case had she gone up against Sylvia Dalton, who was at least as stubborn, if not more.

Thalia disliked the prospect of bloodshed. "I hope you don't intend to get out there all alone and stand in front of a bulldozer or anything," she said anxiously.

Lorraine laughed. "Heavens, no. As it happens, the entire city agrees with me. We're fully prepared to do whatever it takes to block this monstrosity, but there's no need for *you* to worry about it. What do you care if Sylvia's on her high horse?"

Yes, indeed. Sylvia was Luke's problem, after all, so Thalia just shrugged.

Her mother gave her a knowing glance. "Unless you don't want Luke all stressed-out."

"Luke is not my concern."

"I'm not so sure about that. The way he was looking at you—"

"Stop, Mother. To Luke I'm just John's annoying little sister." Time to change the subject. "Where are the hamburger buns? That sloppy joe looks ready to me."

Lorraine laughed heartily. "This isn't sloppy joe, it's spaghetti sauce. But you can pull out a package of pasta from that cupboard over there, and then set the table. After we eat, I want to take you on a tour of the town and point out all the awful things growth has done.''

And so she did.

THALIA WENT TO EMILY the next day for the straight scoop about Shangri-la one and two. ''Read all about it.'' Emily handed over the local newspaper, the *Shepherd's Pass Review*. Between customers, she added her interpretation.

''The Daltons own the land, but the project is the brainchild of a Texas developer named Joe John Jeff Jordan, called Four-Jay by all,'' she said. ''He came in here and charmed everybody's socks off, got the approvals he needed and went to work before anyone really knew what was going on.''

''That's pretty much what Mother and the newspaper say,'' Thalia mused. ''Does that mean the rest of what she said is also true—that everyone in town is against the next phase of the project?''

''Hardly!'' Emily laughed. ''I'd say the town is split right down the middle. There's stiff resistance, led by your mother, and equally stiff support, led by Four-Jay and Mrs. Dalton and Michael Forbes— you remember Mike, I'm sure. He graduated with your brother and Luke. He's a real hotshot attorney now.''

''I remember him vaguely.''

''If you'd like to see them all in action, there's a community meeting set for Wednesday night at seven at city hall. Nothing will be decided, but it would help you get up to speed on the subject.''

Emily laughed. "That is, if you *want* to get up to speed."

Thalia grimaced. "Not really, but maybe I'd better since Mother's leading the charge." She cocked her head. "How about you, Emily? How do you stand on all this?"

"I can see both sides," Emily admitted. "I do think the houses are quite nice, and I understand the next phase will be even nicer—and more expensive. On the other hand, I hate to see things change in our little hometown." She sighed. "It's a puzzlement."

AND SO IT CERTAINLY SEEMED as Thalia made the rounds renewing old acquaintances. Emily was right—sentiment appeared to be very evenly split. She wondered how Luke felt about it, then realized he would surely back his mother. The Daltons, after all, stood to make a great deal of money from this project...not that they needed it. One of the pioneer families of Shepherd's Pass, they were also the wealthiest.

Luke called Thalia Monday night and asked her out to a movie; she turned him down. He called her again Tuesday morning and asked her to lunch; again she turned him down, saying she'd be filling in at her mother's flower shop and couldn't count on getting away for lunch at any particular time.

Still, she was less than surprised when he dropped by at noon with a bag full of sandwiches from the Paper Sack. Refusing to acknowledge the obvious, she gave him an impersonal smile, hands poised over the file drawer.

"May I help you?"

"You sure can." He hit her with a winning smile. "You can help me eat all this food." He held up the bag.

"Thanks, but I'm working."

Miss Pauline, manning the phones at the desk up front, tsked-tsked. "Now, Thalia, you have to eat you know."

"Actually, I already have." She'd gobbled a candy bar on the run an hour ago but saw no need to go into detail. "Sorry Luke, but I've got to make deliveries this afternoon. Mother's finishing up the orders now and I'll be leaving in just a few minutes."

He sighed with exaggerated disappointment. "Okay, if that's how it is. I'll just take one of these sandwiches and leave the rest, in case Miss Pauline or your mom's hungry."

"That's not necessary."

"I know." He reached inside the big bag and pulled out a foam container. "You seem to be keeping busy day and night."

She knew he was thinking about her various rejections, and simply shrugged.

"Any chance you'll be going to the Shangri-la meeting Wednesday evening?" He opened the foam box and hauled out half of an enormous sandwich.

"I haven't decided," she said noncommittally,

although she had. She must support her mother. Lorraine had asked her daughter to go not a half hour earlier and that clinched it. "How about you?"

"Same." He opened the sandwich bag and looked inside. "How's Reckless?"

"Same. We haven't forgotten what you said. We'll bring him in first chance we get."

"Good." Of Miss Pauline he inquired, "How about Gertrude? Is she doing okay?"

"Oh, yes, Doctor. She's her old self again. I can't thank you enough for what you did for her."

"Just doin' my job, ma'am," he said with false modesty and a lot of good humor. "Guess if I can't talk either of you lovely ladies into dining with me, I might as well run along."

"Why, I'll be glad to dine with you," Miss Pauline said. "Pull up that chair and make yourself comfortable, Lucas. That way I can answer the phone and still—"

The bell behind the counter tinkled. Thalia, who'd almost finished the filing, straightened. "That's Mother," she announced. "The order's ready. If you'll both excuse me—"

She wasn't even sure they heard as they busily examined the contents of the bag for the tuna salad Luke was sure he'd ordered.

LUKE FINISHED his second sandwich and patted his stomach. "I can't eat another bite," he declared. He reconsidered and added, "Well, maybe a brownie.'' He fished out a large wrapped square from the bottom of a bag now containing mostly discarded paper and boxes.

Miss Pauline smiled. ''That was quite a nice break in my routine,'' she said. ''Do drop by anytime you like, Lucas.''

''I'll do that.'' He gave her a warm smile and rose. ''I've got to get back to work now. Doc Miller's got late lunch.''

''Of course. You run along.'' She patted daintily at her lips with a paper napkin. ''And Lucas...''

He paused with his hand on the glass door. ''Yes, ma'am?''

''Thalia promised her mother she'd attend that meeting tomorrow night. I heard her. I don't *know* why she said that to you.''

Sneaky, he thought. ''A woman has a right to change her mind, I guess,'' he said, opting for the popular view.

''This is not your typical woman.'' She looked puzzled. ''I've never known anyone who took everything so seriously. I'm certain that to her, a promise is a promise—and she promised her mother.'' Miss Pauline's smile was innocent. ''I mention this in case you might have some particular interest.''

''I'm interested, all right. *Very* interested.'' He waved and pushed the door open. ''Thanks, Miss Pauline. I owe you one.''

He left Lorraine's Pretty Posies shop whistling.

"FANCY MEETING YOU HERE."

Thalia looked up from the water fountain at city hall and into the smiling face of Luke Dalton. A sense of inevitability settled over her. How could she feign surprise?

"Yes, fancy that," she said dryly. "Here to support your mother, I suppose?"

"Here to see you, mostly."

His blunt response shocked her. "Really." She turned back into the council chamber where citizen had followed citizen to the podium for the past hour, taking sides in what was shaping up as a real civic crisis. The seven elected council members had been listening with resigned expressions.

"I wouldn't say it if it wasn't true." He fell in beside her, deftly guiding her into a seat at the back of the room where it would be possible to converse in low tones, as opposed to the occasionally loud tones of those clustered down front. "To tell you the truth, I've tried to steer clear of this scrap," he went on. "I can see both sides. With a little compromise, you'd think…" He shrugged. "From what I've seen so far, neither side seems particularly interested in compromise."

"That about sums it up." A man she didn't immediately recognize had approached the podium. Silver-haired and erect, he carried a white Stetson and wore a western-cut suit and fancy cowboy boots. "Who's that?" she whispered.

"That's Four-Jay himself—Joe John Jeff Jordan, the developer. He's from Texas."

The man began to speak and Thalia grinned.

"I hope to shout, he's from Texas. Listen to that drawl."

Luke grinned back, his smile lighting up an already attractive face. "People get so interested in his accent that they forget to pay attention to what he's saying. He is one sharp operator."

"You can say that again."

The large room slowly quieted as the tall Texan continued speaking in his soothing drawl. Even Lorraine, surrounded by supporters on one side of the aisle, and Sylvia with her faction on the other, paused to listen.

"Who's the guy whispering in Sylvia's ear?" Thalia asked.

"Surely you remember Michael Forbes."

"That's Mike Forbes?" She couldn't help being impressed. "Emily told me he'd become an attorney like his mother before him. I guess *he's* chosen sides without any difficulty."

"You know lawyers."

"I should. I was married to one."

He gave her a sharp glance. "Then don't be offended when I tell you that Four-Jay and Mom showed Mike the money." He leaned closer. "It looks like Four-Jay has deflected fireworks this time, at least."

His warm breath stirred tendrils of hair to tickle her ear. She shivered and leaned slightly away. "Were you here earlier when our beloved mothers spoke their piece?" she whispered back.

"Missed it. It took me longer to get here than I expected."

Four-Jay was winding down. "…and so I say to everyone here tonight, to all the fine residents of Shepherd's Pass past, present and future, old and new, that there is room for compromise. In a free society, we can sit down and reason together." He opened his arms wide, a theatrical gesture perhaps rehearsed. "I am a reasonable man and I'm at y'all's service. Many thanks for your kind attention."

He left the podium to applause from both sides of the room.

Mayor Kelly slammed down his gavel as if relieved to have the opportunity at last to do so. "I think you'll all agree that to follow that act would be folly," he announced. "Meeting adjourned! I suggest you all go home and cogitate on the things that have been said here tonight."

Thalia raised her brows. "That was sudden."

"But not unwelcome. How about you and I—"

"I'm sorry," she interrupted quickly, "there goes my mother, rushing for the door. I need to catch her." Standing, she leaned across him and called, "Mother!"

"Huh? Oh!" Lorraine turned toward the sound of her daughter's voice. "It's you."

"Of course, it's me. Where are you heading in such a hurry?"

"I've got to talk to Four-Jay! I heard him say he was going over to the Watering Hole so—"

"What about me? I don't want to go to a bar and listen to more of this Shangri-la stuff."

"Oh." Lorraine blinked, looked toward the door through which Four-Jay had now disappeared, looked back with a frown and finally brightened. "Luke can take you home, then. Can't you, Luke."

"Sure thing." His smile was benign.

"In that case, I'm out of here. Don't wait up, Thalia."

Lorraine rushed on. Thalia sat back down, feeling grumpy. "Well, for goodness' sake. That was some brush-off from my own mother."

"Not to worry," he said. "I'll see you get home safe and sound."

"I don't seem to have much choice so…thank you."

He laughed. "Gracious, as always."

"Touché." She smiled sheepishly. Together they rose and started toward the door. "I didn't mean to be rude." She looked around the rapidly emptying room. "Where are you parked? If you got here late, you must have had trouble finding a spot."

"No problem at all. I'm parked in the driveway at home."

"But—? What are you saying?"

"I walked."

He lifted a foot and pointed to his jock shoe and for the first time it registered with her that he was wearing sweat pants and a T-shirt. She'd been so dazzled by the man that she hadn't noticed the ensemble.

"Then why did you agree to drive me home?" she demanded.

"I didn't. I said I'd *take* you home, which I will."

"But—it must be two miles!"

"You look like a healthy woman to me. You can walk, can't you? I noticed you had on sensible shoes and it's a beautiful night, so what's the problem?"

She considered. "I guess there *is* no problem," she said at last. "A brisk walk will probably do me good."

"That's what I thought." He held the door open for her. "Lead the way, Thalia."

Taking a deep breath, she did.

THEY STROLLED THE STREETS of Shepherd's Pass, through a business district that quickly gave way to homes. Streetlights and a nearly full moon illuminated their way; glowing windows lined their path. The night was quiet and peaceful and infinitely calm.

It was exactly as he'd hope it would be: Thalia at his side, crisp fall air filling his lungs, competition with no one and nothing for her attention. When he'd decided to walk to the meeting instead of drive, it had been a calculated risk with this in mind—even though he lived a good mile farther than she did from city hall.

"Do you like being a veterinarian?" she asked suddenly, her tone full of sincere interest.

"Yeah," he said, "I do. A lot."

"I was surprised when I heard."

She looked both ways although there were no vehicles in sight, then stepped off the curb to cross a street. He took her elbow, feeling protective on general principles. She gave him a skeptical glance but didn't object.

He remembered what she'd said then and asked, "You were surprised? Why?"

"I thought you were going to be a people doctor. That's what you always said."

"That was my plan. Fortunately, I discovered in time that I like animals better than people."

Her smile was wry. "I see your point."

"What about you?"

"What about me?"

"You work for an insurance company, Lorraine said."

"That's right. I'm an executive at the national headquarters of Insurance World."

"Do you like it?"

"Of course." She sounded a bit touchy.

"Because you like business," he prodded.

"Well, yes."

"Thalia, I heard doubt in those two words."

"No, you didn't—not at all." She gave him another annoyed glance. "I'm crazy about my job, I have an unlimited future, and I'll be going back to it in a few weeks."

"Why?"

"I just told you."

"You certainly did not. You told me a lot of external stuff. What I want to know is why you want to go so far away when your mother and the people who care about you are here, in Colorado. There are jobs here, too—all kinds of businesses to choose from.''

"But—'' She sucked in a deep, agitated breath. "You just don't understand. I—I have a life there. I'm already established. Everything's in order.''

"You're established here, too.''

"I have friends there....''

"So? I didn't say you didn't have friends there. But old friends are the best, Thalia.''

She remained silent for a couple of blocks, both of them striding along in near silence in their athletic shoes. At last she said, ''What's your point, Luke?''

"That there's no place like home, Dorothy.''

Her laughter was sharp and incredulous. "My home is in California now.''

"No, it isn't. Your career is in California. Your home is here.''

"My career is important. I'm serious about my career. I couldn't just toss everything aside and relocate on a whim.''

"Honey, you're serious about everything—too serious, if you ask me.''

"I didn't.''

"So I volunteered an opinion.'' Time to lighten the mood. He didn't want to alienate her any further than she already was. ''Feel free to ignore it.''

"Thank you. I will. Because to walk out on my job and my life and my career in California would be—it would be unforgivable.''

"I'd forgive you," he said softly. "Your mother would forgive you. Emily would forgive you."

"Maybe so, but I wouldn't forgive—"

She bit off her words and glanced at him over her shoulder. It was too dark to read her expression but her tone said *back off*.

He couldn't. "Forgive yourself, right? That's what you were about to say."

"So what? The bottom line is, I don't want to come home—I mean back to Colorado. To stay I mean."

"Aha!" He had her now. "I heard you the first time. You called this place home."

"A mere slip of the tongue."

"No way! You were born and raised here and it *is* home. I feel the same way. I never intended to practice here, but here I am. You, my girl, want to do the same thing. You're just not ready to admit it quite yet, but you will."

They turned right on Heavenly Lane automatically, engrossed in the conversation. She said, "You don't know me well enough to be so sure about what I want. In fact, you don't know me at all as an adult, just as a goofy kid." She gave him a triumphant glance.

"You were never goofy," he said with total conviction. "Trust me on that."

"After what I did?"

"What you did was wonderful." He spoke from the heart. "Your timing was goofy, not what you did."

"Oh, Luke." It was a helpless moan. "I made

such a fool of myself and I *hate* looking foolish. I've regretted it ever since.''

"I'm sorry to hear that,'' he said. He stuffed his hands deep into his pant pockets to keep from touching her. "Everybody looks foolish at one time or another. Believe me, I've been there and done that. You had a great idea, honey, but—you know, yada yada.''

"Too young, too old, too you-name-it,'' she recited.

"Right. But bad timing is no reason to treat me like a pariah. You've avoided me from that day to this.''

"I've hardly seen you from that day to this. I simply went on with my life and tried to forget it had ever happened. I went away to school, got married—''

"Got a divorce.''

"It happens.'' She walked stiffly for half a block, then said, "At least I tried marriage. You didn't even do that.''

"That's true,'' he agreed. "I was engaged, though. Fortunately, she came to her senses in time.''

"I should have been so lucky. The fact that my marriage didn't work out—'' All the bluff and fire went out of her. "The fact that it didn't work nearly killed me. I tried, Lord knows I tried. He tried, too, but after three years it seemed wiser to cut our losses and call the whole thing off.''

"Was he a nice guy?''

"That's a funny thing to ask.'' She seemed to consider carefully. "Yes,'' she said finally, "he was a very nice guy. He's an attorney with an independent movie company. Loves his job, is good at it, works very hard. He worked hard at his marriage, too. We just grew in different directions, I guess."

"I'm sorry," he said. "But I'm glad."

"Glad? I must say, that's the first time my tale of woe has met with that particular response."

"That's because I'm glad you came home, and you wouldn't have if you were still married. Or if you did, you'd bring him and that would be a problem."

"For whom?"

They'd reached Lorraine's house, dark except for the soft glow of the porch light. They turned up the walk and halted at the foot of the steps, pine needles crunching beneath their feet.

He rocked back on his heels. "It would be a problem for me."

"I don't see why."

"Sure you do." Giving up the fight, he put a tentative hand on her shoulder. She stiffened but didn't step away or otherwise react.

"I don't." She sounded slightly breathless, as if she'd been running. Which she hadn't.

"Then I'll spell it out." He lifted his other hand to tilt her chin up. "Because if you'd come home with a husband, I couldn't have done this with a clear conscience."

And leaning forward, he pressed his lips to hers.

# 4

SHE COULDN'T BELIEVE he would kiss her, just like that.

She couldn't believe she would kiss him back, either, which is exactly what she did. Flinging her arms around his neck, she pressed her body against his and kissed him with so much enthusiasm that it shocked her.

This would never do! She tried to dredge up enough self-control to pull away, but unfortunately, her self-discipline seemed to have vanished. Only when a sweep of headlights passed over them did she manage to find the willpower to push herself out of his arms.

Lorraine braked in the driveway beside them and jumped out. "Oh, it's you," she said, as if surprised.

Luke chuckled. "Who'd you expect to find making out at your front door?"

"Nobody, actually." With a wave, she sailed past. "Take your time."

"Mother!"

"You, too, Thalia. Don't let me rush you." She disappeared inside the house.

Luke moved to take Thalia in his arms again. "Where were we when we were so rudely interrupted?" he murmured seductively.

"Stop that!" She batted his hands away. "I was just about to slap your face, is where we were."

His laughter sounded incredulous. "What for?"

"For—for—" She swallowed hard. "For taking me for the kind of woman a guy can just grab and kiss on the spur of the moment."

"Are you kidding?" He stared at her in obvious disbelief. "That wasn't spur of the moment. I've wanted to do that ever since I declined the honor of being your first."

She groaned. "Will you kindly stop referring to that? It's not a memory I want to relive."

"I do, if I can change the outcome."

She took a hasty step back. "Too late."

"Says who? Now that age is no longer a factor—"

"Are you *kidding?*" She stared at him. "Age be damned! You had your chance and you blew it."

"That's a bit inflexible. Everybody deserves a second chance." He edged toward her.

She continued to retreat. "I wouldn't get mixed up with you again for—for a million dollars. You always were a fun-and-games kinda guy, Luke Dalton, and you obviously haven't changed a bit. Well, this time you're barking up the wrong woman."

"How do you know what I'm after?"

Her heels hit the bottom step. "I wasn't born yesterday, you know."

"You're acting like you were."

"After *what happened,* how do you expect me to act?"

"Like a grown-up."

"I am," she insisted desperately. "You're the one acting like a kid. Life is serious business, Luke." She clenched her hands into fists. "I'm simply not interested in you *that* way."

"You were once."

He was crowding her. She stepped up on the first step. "That was then and this is now. Besides, I'm not going to be here long enough for anything to develop so you can just back off."

"Because of *what happened.*"

She lifted her chin, annoyed by his teasing but incapable of backing down. "That's right."

"It looks like you should be over *what happened* by now."

"I would be if you'd quit bringing it up."

He rocked back on his heels, the light casting diabolical shadows across his face. "Yeah, right. Sure you are."

"Darn it, Luke—"

"Okay, okay, calm down. I'll change the subject. You're coming to my birthday party Saturday, right?"

"Yes, as the hired help."

"As a very special friend. And your mom, too."

"Thanks but no thanks. I have no desire to crash your party. I'll help Mother decorate and then we'll—"

"You'll stay."

"I won't."

"Your mother will, if just to annoy *my* mother. Then you'll have to stay to make sure the two don't come to blows."

"Did anyone ever mention you're a rotten listener? My mind is made up."

"You can always change it." Grabbing her hand, he planted a quick, warm kiss on her unprotected palm. "Thanks for walking with me. It was great. We'll do it again, someday."

"We certainly won't," she shouted after him.

Jogging down the driveway, he waved cheerfully without glancing around. Frustrated and well aware that she'd come off second-best in that exchange, Thalia gritted her teeth and turned to the door. Lucas Dalton drove her crazy!

But he sure did know how to kiss.


"LOOK," THALIA SAID, "I don't want you to think there's anything going on."

Lorraine looked up from the cup of hot chocolate resting on the tabletop, cradled between her hands. "Going on where?"

"Between me and Luke." Thalia sat down and reached for the second cup her mother had prepared.

Lorraine feigned surprise. "Something's going on between you and Luke?"

"Mother! I know you saw us when you drove in."

"Saw you doing what? You mean kissing?"

"Of course, I mean kissing. But he was doing the kissing and I was getting ready to give him a piece of my mind, which I did as soon as you went inside."

"Honey," Lorraine drawled, dropping all pretense of misunderstanding, "from what I saw he wasn't doing *all* the kissing. You were doing your share or you're no daughter of mine."

"Mother!"

"Calm down, Thalia honey. Luke's a great guy. You could do worse. In fact, you *did* do worse."

"Mother!"

"Oh, pshaw." Lorraine finished her cocoa and carried the cup to the sink. "I wasn't born fifty-one years old, you know. I was young once. I had a life." One brow rose. "In fact, I still have a life—or will soon, if I'm not mistaken."

"You and Four-Jay?" Thalia stared at her mother, who looked like the cat with canary feathers decorating the corners of her mouth.

Lorraine shrugged nonchalantly. "Who knows? But it'll be fun finding out." She started for the door. "See you tomorrow."

"One more thing before you go—"

"Yes?"

"You won't be staying for Luke's birthday party, will you?"

"Absolutely not." Lorraine shook her red-gold head vigorously. "Under no circumstances. I'm going to work, and then I'm out of there."

"Thank heavens," Thalia muttered to herself.

Until Lorraine's voice sailed through the kitchen door. "Unless somebody gives me a good reason to change my mind, of course."

THALIA HAD NEVER BEEN to the Dalton mansion, as it was generally called. It had been built after she went away to college. Before that, the Daltons had lived in a splendid ranch house five or six miles out of town.

"Sylvia decided she needed the grandest house in town to support her social ambitions," Lorraine explained contemptuously while parking the Pretty Posies delivery truck around back near the service entrance. "Joe built this place for her and then died before he ever got a chance to move in. It was just pitiful."

"You can hardly blame her for wanting to live closer to town," Thalia pointed out in the interest of fairness.

"I didn't care where she lived, so long as it wasn't right down the road from me." Lorraine made a face. "Then when Luke decided to come back here to practice, she practically *forced* him to move in with her."

"She's got the room, that's for sure." Thalia looked around at the impressive three-story stone structure. Surrounded by landscaped gardens and walkways, it really was quite impressive. Over to the far side she could see the matching enclosure, which must shield the pool. Living here alone would certainly be lonely, especially when Sylvia had thought her husband would be here with her. Thalia felt a flash of sympathy, which she carefully hid from her mother.

Lorraine set the brake, then smiled at her daughter. "Are you ready? Sylvia wants a Hawaiian luau and that's what we're going to give her. The flowers alone are costing her a small fortune and the guys over at Bob's Barbeque have dug a pit big enough to cook a whole pig, but what the hell? It's only money."

"I guess so." Thalia took a deep breath, glad it wasn't *her* money. "I'm ready."

"Then let's synchronize our watches and *do it.*"

"LADIES, THE DECORATIONS LOOK great," Luke announced. "Now you've both got to stay for the party."

He looked expectantly from Thalia to her mother and back again, figuring he knew where the power lay. The daughter nodded no while the mother nodded yes.

Lorraine added with a grin, "I thought you'd never ask."

Thalia glowered at her mother. "I'm afraid it's out of the question."

"Why?"

"For openers—" She glanced down at her jeans and sneakers and simple plaid shirt. "I'm not dressed for it."

He laughed. "Don't be ridiculous. You look

great. Of course, if you want to go home and get a bikini—''

"In your dreams."

"Okay, failing that, you're perfect."

"Really, Luke, I wouldn't feel right—"

"Thalia! I'm so glad you're here!" Emily came through the door between the house and the flower-bedecked pool area, carrying a white package wrapped with blue bows. "Isn't this great? Happy birthday, Luke, and many happy returns." She gave him a peck on the cheek. "Where do I put this gift? Mrs. Myers, I'm so glad to see you! What—"

While Emily gushed on, Luke caught Thalia's glance and smiled encouragement. Somehow he didn't think it would be much of a celebration without her.

THE PARTY DIDN'T START winding down until nine o'clock that evening—not a minute too soon, Thalia thought. She'd spent most of the preceding six hours trying to avoid Luke, which wasn't as difficult as it might have been. As the host and the "birthday boy," as his mother announced prior to the cake cutting, he'd had duties of his own. But time and again, he'd appeared at Thalia's side to make sure she had a drink, food, someone to amuse her—simple enough since she knew practically everyone there.

Thalia had tried to make herself useful by keeping an eye on the proceedings: picking up, cleaning up, making sure the dishes and platters were refilled regularly, that no one's glass remained empty for long. Many of the guests came prepared for a dip in the enormous Dalton pool while others were content to lounge in the sun, at the many patio tables or around the bar set up in an open-sided cabana at the far end.

Everybody seemed to be having a good time but no one more so than Sylvia. At one point, she'd surprised Thalia by slipping an arm around her waist and whispering, "Thank you so much for staying. It means a lot to Luke."

Not knowing how to respond, Thalia simply smiled and nodded.

But now, at last, everyone was leaving. She'd help clear the pool area and then maybe she could coax her mother into leaving. Of course, that would only happen if Four-Jay left first. The two had staked out an umbrella table near the bar and held court for most of the evening.

Thalia guessed that only good breeding kept Sylvia from raising a ruckus about that. She had finally managed to coax Four-Jay onto the makeshift wooden dance floor set up at one end of the pool, where a trio looking more western than Hawaiian provided music.

"Hey!" The warm voice in her ear made her jump in surprise and nearly drop the platters she'd been stacking. Hands equally warm settled on her upper arms. "You're a guest. How come every time I see you, you're working?"

"Because—" Thalia caught her breath, intensely

aware of his touch. "I don't feel like a guest. I feel like an employee," she insisted stubbornly.

He turned her to face him, taking the platters from her and replacing them on the buffet table. The two of them were, she suddenly realized, quite alone. In the silence she could hear the water in the pool lapping against the tile, the faint hum of an unseen pump.

He sighed. "You are one stubborn woman," he said regretfully. "Did you have a good time?"

"It was a nice party," she said evasively, thinking she should step away from his light grip but indecisive because that might be construed as more than it was. She licked her lips. "I saw a lot of friends and that was nice."

"I got a lot of nice presents."

That made her smile. He'd got a lot of gag gifts, like the embroidered hat from Emily which read Doggy Doctor in large script.

He touched the corner of her upcurved mouth with his thumb. "There, that's what I wanted to see. A smile."

She tried to stifle it, without notable success.

His voice was low and warm. "I don't have a birthday gift from you yet."

"And that ain't the half of it," she retorted.

He looked hurt. "No present?"

She spread her hands between them. "Do I look like I'm hiding a birthday gift?"

"Well, yes."

She frowned. "I'd like to know where."

"Remember, you asked for it." He stepped closer, until his thighs touched hers lightly. "I've been waiting all evening to collect my birthday kiss."

"Birthday—!" She stepped back, stumbling in her haste. "If you think I'm going to give you a—"

"Watch out!" He made a grab for her. "Don't—"

But it was too late. Her foot bumped against a stack of ropes coiled on the deck next to the pool. Losing her balance, she tipped backward, grabbing wildly for any support. Her fumbling hands touched the collar of his flower-bedecked Hawaiian shirt and clenched tight.

He let out a muffled and surprised *humpf* and together they tumbled into the deep end of the pool. They came up coughing and gasping for air.

Thalia, treading water, shoved hair out of her eyes. "Why did you do that?" she cried.

He moved as easily in the water as he did on land. "I didn't do it. You did."

"I—did, didn't I?" And then she couldn't hold it in any longer and burst into delighted laughter. "I guess that's your birthday gift, then." Flipping over, she took off for the shallow end of the crystal-clear pool, stroking strongly.

"Yes!"

His satisfied shout sent fresh shivers down her spine. She'd never before been in the water fully dressed and there was something downright decadent about it. Fortunately, she was a good swimmer.

But he was better. He caught her just as her toes touched the bottom at the shallow end. She struggled to shake off his hold, impeded by her laughter. He turned her around anyway, his amber eyes gleaming with that familiar mischief.

"Happy birthday to me!"

"That's what you—"

The rest was lost in the pressure of his mouth on hers…his mouth, chilly and wet at first but quickly growing warm and masterful. *It* is *his birthday,* she thought foggily. *One kiss—one little bitty kiss—*

Which led to another, and another—

"Come out of that pool this instant! Honestly, you—" Sylvia's command ended in a shriek of embarrassment. "Oh, Luke, I'm so sorry! I didn't know it was you and…is that *Thalia?*"

Sylvia was no more shocked than the object of her attention. Thalia shoved out of Luke's slack embrace and moved to the ladder as quickly as she could, which wasn't very. Waterlogged clothing and shoes weighed her down, but she managed to drag herself up the ladder.

It got worse. Lorraine stood beside Sylvia. Taking a good look at her dripping daughter, she burst out laughing.

From the pool, Luke intervened. "Back off, you two," he ordered. "Thalia was just giving me my birthday kiss."

"No, I wasn't!" Thalia glared at him. "He was *taking* his birthday kiss. There's a difference."

"Really?" Lorraine sounded suspiciously innocent. "From where I was standing, any difference wasn't immediately discernible."

Feeling cornered and considerably flustered, Thalia glared equally at them all. "Look, I'm not accustomed to being thrown into a swimming pool with my clothes on," she tried to defend herself. "I'm not responsible!"

Luke shook his head sadly. "What happened was, she tripped. I was trying to save her."

"Luke," she yelled at him, "you're not acting like a man who turned thirty-two today!"

"Because I'm not a serious person—capital *S*, capital *P?*"

Both mothers laughed and looked expectantly at Thalia, who lifted her chin haughtily. "I won't apologize for being a grown-up," she announced.

"You're not a grown-up, you're an old lady," he tossed back, his smile never slipping. "You're only twenty-seven and you act seventy."

"And you act like you're thirteen," she retorted.

"Come to your senses before it's too late," he urged, moving through the water toward the steps. "You still have time. Don't you ever want to just let go and *enjoy?*"

"Boy," Lorraine said breathlessly, "I sure do."

"Mother!"

"Lorraine, you're too old for that kind of nonsense," Sylvia inserted. "And in case there's any doubt, you made a fool out of yourself hanging over Four-Jay that way."

"Oh, you think so?" Lorraine got a crafty look

on her face. "Do I hear a little jealousy in there somewhere?"

"Me? Jealous of *you?*" Sylvia drew herself up to her full height, looking even more regal than usual in her imported Hawaiian muumuu and six or eight fresh flower leis coiled around her neck. "That will be the day!"

"Maybe, but it wouldn't be the first time, would it."

While the two bickered, Luke hauled himself out of the pool. His white shorts clung; his flowered shirt did likewise, leaving little to the imagination. Thalia shivered.

"You're cold," he said with quick concern. "Come in the house and I'll find something dry for you to—"

"That's not necessary. I'll just go on home."

"Suit yourself." But his expression conveyed his disapproval. Grabbing a towel from a stack on a nearby bench, he tossed it to her. "At least put this over the car seat to protect it."

"Thank you."

"And Thalia…"

"Yes, Luke?"

"Thanks for my birthday kiss—or maybe we should call that *kisses.* Because no matter how you spin it, you were there, sweetheart."

"That's *your* opinion."

"Sure is," he agreed cheerfully. Unbuttoning his shirt, he dragged the soggy thing off and tossed it aside.

Nice chest. *Real* nice chest.

"Mother," Thalia said forcefully, "are you coming with me? If not, I'd like the keys." She held out a steady hand.

"I'm coming."

"In that case—" Thalia smiled impersonally at Sylvia and her maverick son "—thank you for inviting us."

"You had a lovely time, right?" Luke raised his brows.

"Of course."

"Seriously, if you'd relaxed, you might have enjoyed yourself even more." He cocked his head. "Aren't you ever tempted to give it a try?"

"Absolutely not." But was that true?

Later, alone in the second-story bedroom of her youth, Thalia sat in dark silence staring out the window, her heart full of questions. Maybe she did take everything too seriously. It *might* be fun just to relax and let life happen.

But could she actually *do* that? At this point, she really wasn't sure.

Yet those few minutes spent floundering around completely clothed in the swimming pool with Luke Dalton had been not only fun but exciting and sexy and very, very provocative.

Which was all the more reason to stay away from the man, she decided.

"Look," Lorraine said bright and early Monday morning, "I've got a ton of stuff to do at the shop today since all of Saturday was devoted to the Dalton soiree—"

"I'll help," Thalia cut in quickly. "No problem."

"Great." Lorraine looked relieved. "That's what I was expecting you to say. What I need you to do is take old Reckless to the vet."

Thalia frowned. "Did I just get set up or what?"

"Of course not, dear." Lorraine looked offended. "I'm really worried about that dog. He's been off his feed all week and he just mopes around."

"You take him to the doggy doctor. I'll open the shop for you."

"When did you become a floral designer?" Lorraine's brows rose. "Seriously, if you want to help me, this is what I need you to do. That way I'll have the first wave of orders ready by the time you get there and you can help out with deliveries."

Thalia groaned. "If this is just some trick to throw me and Luke together—"

"Oh, for heaven's sake." Lorraine finished her coffee and rose from the breakfast table. "Why would I do that? For all I know, Luke won't even be there. Ask for Doc Miller, I don't care. Just do this for Reckless, okay?"

"I suppose I can if you insist."

"Great. We'll take him with us, then. You can drop me at the shop and go straight to the clinic. Thanks, honey."

Lorraine bustled out. Thalia sat alone at the table

for a good two minutes, feeling dejected. Doc Miller wouldn't be there, or if he was, he'd be busy elsewhere. She'd have to face Luke again and that was getting harder and harder to do.

Worse. He knew it.

LUKE GAVE RECKLESS a thorough going-over, up to and including the drawing of blood for further tests. Reckless just sat there like a furry lump, sad brown eyes accusing.

What the hell was going on? Luke asked himself for about the twelfth time. This was one miserable dog when he should be in tall cotton. He had a great life: plenty of food, lots of room to run and roam, people around when he wanted attention.

Opening the door to the examining room, he gestured for Thalia to enter. This she did without the slightest flicker of recognition. It was as if she'd met him for the first time five minutes ago.

That made him grin. She sure was working hard to keep things between them impersonal.

And failing.

She sat down in the chair next to the dog. Automatically she began to scratch his ears, then stroked the dog between the shoulder blades. She had a wonderful smile, especially when it was sincere. As now—for a dog, not for Luke.

She looked up and the smile evaporated. "What's wrong with him, Lu—Doctor?"

Luke sighed. "I can't find a thing physically wrong," he said honestly. "There are still a few tests to do and then I'll talk the results over with Doc Miller. The bottom line is, this dog seems perfectly healthy to me.''

Her frown revealed her frustration. ''Mother says he used to be real perky and now he just lies around and sighs.''

''Sighs?''

She nodded solemnly. ''Or as close to a sigh as a dog can get. It's almost like…like he's depressed about something.''

''You know,'' Luke frowned, puzzling over what she'd said, ''you could be right. Maybe what he needs is a new interest in life, something to shake him out of the doldrums.''

''Like what?'' she asked, obviously interested.

''I don't know, like—'' Luke slapped his hand alongside his temple. ''Of course, why didn't I think of this before? Thalia, Border collies are working dogs.''

''Yes.'' She frowned. ''And your point is…?''

''Your mother got him from a rancher, right?''

She nodded. ''A sheep rancher, actually.''

''Then that's it.'' He ruffled Reckless's furry black head.

''What's it?''

''He needs a job. He needs sheep to herd.''

Her eyes widened. ''You mean Mother's pet needs pets of his own?''

Luke threw back his head and laughed. ''Exactly. A few sheep to herd around in circles could give purpose to his days.'' He looked at her then through half-shuttered eyes. "How about you, Thalia? Do you need new purpose to your days?"

She met his gaze squarely. "I don't need new purpose, Luke," she said too sweetly. "I'm happy with my days exactly as they are."

As if he believed that. Amused, he showed her and the depressed Border collie from the office, promising a report on the dog's tests in a day or two.

And already scheming to get her alone to deliver them.

THAT NIGHT AT DINNER, Thalia innocently repeated Luke's remarks to her mother, and then only in passing. Therefore, no one was more astonished than she when two sheep were delivered a day later.

# 5

"UH...HENRY?"

"What is it now, Joyce?"

"Do my eyes deceive me or are there really two sheep grazing in that pasture across the road?"

Henry Brown squinted. He was sitting on a patio chair on his deck across the street from Lorraine Myers's place, so he didn't have to go to much trouble. After a moment he said, "Yep, that's sheep all right."

Joyce harrumphed. "That woman must be crazy! Sheep aren't allowed in Shangri-la."

"Well, now, she was here before anyone ever heard of Shangri-la, Joyce."

"There you go, taking her side again. We didn't pay this kind of money for a home in Shangri-la so we could live across the street from sheep—smelly, ugly, noisy, dirty sheep."

"That's your daddy talking, hon," Henry said, trying to soothe her. "You don't like sheep because he was a cattle rancher."

"I don't like sheep because they kill the grass. Where they've been, not even a weed will grow and no self-respecting cow will ever go."

"That's an old wives' tale."

"Watch who you're calling an old wife. I tell you, those sheep have got to go! Lorraine Myers is doing this just to annoy us, you know she is. She's against Shangri-la number two and this is her way of—"

"Joyce, Joyce, I can't believe she'd—"

"Cows are approved in Shangri-la. Horses are okay, too. But sheep and pigs and chickens are out—*o-u-t*, out. They simply aren't class enough."

"Calm down, honey. You're getting all worked—"

"I'm calling Joe John Jeff Jordan and then I'm calling Mayor Kelly. This has got to be nipped in the bud. It's bad enough that she refuses to sell out so we're forced to look at that awful island, that eyesore in the middle of the nicest development in—"

"Her property's not an eyesore, sweetheart. Actually, it's quite a nice old Victorian, and she keeps it up real well. Just because it isn't new like all the rest of—"

"That's right, it isn't new. It's an eyesore, just like I said. Maybe we have to put up with *that* but we don't *have* to put up with sheep!"

Joyce stomped back inside the ersatz Tudor. Henry sat there alone on the wooden deck, listening to birds sing and watching a furry black streak maneuver two woollies. Sipping his coffee, he thought about the fact that his wife was on a rampage and he hadn't even had breakfast yet.

He *sure* didn't deserve a range war over sheep at this hour.

ANTICIPATING A SLOW DAY at the shop, Lorraine decided to pop into Denver to visit wholesalers, leaving her daughter and Miss Pauline in charge. With the pickup in the garage for service, Lorraine bubbled with excitement about the sheep while driving her daughter into town.

"Did you see how Reckless perked up?" she demanded for the third time. "He's already a new dog."

Thalia had to admit it was the truth. No sooner had the two fat white sheep been unloaded than Reckless had bolted upright, ears and eyes suddenly alert. When Lorraine waved the dog forward, Reckless was off like a streak.

For the next hour, the dog shoved those balls of fluff from one end of the pasture to the other, his tongue hanging out in happy pants with the effort. He was obviously in his glory.

Thus Thalia entered the flower shop already smiling. She supposed she really should call Luke and tell him how brilliantly his suggestion had worked. She knew he'd been kidding around about the sheep but still—

Miss Pauline looked up from the receptionist's desk, her normally placid face flushed. She held several slips of paper in her hand and others littered the desk.

"My goodness." Thalia's smile slipped. "What's the matter?"

"It's those sheep," Miss Pauline wailed. "Honestly, Thalia dear, what *has* your mother done this time?"

THALIA DIDN'T WANT or need a brand-new crisis while her mother was out of town. All Thalia wanted was to be left alone, without involvement with anyone or anything. She would be leaving Colorado soon. Conflict and confrontation was not what she wanted in her life.

That's what she was getting, though. All hell had apparently broken loose in Shepherd's Pass over the presence of sheep in Shangri-la, or near it, as the case might be. Thalia hadn't even made it through the telephone messages when Emily rushed through the front door.

"Hi, Miss Pauline," she greeted the elderly lady before zipping past to lean breathlessly over the counter where Thalia was reading the messages spread out before her. "Is it true?"

Thalia grimaced. "Is what true?"

"That your mother is starting a sheep ranch at her place."

"A sheep ranch!"

Emily nodded. "I hear she's already got a contract to sell wool to a big sweater manufacturer. She's got a flock of fifty sheep with more to come and—"

Thalia burst into incredulous laughter. "She's

only got two sheep! She bought them to give old Reckless something to do.''

"Her dog?" Emily frowned. "Only two?"

"Right, and right." Thalia shook her head helplessly. "How do these stories get started?"

"Usually with a little grain of truth that quickly becomes the oyster that ate Cincinnati." Emily propped her elbows on the counter. "I don't know if you're aware of it, but this news is literally sweeping through town like a wildfire."

"I'm aware of it, all right." Thalia glanced ruefully at the phone messages. "And as you'd expect during a crisis, Mother's out of town for the day. I don't know what *I'm* supposed to do about this."

"You might start by ducking." Emily rolled her eyes toward the front door. "Because here comes our esteemed mayor now, and I don't think he wants to make you citizen of the day." She backed away. "See you!"

"Emily, don't leave me!"

"Sorry, I've got to get back to my own job." With a wave for Thalia and another for Mayor Kelly and Miss Pauline, she retreated.

Mayor Kelly's ruddy complexion was even redder than usual. He gave Thalia a resentful look. "Young lady, what has your mother done this time?"

"This time?" It was a squeak of dismay.

The mayor nodded. "Whenever we have trouble in this town, we always find Lorraine Myers right smack-dab in the middle of it. But I sure didn't think she'd stoop low enough to terrorize the residents of Shangri-la with sheep!''

A cattleman, huh. Just what Thalia needed. "Look, Mayor Kelly, Mother brought in two sheep—just two. Her reasons had nothing to do with Shangri-la.''

"I find that difficult to believe.''

"Why? Mother isn't interested in annoying her neighbors.'' Thalia hoped. "Just because she's opposed to the second phase of that project doesn't mean—''

"Tell that to all the residents of Shangri-la who have been bombarding me with calls.'' Mayor Kelly thrust a distracted hand through his thin brown hair. "However, I didn't come here to argue.'' He looked around. "I'll have to take this up with Lorraine directly. Is she here?''

"I'm afraid not. She's out of town for the day.''

"Figures.'' He grimaced. "When you see her, tell her that her neighbors are just about ready to send out a posse to take care of those sheep themselves. Sheep are definitely not allowed in that area. Something will have to be done immediately.''

Thalia was getting annoyed. "The rules for Shangri-la don't apply to my mother's property,'' she said stiffly. "I'll give her your message, but I wouldn't hold my breath waiting for her to see it your way.''

"Time will tell.'' Turning, Mayor Kelly marched out of the shop.

"Oh, dear." Miss Pauline looked genuinely distressed. "I can't imagine—"

The telephone rang, cutting her off. Thalia could tell it was another irate caller looking for Lorraine.

Thus it went for the rest of the day. By the time Thalia locked up at five o'clock, she and Miss Pauline were both exhausted. Now she had to walk home, because the pickup wasn't ready and her mother had left a message saying that she wouldn't be home until—

"Can I give you a lift?"

Startled, she looked up into the handsome smiling face of Dr. Luke Dalton. "I don't want to put you out," she said.

"I go home right past your house," he reminded her. "I wanted to stop and make a house call anyway. If I don't miss my guess, I'm going to find one very happy Border collie guarding his own little flock."

Her shoulders slumped. "You heard."

"I think everybody in town knows about this. I was kidding when I suggested sheep, but apparently your mother recognized a good idea when she heard it." He opened the passenger door to his Cherokee and she climbed in.

When he was behind the wheel, she burst out, "Has the world gone mad? You'd think Mother had imported a whole herd of—of buffalo or something, instead of two nice fluffy little sheep. What's up with that?"

"Apparently the homeowner covenants forbid

sheep,'' he said, giving her a sympathetic glance. ''Also pigs and chickens.''

She groaned. ''Don't tell Mother, whatever you do. If they rile her enough, it'd be just like her to go out and bring in anything she can find that's guaranteed to annoy her neighbors.''

''Like pigs and chickens?''

''Exactly like pigs and chickens. But in her defense, she was living there a long time before that housing development was ever built. How can they expect her to abide by their rules?''

He shrugged, but his expression was understanding. ''Don't ask me,'' he said. ''I'm just a simple veterinarian. I like all animals, including sheep.'' He braked at Lorraine's curb. ''Let's go see how Reckless is feeling today.''

''Okay, but I'm not getting close to any more telephones,'' she said, and meant it.

THAT BORDER COLLIE WAS BORN to herd sheep, Luke thought admiringly as he watched the black-and-tan dog maneuver his small flock toward them. The dull eyes and hangdog expression had been replaced by sparkling excitement. As was common with his breed, Reckless slunk along behind almost on his belly, ready to dart right or left to ''reason'' with troublemakers by ''gripping''—snapping at their heels.

Thalia gave Luke a helplessly confused look. ''Did you ever see a happier dog?''

He had to admit, he never had. Reckless came

obediently when called, suffered a swift examination, then, when released, took off after his charges like a streak of black lightning.

Thalia said dryly, "I'd call that a miraculous recovery."

"Yes." They turned back toward the house. "That's all I'm interested in." He slanted an amused glance at her. "Another brilliant diagnosis on my part, you'll notice."

"Brilliant except for the dissention it's created in town. According to Mayor Kelly and my mother's phone calls—"

They rounded the corner of the house and stopped short. Four very large black automobiles lined the street. She turned to Luke in confusion. "What in the world?"

"Unless I miss my guess—" Luke watched his old friend, Mike Forbes, walk toward them across the yard. "Yeah, it's the lawyers. Jeez, they outnumber the sheep. Sorry about that."

"It's not your fault." She frowned. "Is it?"

"Well, it's my mother's fault, I expect. Mike's her attorney—one of them, anyway."

"Good grief, I should have known." She stopped and waited for the lawyer to reach her. Four other, older, men, all carrying briefcases and wearing grim expressions, also closed in.

Mike approached with a cautious smile. "Hi, Luke, Thalia. I saw you two at the meeting the other night but didn't have a chance to say hello."

She nodded. "I saw you, too. Now that the pleasantries are out of the way, I should tell you not to waste any more breath. I have nothing to do with this sheep business—you are here about the sheep.''

''That's right, but—''

''Forget it.'' She backed away, shaking her head. ''You need to speak to my mother.''

''Who is—?''

''Out of town for the day. You'll be able to reach her tomorrow, I expect.''

''I see.'' Mike waved off the rest of what looked like his legal team. ''I'm sorry we bothered you, then, but we wanted to nip this sheep thing in the bud before it went any further. They're illegal here, plain and simple. I'm sure once your mother realizes that, she'll do the right thing.''

''Who do you represent in this, Mike?''

His calm expression gave nothing away. ''Mrs. Dalton and Joe John Jeff Jordan. My colleagues over there represent some of your neighbors.''

''I see.'' She glanced at Luke accusingly. ''Maybe it's time my mother got her own lawyer.''

Mike laughed easily. ''Not over this. It's pretty cut-and-dried. Sheep aren't specifically allowed anywhere inside city limits, so it doesn't actually matter whether this land is in the Shangri-la acreage.''

''It matters to us,'' Luke said.

Mike looked flustered for the first time. ''You're dealing yourself in, Luke?''

"I've almost got to, since the sheep were my idea."

"*Your* idea?" Mike looked taken aback for the first time.

"That's right, and you can pass that word on to your clients. Now if you'll excuse us, Thalia and I have more important things to do." Taking her arm firmly, he escorted her along the walk, up the porch steps and into the house.

Once inside, she turned to him. "Thanks, but I'm as curious as Mike to know what more important things we have to do."

"Just this," he said, pulling her into his arms. "I didn't get to finish my birthday kiss and I'm getting older every day."

SHE COULD GET USED TO THIS. She could get used to being in his arms, to lifting her face for his kiss. She could probably get used to a whole lot more than that if she didn't get hold of herself.

Which she finally did. Stepping back, she said in a breathless voice, "Happy birthday—again. Now can we possibly move on to more important things?"

He looked hurt. "I can't think of much that's more important than that."

"Then you're not trying very hard." She turned away, unnerved by the sight of him all tall and strong and handsome. "About those lawyers—"

"I'll talk to my mother, but they weren't all representing her."

"I know." She added plaintively, "What's so bad about a few sheep, anyway? Why are people getting so excited?"

"Probably because this is just the latest in an escalating difference of opinion. If either side would compromise...but nobody's shown any interest in that approach so far."

She turned back to face him finally, feeling calmer. "Maybe there's a way."

His brows rose. "You've got an idea?"

"No," she admitted, "but maybe if we both thought about it—"

"Thought about what?" Lorraine burst through the front door, lugging a large tote bag overflowing with ribbon and paper.

"Thank heaven, you're home!"

"Uh-oh." Lorraine stopped short. "Something's happened."

"Your sheep happened, Mother. The entire town is in an uproar. I've spent the day fending off politicians and lawyers and neighbors."

"Surely you're exaggerating." Lorraine dropped her bag onto a chair. "I'm starved. I hope you've fixed something for dinner."

"I haven't had time! Luke drove me home because the truck isn't ready yet. We were met by a whole pack of lawyers who—"

The telephone rang. "Hold that thought," Lorraine said, picking up the handset. "Hello? Oh. It's for you, Thalia."

"Me?" Thalia frowned. "If that's more of this sheep business—"

"It's Emily."

"Oh, okay." Thalia accepted the handset. "Hi, Em. What's up?"

"A bunch of us are meeting later at the Watering Hole. I thought you and Luke might like to join us."

"I don't think so—and how did you know Luke was here?"

"I saw him pick you up downtown." Emily giggled. "I didn't mean *pick you up,* I meant give you a ride. Can I speak to him?"

Thalia handed the phone to Luke, who uttered a few noncommittal "uh-huhs" before hanging up. He looked at Thalia expectantly and said, "I told her we'd see her later."

"Forget it. I already told her I wasn't interested."

"You are, though. It's just a bunch of old high school pals getting together for a little drinkin', dancin' and devilry. What's not to like?"

Lorraine looked pleased. "This is just what Thalia needs," she confided in Luke. "What time will you pick her up?"

"Around eight."

"Great. She'll be ready."

"Now wait a minute—"

The phone rang again, and again, Lorraine answered.

Luke said, "I'd better run along. You're busy."

Thalia wanted to urge him to stay but caught herself up short. He was, after all, the son of the enemy. She also had to bring her mother up to speed on the day's events. "All right," she agreed. "Thank you for the ride, and for standing up for me with those lawyers."

"It was nothing," he said modestly. "I was just glad to see old Reckless in such high spirits. See you later." Looking very pleased with himself, he turned and disappeared through the front door.

Lorraine was grinning broadly by the time she hung up the phone. "There!" she said. "The whole town's behind me on this."

"Are you kidding? The whole town's being torn apart by this. You weren't here all day. You didn't see—"

"Thalia, dear, you're a worrywart. That was my Shangri-la It Ain't co-chair and she says we've got 'em on the run. All we've got to do is stand fast."

Thalia groaned. "Believe me, it's not that simple."

"It *is* simple." Lorraine looked suddenly serious. "Thalia, I didn't get those sheep to annoy anybody. They're wonderful animals—gentle as..." She laughed. "Gentle as lambs. I got them to improve the mental health of old Reckless. Speaking of which, how is old Reckless? I hope Luke wasn't making an emergency call."

Thalia shook her head. "He says Reckless has never looked better. That dog spent the day herding those poor sheep from one end of the pasture to the other. At this rate, they'll starve to death by Friday.''

''Wonderful. That was the whole point, wasn't it?''

''Yes, but—''

The telephone rang.

''Let it go,'' Lorraine said blithely. ''I've got to change and then figure out what to fix for supper.''

''I can't stand to hear a phone ringing.''

''The machine will pick up. Don't worry about it. We won't miss anything.'' Lorraine turned to the stairs.

The machine picked up. ''Lorraine Myers, how can you do this to your neighbors? Those sheep have got to go! We won't stand for this—''

Thalia turned abruptly and walked into the kitchen, then out the back door. She felt off stride, out of kilter. It wasn't just the sheep, or the ensuing community uproar; in fact, that was the least of it.

It was Luke.

It was his kiss and his embrace, his sparkling eyes and enticing smile, the warmth and strength of his arms. He was getting to her and she didn't know what to do about it.

Sitting down on the swing suspended between two tree limbs, she slumped dejectedly. Reckless left his miniflock to wander over and lie down at her feet. The look he gave her was triumphant. She suspected it might accurately be the opposite of her own.

And then he got up and loped back to his sheep.

Reckless knew what made him happy. She should be so lucky.

She sighed. She dared not get involved with Luke Dalton! She seemed to lack both willpower and self-discipline where he was concerned. He would break her heart. It had been ever thus.

Leaning back, she clutched the swing chains tightly and pushed off with her feet. She would like to see old friends again. Most of her school memories were happy ones, after all.

She'd been a big fish in a little pond in those days, scurrying around with a serious intent to reform student government—as if it needed it!—and square away every organization to which she belonged. A natural-born reformer, she looked around one day and realized that everybody else seemed to have taken a different path.

*Her* path led to straight A's on her report cards, the presidency of the student council, and leadership positions in every do-gooder project that came along. *Their* paths seemed to lead to "adulthood"; first loves and first lusts.

Best friend Emily had assured Thalia she was simply a late bloomer. "I am, too," Em had confided. "The difference is, I don't care and you do. I'm willing to wait for the perfect romantic hero. You, on the other hand, want to be first—in everything."

Being first among Shepherd's Pass sixteen-year-olds in a race to "adulthood" was out of the question; Thalia had already lost that one. But that didn't mean she hadn't tried to catch up, once she'd realized she must be missing out on something.

She had brooded about it for months before coming up with a plan. She'd turn to Lucas, her brother's best friend, to make her a woman.

Rocking gently on the swing, she closed her eyes and let her head drop back. She could hardly believe what she'd done next—and neither could Luke when she went to him in a completely businesslike way and stated her case.

"I'm probably the last sixteen-year-old virgin at Shepherd's Pass High School," she'd said, adding quickly in the interests of veracity, "or second to the last, at the very least. All I'm asking is your cooperation in overcoming this little...uh...flaw."

"Me?" He looked horrified.

She'd nodded. "I trust you, Lucas. You'd never let anything bad happen." Honesty made her add, "Besides, there's no one else I can turn to."

"Ah, gee, that's a relief." Then he had looked disgusted.

"Then you'll do it?"

"No way! Not a chance!" He'd shaken his head violently from side to side. "You're out of your mind, Thalia. That's not the way it's supposed to happen."

"But I feel stupid! All the other girls are talking about...you know, their love life. And I don't even have a steady boyfriend."

"You don't need a steady boyfriend. You've got lots of time to wait for the right guy to come along.

Don't throw yourself away before you're old enough and smart enough to know what you're doing.''

At that point, it had all become clear. ''I'm not sexy enough,'' she'd said.

''It's not that.''

''I'm not pretty enough.''

''Thalia, you're gorgeous. That has nothing to do with it.''

But she hadn't believed him. She might not be sexy or beautiful but what she was was smart. She'd ambush him, she'd decided. She'd catch him off guard in a situation where he wouldn't be able to turn her down and—

''Thalia! Supper's ready.''

''Coming, Mother.''

She put her feet back on solid ground and stood up. Nothing had turned out the way she planned then, as nothing would turn out the way *he* apparently was planning now.

Sure, she'd go to the Watering Hole with him. She'd laugh and talk with old friends and probably have a terrific time.

What she wouldn't do was pick up with Luke where they'd left off at the Dalton cabin on that long-ago day.

She'd try hard to convince herself that's the way she wanted it.

# 6

"Look, everybody! It's Luke and Thalia!"

Nearly a dozen people looked up from the two large tables pushed together at one edge of the dance floor at the Watering Hole, not the classiest joint in Shepherd's Pass but apparently the most popular. It was so dark Thalia had trouble making out who was there, but when they got closer, she realized that she did, indeed, know just about everyone.

Emily jumped up and made room for two more chairs to be dragged up to the table. "I knew Luke would talk you into coming," she said to her friend. "What'll you have?"

"White wine." Thalia took a seat, waved and smiled at Angeline Adams directly across the table.

"A beer." Luke looked around, one hand on the back of his empty chair and the other on the back of Thalia.

"Hi, Thalia!" Several people left their seats to approach. All were from her high school days. "I heard you were back...Mom told me she saw you the other day. So how long will you be staying?"

Thalia answered the questions with good grace,

although she didn't as a general rule like being questioned this way. But for some reason, it seemed right under these circumstances. She'd known these people forever and she didn't doubt the sincerity of their interest.

Or the sincerity of their curiosity as they zeroed in on Luke's proprietary touch. Thalia supposed she should shrug away from his hand, or even stand up, but there was something infinitely reassuring in his touch.

A three-piece western band struck up a lively tune and Luke's grip tightened. Leaning down, he said, "Let's dance."

Startled, she jerked around to look at him questioningly.

He grinned that coaxing grin. "Please?"

"I...sure. Why not?" With an apologetic smile for the others, she rose and let him lead her onto a dance floor not yet overcrowded with couples. At least the music was fast...but changing, even as he opened his arms to her. She went into them stiffly, wondering if he'd given the musicians some kind of signal.

His arms closed around her tense shoulders and he chuckled deep in his throat. "Relax," he said into her ear, so close the warmth of his breath made her shiver. "I don't bite."

"That's what you *say*."

She couldn't relax when she was this close to him. Impossible. This was the first time they'd danced together and she felt as anxious as a teenager. She was going to step on his foot, she just knew it. She was making a fool out of herself and she was doing it in public.

But something was happening, something she couldn't explain. As he brought her closer, feet that had seemed at odds were suddenly in sync; the metal rod in her back disappeared and she found herself fully in his embrace, moving with him as if she'd been doing it for a lifetime.

"See?" he murmured, and although she couldn't see his expression she could hear the smile in his voice. "Dancing with me isn't all *that* scary."

"That's what you think," she muttered, but she didn't pull away. This was too nice. She'd never danced this well in her life and it had to be her partner. "What are you, Fred Astaire or Svengali?"

"Neither. I'm plain old Luke Dalton, the object of your teenaged affections."

"I wish you wouldn't keep bringing that up."

"Why, when I'm fully prepared to turn the tables on you?"

"Meaning?" The music stopped and so did she. Stepping back, she frowned, trying to figure out—

Emily interrupted the moment, stepping to Thalia's side and clapping enthusiastically. "I love this band," she exclaimed, adding, "Thalia, do you remember Juan Martinez? He was a year ahead of us in school."

Thalia smiled at the darkly attractive man at Emily's elbow. "Of course. Good to see you, Juan."

"Thalia." Juan nodded. "Luke."

"How's your mom's fish?" Luke asked.

"Fish?" Thalia echoed.

Juan laughed. "Goldfish. She took it in to Luke because she said it looked pale. It still looks pale, but at least it hasn't gone belly-up."

They moved off the dance floor in a group, returning to their tables where lively conversations abounded. With a wave, Juan returned to his seat at the other end and the three sat back down.

"Hey, pay attention!"

It was Bill Lovett, who was, according to Lorraine's update, an officer with the Shepherd's Pass Police Department. He stood, holding his beer high while Angeline tried to tug him back down. "In case nobody knows, today is Angie's birthday and she's twenty-*umhpf!*"

For Angie had leaped to her feet and slapped a hand over Bill's mouth.

Thalia joined in the general laughter and well-wishing that was going on, thinking that Emily was right; it was good to be here. These people accepted her back as if she'd never been gone. Maybe there really *was* no place like home.

And then she glanced at Luke and forgot everything else.

SHE WAS HAVING A GOOD TIME.

Nursing a beer, Luke kept a wary eye on Thalia. He didn't want her to be lonely or bored or offended or anything else the least bit negative. He wanted her to have a great time, so she'd realize that this was where she belonged, not back in *California.*

He smothered a smile. It wasn't as if California was a foreign country or anything, but she looked so comfortable and at home trading one-liners with friends and laughing uproariously at—

"So what's funny?"

Luke looked around and saw Mike Forbes standing there, a quizzical expression on his face. Luke shrugged. "Nothing. Everything."

"That covers most of the bases."

"Care to join us?"

"Maybe not. I'm not too popular in some circles."

"You mean because of the sheep?"

"That and...other things." Mike's gaze shifted and he nodded. "How's it going, Emily?"

"Fine," Emily said from behind Luke's shoulder, "no thanks to you."

Luke laughed. "So that's how it is."

Mike shrugged. "What can I say? Maybe she just doesn't like lawyers."

"Lorraine Myers is not too crazy about you these days, either."

"That's a shame," Mike mused. "I always liked *her.*"

"Uh-huh. Tell me the truth, Mike. Are sheep really on the hit list in Shangri-la or are you just trying to scare Lorraine?"

Mike's grin didn't falter. "Sorry, you'll have to

read the covenants yourself or hire your own lawyer to tell you that."

"You're my mother's lawyer. It's the same thing."

"Not quite." Mike backed away, shaking his head.

"Okay, make it hard. But I *will* find out."

"Whose side are you on in this, Luke? Your mother—"

"Are you still here?" Emily glared at Mike again over Luke's shoulder. "Sorry—" she said a hand on Luke's forearm "—but I need to talk to Luke."

"Be my guest." Mike turned away and moved toward the bar, where it appeared he had friends waiting.

Luke looked at Emily, curious about her attitude. "You don't like him much, do you."

She shrugged. "What difference does it make? What I wanted to say is, thank you for getting Thalia here tonight."

"You're welcome."

"She wouldn't have come if you hadn't put on the pressure. I think it's good for her to get out and about, don't you?"

"Yes, but why do you say that?"

"Well, you know—the divorce and all."

"Did you know her husband?" He shouldn't have asked that, just because he wanted someone to assure him that unknown gentleman was a son of a bitch.

"No, but I hear he was a real nice guy."

"Then what went wrong?"

She shrugged. "Irreconcilable differences, I guess. They're still friendly, or at least civil, but that's about it."

That was enough for Luke. He sure didn't want Thalia pining after her former husband.

Strictly for her own good, of course. His motives were pure.

More or less.

"THAT WAS *REALLY* FUN." With a satisfied sigh, Thalia relaxed back against the seat in Luke's Cherokee. "Thanks for badgering me into coming."

"I badgered you? I don't think so." Starting the engine, he backed out of the parking lot of the Watering Hole.

She laughed, feeling more relaxed and at ease than she'd felt in a long time…months, maybe even years. "You know you did, but it's okay. Just don't do it again, okay?"

"I can't do again what I never did in the first place." He glanced toward her, but she couldn't see his expression in the dark interior. "But I'm glad you had a good time."

"I did." *And a lot of it was dancing with you,* she thought. "Did you know Bill and Angie were engaged a while back?"

"I think I heard something about that."

"They called it off, but they seem to be getting back together again. I hope so. They're nice people. They deserve to be happy."

"Everybody deserves to be happy. Me, for example, you for another example."

"I'm happy enough," she said, but she recognized that warning edge to her tone.

He made a right-hand turn. "Why the qualifier—happy *enough?*"

"A figure of speech," she said airily. "I'm deliriously happy. I'm on the fast track, career-wise. I have a mother and a brother I love. My future's bright."

"Your future's lonely. Don't try to kid a kidder, Thalia."

She sat up straight, suddenly annoyed. "I wish you'd quit harping on that, Luke. I'm not lonely. Just because I'm not married…" But then she stopped, because he wasn't talking marriage, he was talking significant other. Or significant lover. Or insignificant one-night stand. Or—

She pressed the heels of her hands to her temples. "I think I'm tipsy."

"*I* don't think so. You couldn't have had more than two glasses of wine over a three-hour period."

"If I'm not tipsy, why do I feel so…so light-headed? I'm…I'm talking silly." *And my thoughts are sillier still.*

"Maybe it's the company you keep."

He pulled over to the curb and she saw they had reached her mother's house. Shutting off the engine, he turned in his bucket seat. She wished she could see his expression, but it was much too dark.

She licked her lips. "I don't know what you mean."

"Sure, you do." He reached for her, cupping a hand possessively over the curve of her shoulder.

This was getting dicey. She grabbed for the handle and flung open the door. "Whatever. Thanks for the ride. I had a really nice time."

"The *ride?*"

His car door slammed. He was coming after her. Heart fluttering in her throat, she skipped through moonlit shadows toward the porch—where he caught up with her and swung her around and into his arms.

"Not so fast. I'm not leaving until I get my goodnight kiss."

"You got fifteen birthday kisses," she said breathlessly. "Let's call one of them your good—"

"Thalia, Thalia, don't be stingy. There's plenty more where they came from."

He tilted her chin and at last she could see his expression, full of humor and determination and...and...she gulped hard. And passion. The same passion she was fighting.

He lowered his mouth to hers and she stood as still as an ice sculpture, an ice sculpture quickly heated to the melting point. When he grabbed her by the waist and hauled her hard against him, she flung her arms around his neck and hung on.

And she kissed him back, as always. It was impossible to do anything else.

At last he lifted his head. "Damn," he said in

an awed tone, "that sure puts the frosting on the cake." Bending, he nuzzled the curve of her shoulder.

"Luke—what are you doing? You can't—"

"I can't?" He left her shoulder to return to her mouth for another soul-searing kiss. "This could be habit-forming, Thalia."

"Unfortunately—" she wrestled her way out of his embrace, breathing hard "—it *can't* be habit-forming. There isn't time."

"I can work fast, when I want to."

"Absolutely not. You're already working too fast for me."

"Ha! I heard what you said."

What *had* she said? She searched her shattered memory banks. "I have no idea what you mean."

"You said unfortunately. *Unfortunately,* it can't be habit-forming. I'm saying, *fortunately,* I'm a fast worker." He took a step toward her, his eyes gleaming even in the uncertain light.

"Luke—"

"Thalia—"

"I've got to go in."

He sighed. "Okay, if you insist. How about lunch tomorrow?"

She was shaking her head before he finished the question.

"I can kiss you until you give in," he threatened.

She couldn't help registering the alarm that possibility gave her, then was humiliated when he chuckled low in his throat. "Oh, all right," she said crossly. "But just lunch, nothing more. You can pick me up here at…is twelve-thirty all right?"

"Absolutely."

"If anything comes up, I'll call. Mom may need me at the shop or…or something."

"Fine."

"It could be late. Two or three, even."

"Thalia, I don't care if you want lunch at nine or at four. Name your time and I'll be there."

She groaned helplessly. "You're a hard man to fight, Luke Dalton."

"Then—" he stepped forward to drop a gentle peck on her flinching cheek "—don't fight me."

She stood there helplessly while he turned back to the Cherokee, moving with a happy nonchalance that made her want to scream. If this was a battle of wits, was she losing ground?

On that scary thought, she dragged herself up the steps and into her mother's house.

"I DON'T HAVE TO ASK if you had a good time."

Lorraine's voice came out of the dark parlor. Thalia, hand on the wall switch, started; light flooded the room.

"Mother! You *scared* me!"

"Sorry." Lorraine stood in the middle of the room, clutching a light seersucker robe around her waist. "I was out back checking on the dog and the sheep when I saw you and Luke drive up. I didn't want to disturb anything."

Thalia groaned. "You're creeping around in the dark so as not to disturb me?"

"No, honey, I'm heading upstairs to bed. I've lived in this house so long I don't need to turn on lights to find my way. So did you?"

"Did I what?"

"Have a good time at the Watering Hole." Lorraine winked one blue eye knowingly. "I know you had a good time once you got back home."

"You were spying on me? I can't believe—"

"Give it a rest." Lorraine brushed aside all opposition. "Why do you think I always left the porch light on when you were out with boys, because I like drawing bugs? Of *course* I spied on you. I'm a mother. It's my job."

Thalia sighed. "At least you're honest."

"What do you mean, at least?" Lorraine laughed. "Seriously, I like seeing you with Luke. He's a great kid."

"He's no kid. Trust me on that." Thalia started for the kitchen and Lorraine followed.

"That's true. How that obnoxious Sylvia could have such a terrific son is beyond me."

"Speaking of Sylvia—" Thalia poked around in the refrigerator and pulled out a bottle of water. "I'd think you'd just as soon Luke stayed away while this sheep controversy is raging."

"Why ever would you think that?" Lorraine looked honestly astonished.

"He is her son, after all."

"But he's on *my* side."

"Against his own mother? I don't think so."

"He's not against his mother, he's for truth and justice. That means he's on my side." Lorraine looked extremely pleased with her conclusions. She headed for the kitchen door. "That being the case, you can kiss him all you want."

*No, I can't,* Thalia thought, glaring at the doorway. *If I did, I'd never get anything else done.*

LUKE LET HIMSELF INTO the house through the back door as quietly as he could, not wanting to disturb his mother. He might as well not have bothered, because there she sat at the kitchen table, a magazine open before her and a cup of something beside it.

She looked up with a bright smile. "Hello, dear. You're home early."

"Not that early." He crossed to the industrial-sized stainless steel refrigerator and looked inside, grabbing a can of soda.

"How's Thalia?"

"She's fine." He popped open the tab on the top of the can and took a big swig of soda. He'd been waiting for his mother to protest his interest in her worst enemy's daughter. Not that Sylvia didn't like Thalia; he was pretty sure she did…at a distance, anyway.

That distance, he thought smugly, was considerably less than it had been.

"She's a nice girl," Sylvia said.

"Go on."

She frowned. "I don't know what you mean."

"I'm waiting for the 'but.'"

She looked offended. "There are no buts."

"Even though she's Lorraine Myers's daughter?"

"Even though." She nodded firmly.

"Now I've heard everything. I thought that at least while this sheep controversy was front page, your feelings would be less than charitable toward that family."

"Silly boy!" Her smile sparkled. "If anything, Thalia's an ally. She'll see the fairness of my cause, I'm sure, and then she'll help bring that stubborn, pigheaded, unreasonable—"

"Easy, Mother, you're hung up on technicalities."

She let out an annoyed breath. "I'm afraid you're right. I just meant to say that when the chips are down, so to speak, Thalia will stand for principle— which is to say, for me."

"I don't believe I'd go that far. Her mother—"

"Don't worry about her mother. I'll take care of Lorraine Myers." Sylvia rose and stood on tiptoe to kiss his cheek. "Good night, sweetheart. I'll see you tomorrow."

Luke watched her go, wondering where all this was going to lead. Because he was relatively certain that Thalia *wasn't* on his mother's side any more than he was. On the other hand, neither of them were exactly on Lorraine's side, either.

There had to be a happy medium somewhere, but he wasn't going to worry about it tonight.

Tonight he was going to take a cold shower and try not to think about Thalia, all warm and wonderful in his arms.

THALIA CHALKED UP her restless night to spring fever. Yes, it was fall instead of spring, but she felt exactly as she had as a teenager staring at the moon and fantasizing about love and romance and a future filled with both.

Only now she knew what "love and romance" included. Pacing around the small bedroom in which she'd grown up, she struggled against images of Luke Dalton...Luke, grinning at her...pulling her into his arms to dance...pulling her into his arms for a kiss....

She groaned and threw herself across the bed. Every molecule in her body tingled with longing. Worse still was the ache in the deepest part of her. Luke had put it there a long, long time ago, back when she didn't even know what it meant.

Now she did, and it was driving her crazy.

LUKE TOOK THALIA to Bob's Barbecue for lunch.

"Not classy," he said cheerfully, "but it's the best food in town."

"I've done classy," she reassured him, reaching for the plastic-coated menu. "This is fine. What do you recommend?"

"Everything." He watched her peruse the menu,

enjoying her enthusiasm. He'd had warm feelings for her for years, but those feelings seemed to be heating up quickly, if something this simple could bring him such pleasure. Clearing his throat, he turned to his own menu.

The middle-aged blond waitress appeared beside the table. "What can I bring you to drink?" she inquired, following that up with, "How's it goin', Doc Dalton?"

He grinned up at her. "Just fine, Jackie. You?"

"Fine," she echoed. "Jeffie's hamster recovered, by the way. That's why we didn't come back."

"I'm glad to hear it. Thalia, what would you like to drink?"

"Iced tea would be fine."

"Make that two. Are you ready to order?"

Thalia closed the menu. "I think I'd like the baked potato with the barbecued pork on top."

"And I'll have the chili and barbecue sandwich special."

"Comin' right up." She ambled away.

Thalia looked around the restaurant, taking in the wooden picnic tables and the checked oilcloth coverings. The only other customers were an elderly couple on the far side of the room.

"At least we missed the noon rush," she said.

"Yes." He leaned forward, hands clutched together on the tabletop to keep from covering her hand with his. "Thalia, I checked with an attorney about the Shangri-la rules and regulations."

She perked up noticeably. "And discovered that—?"

"There's no mention of sheep, pro or con. Horses and cows are on the approved list. Pigs and chickens are on the shi—on the *not* approved list. But sheep aren't mentioned in any way, shape or form."

"Aha!" She pounded a fist on the table. "That means Mom's got it right this time."

"Not exactly. There's the little matter of standard practices. If the majority of the residents of Shangri-la don't want sheep…well, you get the idea."

"But Mom's not even in Shangri-la."

"True, but sheep aren't specifically allowed in town, either. Still, she might win the sheep issue in the end, if she's willing to carry the fight that far. To do that would cost a lot of money and create a lot of hard feelings—make that a lot *more* hard feelings."

"I see what you're getting at." She grimaced. "Honestly, I didn't come home to get all tangled up in sheep and dogs and mothers."

"I sympathize," he said, and he really did. It would be much easier to seduce her…to court her…to do whatever it was he intended to do if she weren't distracted by all those peripheral issues. "I'm having as much mother trouble as you are, if that's any consolation."

She laughed. "It isn't, but thanks for trying. Honestly, Luke, I don't know what I'm going to do with my mother. She seems to be sailing along in

her own little world. Who else would buy pets for
her pet?''

''Someone who listened to her friendly local veterinarian?''

His smile was infectious. ''Or a daughter who
would repeat what was obviously a joking suggestion? I'm not going to blame you for this.''

Jackie arrived with their drinks, shortly thereafter
with their food. Only after they'd eaten did they
return to the question of mothers.

Thalia broached the subject. ''I meant it when I
said my mom's a real problem. I love her and want
to support her, but I don't think she's *entirely* in
the right this time.''

He nodded, equally serious. ''Same with my
mother. Too bad neither one is interested in compromise. It's shaping up like a battle to the end.''

''I'm afraid so,'' she agreed miserably. ''Honestly, I don't know what to do with her.''

Struck by sudden inspiration, he straightened.
''Damn, I've got the answer. I know exactly what
I'm going to do with my mother.''

She looked at him with admiration. ''This I can't
wait to hear.''

He grinned. ''It's simple. I'm going to buy a
house of my own. I should have done that long
ago.''

''That may work for you, but it won't do much
for me.''

''Sure it will.'' Taking a deep breath, he also
took a leap of faith. ''Would you like to be my
roommate?''

# 7

"WOULD I...WHAT?" Thalia stared at Luke uncertainly.

"Move in with me." She hadn't gone ballistic, so he might be on to something here. Luke gave her a cocky smile that didn't entirely reveal his true feelings. "Of course, you couldn't have your own room, but anything else you want would be—"

"Of all the nerve!" She flattened both palms on the tabletop, her eyes flashing. "I was trying to discuss a serious problem and you have to get funny."

"I'm not being funny," he protested. "Trust me—I'm dead serious."

"Not if you know what's good for you." Her blue eyes had turned frosty. "Lucas Dalton, you're incorrigible!"

"Yeah." He cocked his head and regarded her hopefully. "It occurs to me that the lady is protesting entirely too much. In fact, unless I'm completely off base—and I rarely am—you're just as hot for me as I am for you, Thalia Mitchell. And you have been for years. Surely you recall wrapping yourself in that shower curtain and—"

"I *have* forgotten that," she yelled at him, "and

I'd thank you to do the same. I am *not* hot for you! Maybe I was once, a long time ago, but I was young and foolish. No way will I make a fool of myself all over again.''

"Really?'' He regarded her dubiously. "Or is it that you're so unaccustomed to being spontaneous that you don't have the guts to go for what you really want.''

"I'll show you what I really want.'' And she stormed out.

But she still didn't convince him.

LIFE IN SHEPHERD'S PASS was not the peaceful bucolic vacation Thalia had imagined when she gave in to her mother's pleas. Not only was the sheep rebellion picking up momentum, Lucas Dalton was exerting implacable pressure on her, even when he wasn't around.

Okay, she argued with herself, Luke was exciting and interesting, but then, she knew that a long time ago. What she hadn't recognized in her youth and naiveté was how truly sexy he was. In fact, he was the sexiest man she'd ever met and so much fun to be with that it scared her.

Why was he interested in her, anyway? Probably because he knew she'd be leaving soon and he could come on to her without fearing the nearly inevitable "strings.'' A summer romance…autumn romance…whatever.

She paused with one hand poised over a doorbell, a brilliant assortment of roses and baby's breath in the other. Could Luke be right? Could she be passing up the opportunity of a lifetime to assuage her battered ego in the aftermath of divorce? Was great sex exactly what she needed at this particular point in—

"Hi, Thalia. Are those flowers for me?"

Thalia pulled herself back to the present and thrust out the bouquet with a bright smile. "Happy birthday, Mrs. Pulaski, and many happy returns."

Walking back to the delivery van, she wasn't thinking about Mrs. Pulaski. She was thinking about Luke and what it would be like if she gave up and gave in.

THALIA SAW HIM everywhere she turned. He dropped by the flower shop nearly every day, true, but he was also at all the public meetings on the sheep issue. He drove up to the Chinese restaurant as she walked out with a bag full of Moo Goo Gai Pan; he was already at the gas station when she drove in and at the post office when she drove out.

She'd think he was deliberately harassing her except that wasn't possible, considering the circumstances. It seemed strangely serendipitous, actually, and this possibility made her heart beat faster. She didn't welcome the feeling of inevitability that was slowly settling over her.

Sharing a brown-bag lunch with Emily at the Sew Bee It, Thalia tried her best to appear carefree and relaxed, but her friend wasn't buying it. After a few desultory tries at conversation, Emily put down her peanut butter and jelly sandwich and pursed her lips.

"Okay, out with it. What's got you so distracted?"

"Nobody—I mean, nothing."

"Aha! Then it is Luke."

"It isn't Luke." Thalia's shoulders slumped dejectedly. "Or maybe it is."

"I hear he's looking for a place of his own," Emily said, picking up her sandwich again. "Wonder how that sits with his mother."

"That's why he's doing it."

"Really? Funny you'd know that when you've gone to such pains to avoid him while insisting there's nothing going on between the two of you."

"There isn't, Em, honestly."

"If you believe that—" Emily's expression plainly said that only a self-deluded dingbat would believe such a story. Her smile lightened her words. "I'm not trying to give you advice, or maybe I am, but I think Luke's got to you big time. Maybe you should do something about that."

"Such as?"

"I have no idea, Thalia. Only you can say how far you're willing to go. But I do know that if you don't work this out, it's going to completely ruin your vacation. I'd really hate to see that happen."

Thalia would hate that, too. Slowly she formed her thoughts into words. "I'm restless, Em." She sighed. "Maybe I really do need a mad fling, a wild adventure to remember in my old age."

"Is that what you think is going on here?" Emily shook her head in disbelief. "Thalia, we're talking about a journey you mapped out on your sixteenth birthday, not some quickie affair."

Where had that sense of inevitability come from? "I seem to remember you egging me on the last time, too," Thalia said glumly.

Emily laughed. "I was young, too, not to mention romantic. I still am—romantic, I mean. Besides, Luke's a great guy. I wouldn't mind seeing two of my favorite people getting together."

"Temporarily."

"Or permanently."

"Forget it." Thalia picked up her empty paper sack and crumpled it in her hands. "I'm going back to California in a matter of weeks. Nothing could come of it."

"Maybe nothing would come of it, regardless. Or maybe something will." Emily shrugged. "Can you leave here not knowing?"

*CAN I?* Thalia wondered on her way back to Lorraine's Pretty Posies. *Can I leave and never know what it would be like...with Luke?* Maybe she should sleep with him, if only to get over this itch before she went back to her real life—

"Hi, Thalia. Have you had lunch?"

At the very first word, a shiver of awareness shot through her. Slowly she turned to face Luke, just exiting the Paper Sack. "I ate with Emily."

"That's me, a day late and a dollar short."

Not where she was concerned. To her, he was cutting edge and plenty solvent. "Not hardly," she said.

"If that's a compliment, I thank you." He fell in beside her, swinging the paper bag. "Can I walk you back to the shop?"

"All right."

"How's everything going? I haven't seen much of you lately."

She gave him a sharp glance. "Are you kidding? You seem to show up everywhere I go."

"That doesn't count. I mean I haven't spent any time with you."

"Everything's going fine."

"I *want* to spend time with you. Let's go to a movie tonight."

"I don't think so." Weak. She was weak.

"We could go out to dinner."

"I promised Mother I'd cook tonight."

"I could drop by there, then. Have dinner, take a look at Reckless—"

"You know Reckless is doing great."

"Yes." He frowned. "Thalia, I don't know what good it does to have you back in town if you're going to avoid me."

They'd reached the door to the flower shop. She turned to face him, too aware of his closeness. His skin was smooth and tanned, his eyes clear and probing. She could get lost in those eyes. She took a hasty breath. "You make me nervous, Luke," she burst out.

"You're kidding." He looked honestly shocked. "How, when we've known each other forever?"

"Not as adults," she blurted.

"Ah." The light dawned. "You're talking sex, and the fact that you'd like to sleep with me but, for some reason I've been unable to fathom, have decided to be stubborn about it."

"Believe me, it's not mere stubbornness. It's…"

Fear. It was fear. She was afraid to let him get any closer to her—emotionally or physically—because she wasn't about to change her life plan to accommodate his presence in it.

"What, Thalia? What were you about to say?"

"Nothing," she said, hastily turning away, too aware of the agitated pace of her breathing. "You can drop by after dinner and have dessert with Mother and me, if you want to."

"I want to."

"See you later, then." She entered the shop, feeling as if she were leaving the field in utter defeat.

THALIA ROASTED A CHICKEN and made a huge salad for supper. For dessert, she baked a pineapple upside-down cake, John's favorite. If her brother liked it, Luke probably did, too.

She'd stopped kidding herself that she didn't care about Luke's likes and dislikes. He'd invaded her consciousness to an appalling degree. More and more, she was taken with the notion of simply sleeping with him and getting it over with.

She laughed out loud and Lorraine, just entering the kitchen, gave her daughter a curious look.

"Something's funny? I could use a laugh."

Thalia shook her head, still amused at thinking of sex with Luke in terms of "getting it over with." In all likelihood, she never would. But her mother looked unhappy so she said, "Now what?"

Lorraine sighed and took a seat. "Just more of the same. Those Shangri-la people are impossible. Greed, that's all it is. Greed."

"Surely there's room for compromise." Thalia lifted the golden brown chicken onto a platter.

"Not in this lifetime." Lorraine gritted her teeth ferociously. "I'll fight them to their last breath, I swear I will."

"You *do* need a laugh," Thalia countered. "Maybe if both sides would lighten up, this could be resolved."

"Lighten up! None of those people know how to lighten up, starting with that Sylvia Dalton."

"How about Four-Jay? He looks like a man who'd enjoy a good laugh."

Lorraine looked confused. "You're right. He does. I'm not sure about him, to tell you the truth." Her ferocious expression returned. "But I'm not holding my breath as long as he's mixed up with *her.*"

No need to ask who *her* was.

THALIA AND LUKE SAT on the front porch glider to eat their pineapple upside-down cake. Lorraine had already had her dessert and excused herself to work on "the sheep question."

Luke looked pleased. "You remembered," he said, then took a big bite of cake.

"Remembered what?" His shoulder pressed against hers, warming her—surprising her. She hadn't thought the glider was so small.

"That this is my favorite dessert."

Her glance was doubtful. "It is?"

"Don't pretend you forgot," he teased. "I don't believe in coincidence, do you?"

"I did until recently." The cake was good. She licked crumbs off her fork, concentrating on that. Trying to concentrate on that.

Luke finished the large square of cake in about four gulps. "Can I have more?"

She laughed. "You can have all you want."

"Would that it were true." And suddenly they weren't talking about cake any longer. He curved a hand over her denim-clad thigh.

She started but didn't otherwise repulse his move. Instead she avoided looking at him by focusing all her attention on the growing shadows beyond the porch.

After a moment, he said, "Tomorrow's Saturday and Doc Miller's on call. Let's go for a drive."

Surprised, she faced him. "A drive? Where?"

He shrugged. "Anywhere. Into the mountains. Somebody told me the other day the aspens are beginning to turn."

"Already?"

"It's October—later than you think." Silence quivered between them for a few moments, and then he said gently, "So would you like to go?"

And she said equally quietly, "Yes, I think I would. Thank you for asking." She met his gaze squarely, not retreating from what was going on. Even when his hand tightened slightly on her thigh, she didn't react.

A NERVOUS THALIA PACKED a lunch and was waiting when Luke drove up in the Jeep Cherokee the next morning. Lorraine had already gone to the shop so there had been no one to see her anxiously pacing while she waited.

His smile warmed her, calmed her. "All ready?"

"All ready." For anything.

She hoped.

THALIA HAD SUPPOSED he'd head straight for the Dalton cabin overlooking Shepherd's Pass, but he didn't. Instead he pointed the Jeep north into the highways and byways that led through mountain passes and valleys.

Green and gold beauty surrounded them. Rushing streams appeared and disappeared beside the road, a stark contrast with the dry and rocky creek beds she'd become accustomed to seeing in Southern California.

Dorothy had it right; there was no place like home.

"Oh, look!" She pointed toward a deer disappearing into the trees, its white tail waving high. Immediately he pulled to the side of the road and she jumped out. The deer was gone, but beaver dams on the other side of the water were equally interesting.

He touched her arm and pointed to the sky. Above the treetops, two eagles soared free.

Her heart soared with the majestic birds. *This is so right,* she thought with a certain resignation. *Whatever happens, this is right.*

The aspens were just beginning the annual change from green to gold, but whatever their color, they were gorgeous with their quivering leaves and slender white trunks. Walking among them, she felt a sense of calm engulf her.

It was the same inevitability that had grown on her since her return. Now she had to wonder if she'd come back to Colorado for Luke, even more than for her mother. Maybe this was where she was supposed to be.

Now, anyway. Don't forget that, she warned herself. Nothing's changed, in the long run.

From the position of the sun, she sensed the change of direction as he drove in a wide circle back toward Shepherd's Pass. Still, she wasn't quite prepared when he turned down a small, unpaved road and drove into the clearing before the Dalton cabin.

"Well, look where we ended up," he drawled, a grin hovering around the corners of his mouth. "Does that beat all or what?"

She could laugh or yell. She laughed. "What a surprise. Do I get to go inside and look around? I didn't have much of a chance to do that the last time I was here."

She could tell she'd surprised him and it pleased her. "I was hoping you'd ask," he said. "Here's the key." He pulled the key ring from the ignition and offered it to her. "Help yourself."

She took it, her fingers brushing his. Now that she was no longer fighting her natural inclinations, she could enjoy the byplay between them. He followed her to the front door of the log cabin, as she knew he would, and then inside. While she passed through the rustically furnished living room, he turned right into the kitchen and let her explore on her own.

She knew her brother John had been to the cabin many times—right up until he and Luke got into trouble for holding a beer blast here when they were seventeen. That had pretty much cut off John's visiting privileges.

The only time Thalia had been here, she'd been so nervous she barely remembered anything about the living room, the kitchen, the two bedrooms. What she really remembered was the bathroom, where she'd fled, naked, upon hearing Luke's step on the porch.

She'd planned to greet him in the altogether, thus inflaming his animal passions to the point where he'd be putty in her hands. At the last moment, she'd lost her nerve and run into the bathroom.

There she'd dragged down the vinyl shower curtain to wrap around her shivering frame.

Once so decorated, she got hold of herself again. She could clearly remember herself thinking that this was even better. There had to be something sexy about a naked girl in a shower curtain, right? It could still work. She had heard him outside the door, calling cautiously, "Who's in there? Speak up—"

How had he known she was in there? She'd hidden her mother's car a mile down the road, in the trees. But he was sounding more and more angry, so she'd figured she better do something.

That's when she'd flung open the bathroom door and jumped out, clutching her shower curtain and shouting, "Surprise!"

He'd taken one look at her and exploded into laughter, laughter quickly gone when she angrily dropped the shower curtain.

But that was then and this was now. She'd been humiliated, but it was time to let it go. Otherwise, she wasn't going to be able to pull off what she'd decided to do.

Besides, the bathroom curtain had been changed. Gone was the clear blue vinyl. In its place hung an elaborate brown fabric curtain.

Where had that been when she needed it?

She found him in the kitchen, poking around at shelves and cabinets. When she entered, he looked around with a cautious smile. "Everything like you remembered?"

"All except the shower curtain. That's different."

"I guess so." He seemed to relax, then, as if they'd passed some hurdle. "I'm sorry I laughed at you, Thalia. It was rotten of me, but I was just so surprised. I didn't know what else to do."

She smiled, although she felt her cheeks warming. "In retrospect, I guess I can't blame you. I'd planned such a careful seduction, but I panicked when the time came. I must have looked pretty silly, wrapped in plastic that way."

"*Silly* wasn't the word that leaped immediately to mind." He leaned back against a counter and crossed his arms over the red plaid shirt. "You'll never know how tempted I was, Thalia."

"You're right, I'll never know. You didn't look tempted at all, to me."

"I *was*." He said it with explosive emphasis. "Hell, most kids are easily tempted. But it was more than that," he added. "I'd never thought of you...that way. It was a shock to realize you were more than my best buddy's little sister. Much more."

She liked the way he said it: *much more*. "Not enough to get my way," she countered.

"I don't go around deflowering virgins," he said, sounding a little stiff for the first time. "Don't get me wrong, I was flattered. But, jeez, I was too old and—"

"—I was too young, yada yada. Spare me." She waved away the rationalization she'd heard so many times. "It was a dumb idea anyway."

"It was a *young* idea. I never held it against you."

"Why would you? You *should* have been flattered. I, on the other hand, was crushed."

"Was there a way I could have handled it differently, then? I've wondered. I mean, the laughing wasn't cool—"

"It certainly wasn't." She rolled her eyes. "I should have taken the hint and kept my mouth shut."

"Not you. You had it all figured out. Even back then, you were serious with a capital *S*. I could tell you'd rehearsed exactly what you wanted to say."

"I admit it." How young and innocent that girl had been when she arrived at this cabin—and equally young and innocent when she left. "I also admit I felt like the most total fool in the world when you patted me on the head and told me to run along." She grimaced. "Do you suppose it's time for me to let go of my disgrace and move on?"

"Depends on what you mean by 'move on.'" He straightened away from the counter, suddenly alert. "If you mean let go of the past, I'd say yes."

"That's what I meant, all right." The air in the kitchen seemed suddenly thicker. Licking her lips, she glanced at the picnic hamper on the table. "Good," she said brightly. "You brought in the food."

"You're thinking about food?"

"It's past lunchtime, so…yes, I'm thinking of food. You brought drinks?" She walked to the table and put a shaky hand on the basket of food.

"I'll get them, if you insist."

"I insist." She took a deep breath. "I need a little time, Luke. Let's have lunch, okay?"

So they had lunch.

SHE'D BROUGHT THE LAST of the pineapple upside-down cake. Luke figured that was some sort of signal, that and the fact that she'd come here at all.

She seemed different, he thought, picking up a sticky chunk of cake. Easier, more relaxed. Never in his wildest dreams had he ever imagined they'd be able to talk about what had happened—and do it at the scene of the crime, no less.

She'd reached some sort of decision, he realized as they ate and talked and laughed. Either she would or she wouldn't and he'd soon know which.

He finished the cake and licked his fingers. "That was great," he said.

"Thank you."

They were silent for a few moments, and she began to gather plastic wrappers and cardboard containers to return to the basket. He watched for a moment and then he blurted, "About what I said the other day—"

She stopped short, her hand poised gracefully with a crumpled napkin above the basket. "What?"

"The other day when I said I was going to move out of my mother's house and into my own."

She nodded and said a questioning, "Yes?"

"And I asked you to move in with me. You do remember that, right?"

"I remember." She clamped her lips together.

"I wasn't just being a smart-ass."

"If I'd thought that, I wouldn't have been so annoyed."

"You weren't annoyed, you were upset." He cocked his head and looked at her through shuttered eyes. "Because I meant it and you knew that."

"I suppose I did." Her lashes fluttered down to shield her eyes.

"I didn't intend to insult you or...or anything." He hesitated. "But I don't know why that made you so mad, to be perfectly honest."

"Is that an apology?"

"Yeah, I guess it is. Sort of."

She looked up suddenly, and she was smiling. "Then I accept."

"Okay. So you gonna tell me why you were so mad?"

"Because I'm not going to be around long enough to move in anywhere with anyone—not that

I would anyway. I was shocked you'd even suggest it. Shacking up is not my thing.''

He winced. ''Jeez, hit me again.''

''When I move in with a guy,'' she continued implacably, ''it'll be after I get a ring on this finger.'' She pointed to the third finger of her left hand. ''I'm in no hurry to do that, you understand.''

''Shacking up, huh.'' That one stopped him even colder than the reference to marriage. ''That means living together. Does it also cover a little messing around?''

She drew in a deep, forceful breath. ''If it did, would I be here, Mr. Dalton?''

It took an instant for that to sink in. When it did, he surged to his feet and in a second, had her in his arms. ''Does that mean what I think it means— damn, what I *hope* it means?''

Her mysterious smile rocked him. ''What do you think…and hope…it means?''

''That you've finally faced facts. You and me…happily horizontal and all that.''

She laughed. ''Oh, Luke,'' she murmured, ''shut up and kiss me.''

He didn't need a second invitation. Sliding an arm around her neck, he took her mouth in a kiss that seared him—her, too, judging by her response.

She moaned and pressed her forehead into the curve of his shoulder. ''I can't believe we're here and in each other's arms,'' she murmured, turning her head so her lips brushed against the supersensitized skin of his throat. "There was a time when I thought we couldn't even be friends."

"Will wonders never cease." He tilted her face so he could kiss her eyelids, her cheeks. "Thalia, I want you—"

A ringing noise cut into his impassioned words and she murmured, "I'm hearing bells. Isn't that supposed to mean something?"

He touched her breast lightly. "I think it means you're in love, or at least in serious like."

"Yes, that's what—" She heard the sound again and straightened slightly, frowning foggily. "What *is* that?"

Reality hit him and he drew a shuddering breath. "I think it's my beeper."

"Oh, Lord." She pushed tousled blond hair away from her flushed cheeks. "I guess you'd better answer it."

"Do I have to?" But of course, he did have to. Lives could depend on it.

SO WHAT WAS SHE GOING TO DO when he came back to take up where they'd left off? They'd been about two steps away from the bedroom and it was as much her doing as his—more, actually. She'd made up her mind to do this thing, but that was in the coolness of rational thought. Lost somewhere between that and the heat of passion, she wasn't at all sure which way she was going to jump.

He reentered the room, his expression dark.

"What?" she asked.

"Emergency. One of Emily's cats just met a very large dog up close and personal. Doc needs me to do the surgery."

Her heart dropped; her heart soared; her stomach clenched. She was both relieved and bitterly disappointed, but she nodded as if it didn't matter one way or the other.

# 8

EMILY WAS PACING around the waiting room at the animal clinic when Thalia and Luke entered. She rushed forward, her eyes wild.

"It's Rosie," she cried, clutching Luke's sleeve. "Poor baby. She was minding her own business when this awful *dog* attacked her." She said *dog* as if it were an expletive that should be deleted. "Doc Miller says she's pretty beat up. You've got to save her, Luke! You've got to!"

"Take it easy, Emily." He patted her hand, his manner and voice calm and reassuring. "How about letting me take a look before I give you a prognosis, okay?"

"Of course." She drew a trembling breath, seeming to take heart from his unruffled strength. "I'll wait right here."

"I'll wait with you," Thalia promised, prying Emily's hand from Luke's arm. "You've got to let him do his job now."

"Yes." Emily's mouth trembled. "Luke, you'll tell me as soon as you know, won't you?"

"Absolutely." He cast a grateful glance at Thalia

and hurried through the door leading to the examining rooms.

Thalia drew Emily toward a chair. There were only two other people in the waiting room and they watched with silent sympathy.

Emily sank into a chair and covered her face with her hands. "I just hate dogs," she moaned, her voice muffled. "All they do is *bite* things."

"A few of them herd sheep," Thalia said, hoping to lighten the situation.

"Yes," Emily snapped, "and they bite the sheep while they're at it." She dropped her hands into her lap and drew a shaky breath. "I'm sorry, Thale, that wasn't fair. Your mom's dog is very nice, as dogs go. But this dog—" She shuddered. "He's a big ugly stray. He caught Rosie in the front yard, in the open—no trees handy for escape. I had an awful time driving the vicious beast away."

"You're lucky you weren't hurt doing it," Thalia said, alarmed.

"Ha! I wish he *had* bitten me. Then I could have him sent to the dog pound where he belongs. As it is…" She drew a great shuddering breath. "Poor Rosie is in there fighting for her life and that monster is running around free as the breeze. It's not fair!"

"Few things in life are."

"Oh." Emily frowned. "Uh, you were with Luke when he got the call?"

Thalia nodded.

"Doing what?"

"Emily!"

"No, I mean—where were you?"

"That's an even more provocative question."

"I don't see—" Emily's eyes widened. "Thalia Renee Mitchell, were you at the Dalton cabin?"

"I cannot tell a lie—yes."

"Oh, my gosh!" Emily jumped up, then sat down again. "I don't believe it. You...Luke...the cabin where...and I interrupted..." She looked on the verge of tears. "I am *so* sorry."

Thalia patted her friend's hand, grateful that at least she seemed momentarily distracted. "Not to worry. You didn't do it on purpose and neither did Rosie."

"Even so—"

"Emily, I've looked at Rosie and—"

At the sound of Luke's voice, all color seemed to drain from Emily's face. "Oh, God, will she be okay? Please tell me she'll be okay!"

"She'll be fine, once we get her patched up. She's got a busted foreleg and one of her ears was nearly chewed off. She's got a wound..."

While Luke explained, Thalia sat there holding her friend's hand and marveling at Dr. Lucas Dalton, D.V.M. He spoke with such confidence, such calm authority, that it would be impossible not to be comforted. Stealing a look at Emily, Thalia saw her friend begin to relax.

And this was the same man who'd held Thalia in his arms and swept her away on a sensuous tide of emotion. She closed her eyes, remembering the way he'd made her feel: completely out of control and in his power.

This would never do. As Rosie the black cat had escaped the jaws of disaster, so had Thalia. She was not emotionally ready for an affair. She'd never had one and now she knew why: she couldn't handle it. She needed the safety net of commitment and there'd been no talk of that with Luke, fortunately.

*Because she was going back to California.*

End of discussion.

EMILY WOULDN'T LEAVE until she could see Rosie for herself, cast and all. The cat was still groggy, but Em didn't care, showering Luke with gratitude and thanks.

Which always made him uncomfortable. He was a doctor, not a god. But he tried to be gracious, finally sending her on her way with promises of a speedy recovery for her feline friend.

When he waved Thalia into his office, she came willingly. Good sign, he tried to convince himself, although there was something different about her. Something had changed between the cabin and this moment and he didn't think the change would be in his favor.

He closed the door and tried to take her into his arms—tried and failed, for she stepped away adroitly. He frowned. "What's going on?" he asked, his tone more blunt than he'd intended.

"I'm not ready to have an affair," she said, just as bluntly.

"A moot point if Emily's cat hadn't run afoul of that dog, resulting in a really unfortunate interruption."

"But she did and it wasn't." She half turned. "It was a lucky break for me, Luke. It gave me time to realize I'm just not ready to take our...our relationship beyond friendship. I won't deny that I find you...almost irresistible...but—" She squared her shoulders, the old determined Thalia he knew resurfacing.

"You're resisting me." He advanced upon her.

She retreated. "Don't think it's easy."

"I don't want it to be easy. I want you, and I'm gonna have you."

"Luke, I warn you—" She faced him, eyes darting sparks.

He held up his hands, all innocence. "You don't need to warn me. I'm not going to make this decision, you are. But I might point out while we're chatting, that your protests are too little and too late. We both confronted the truth up there at that cabin not three hours ago. Don't try to sell me a line of bull, sweetheart."

"I never would," she lied with dignity.

"I'll return the favor by promising you that I *will* show you the error of your ways, with your full compliance, of course. We've got unfinished business, Thalia. I mean to correct that before you—" He stopped short, realizing he didn't want to acknowledge the possibility—she would say certainty—that she would be leaving again in just a few weeks.

He'd thought he'd reconciled himself to her eventual departure. Now he realized this train of thought had been derailed when he wasn't at the switch.

THALIA KNEW Luke was turning up the heat.

The looks he gave her, public and private, sizzled; she began to worry that everyone would notice and start talking. Everything he said to her was filled with double entendre, every touch intimate and promising more, no matter how innocent or helpful it might seem on the surface.

At what had turned into a weekly public meeting about the Shangri-la situation, he slipped into the seat next to hers and his thigh brushed hers, setting off warning alarms. When they rose to leave later, he touched her elbow courteously, and it was all she could do not to lean into him for more of that glorious contact.

He'd turned their former tension-packed relationship up another notch. It was almost more than she could bear. So she turned to Emily, who was still ecstatic with the release of her cat from the hospital.

"Emily, I've got this problem—"

"You've come to the right place. Just let me make sure Rosie's all right. Isn't it incredible, the job Luke did? He saved her life, Thalia, he really did. There's nothing I wouldn't do for that man. Honestly, he's the best veterinarian in the world and

I'll never be able to repay him for saving my cat. Now, what can I do for *you?*''

"Nothing." Thalia sighed. "I was just wondering whether to fix lasagna or enchiladas for dinner..."

*...and whether I should give in and sleep with the doctor you're canonizing.*

A WEEK LATER, that decision was made. She couldn't go on like this any longer. She'd spoken to her office and knew she'd be returning to California near the end of October or the first of November. With that finite date staring her in the face, she finally managed to convince herself that if Luke wanted to be used that way, who was she to say nay?

With that rationalization squarely in mind, she made her way to his office on a Friday evening just about the time she knew he usually finished for the day. Sure enough, she was waiting when he walked out the door and headed for the parking lot.

She stepped to his side and took his arm. "Can I buy you a drink, big boy?"

He gaped at her as if he'd never seen her before. "Is that you under there somewhere, Thalia?"

She laughed. "Sure is. I've got a proposition for you and I think it'll best be made over a drink."

"The last time you made me a proposition, I bungled it so bad that it took us years to get over it—if we are."

"That's because I didn't get the answer I wanted. This time will be different."

"You sure?" But he let her lead him toward the Cherokee.

"Pretty sure. Let's go to the Watering Hole and find out."

So they did.

"*I'LL* TAKE THE CHECK." Thalia snatched the slip of paper off the small tray the waitress had automatically set in front of Luke. "This was my idea."

Luke, still reeling from what appeared to be a change of fortune, gave her a cautious smile. "Not the only one you've had lately, obviously."

"That's true." She picked up the glass of red wine and sipped, then sighed. "I needed that."

"Yeah, well…" He, too, drank, but warily. He didn't want to rush her into anything—at least, he didn't *think* he did. "Nice weather we've been having lately."

"Very nice. I'll bet the leaves at the cabin are beautiful."

"Probably." What was she getting at this time? He stared at his beer as her answer slowly sank in. "What did you say?"

"That the leaves—"

"You want to go back to the cabin?"

"I've thought about it."

"Even if you've never known that place as anything but a passion pit?"

She laughed, but didn't back off. "Yes."

"With me?"

"Well, not alone!" For the first time she seemed a little flustered and her cheeks grew pink.

He was still having trouble taking in her change of attitude. He leaned back against his chair, keeping his attention square on her. "Keep talking."

"Yes, well…" She bit her lip. "I want to sleep with you, Lucas."

The calmness of her reply made his gut clench. She'd obviously given this a great deal of thought. He swallowed hard. "I wouldn't mind sleeping with you, either," he said in a gravelly voice.

That brought a tilt to her full lips, but she wasn't finished yet. "Specifically, I'd like to spend the weekend with you at the cabin."

"Done."

"Not so fast. I'm not looking for, nor do I want, some romantic interlude."

"You don't? Then what?"

She shook her head firmly. "What's going on between us is strictly sex, Luke. You know it and I know it."

"Maybe you know it, but I…I don't know sic 'em at this point. You've blindsided me, lady."

"Well, good for me," she drawled. "It's not often I get the upper hand with you."

"You've got the upper hand now," he said fervently. "So you want a hot and steamy weekend of unbridled sex. Do I have that right?"

She nodded. "We're going up there to finish what we started more than ten years ago, and then—that will be that.'' She sounded grim, as if this were an onerous duty but somebody had to do it.

She wanted to sleep with him and then kiss him off? She wanted to scratch her itch and then wave bye-bye? Another man might be pissed off about that. Another man might tell her two could play that game.

Another man might not be in love with her. That realization sent a jolt all the way down to the soles of his feet. Another man might not even have a plan like the scheme that burst full-blown into Luke's muddled head.

What he said to her was, "Tomorrow's Saturday. Is that too soon?''

And was gratified by the way she caught her breath and how her voice trembled when she said, "Tomorrow will be f-fine.''

THALIA INSISTED ON DRIVING her own car up to the cabin.

No way did she intend to be at his mercy. If this didn't work out, she wanted her own wheels nearby so she could get away.

Nervous as she was on the drive up the mountain, she might decide to bolt before she even got in the door. This was crazy and she was crazy to suggest it. But what else could she do when he was like a flame to her moth?

Well, in all honesty, she could go back to California early. Why hadn't she thought of that before?

Her mother needed her, of course. That was the reason she hadn't already flown away. With this sheep controversy picking up steam, Thalia needed to hang around as long as she could. Yes, that was it.

She pulled into the clearing before the cabin and parked next to Luke's Cherokee, turning off the engine of the car she'd borrowed from her mother. Lorraine was driving the ancient pickup truck today and had no idea what her daughter was up to. Not that she'd object. She'd probably celebrate.

Gritting her teeth, Thalia stared at the cabin. Framed by autumn's blazing colors, it looked like a fairy cottage in the wood. Inside, it was simply a plain old cabin, she reminded herself, a little musty from disuse, a little dusty from neglect.

Just the way she wanted it. No frills, no romance, just sex. Taking a deep breath, she threw open the car door and climbed out.

At last, she thought. Finally.

This was no time to chicken out.

She barely paused at the front door, just jerked it open and rushed inside. She didn't want to think anymore. She was all thought out. It was time for action. It was time—

To stop short and stare.

HE'D THROWN CAUTION to the wind and gone all out.

Sure, he'd heard her conditions: no romantic interlude, just sex. Early on he'd decided, to hell with that! He'd do this his way and she could like it or lump it.

But he was sure she was going to like it, after she got over being mad.

Still, he hadn't expected her utter shock as she took in his "improvements"; containers of flowers everywhere, boxes of chocolates strewn around, fresh strawberries heaped in plastic bowls—the only kind of bowls he could find in the kitchen. There was also a bottle of champagne chilling in a tin water bucket, and plenty more where that came from.

"*Lucas!* How could you?"

"It was easy," he said. "I got the flowers from your mom and the chocolates came from—"

"That's not what I mean and you know it." She looked on the verge of tears, not exactly the reaction he'd wanted. "I told you I didn't want anything special."

"Honey…" He let the word roll out rich and full. "*This* isn't special. You're special. And me, too—we're special. This is just window dressing."

"Whatever you call it, I didn't want it." But even as she spoke, she reached out to stroke the velvety petal of a long-stemmed red rose, one of a cluster propped up in a recycled mayonnaise jar.

She'd said "didn't," not "don't." This was going to work. Women were suckers for the trimmings.

Stepping up behind her, he put his hands on her

elbows and his chin on her shoulder. "Let's forget what you don't want and get to what you do want."

He felt the shiver that passed through her. "Not so fast, okay? Give me time to catch my breath."

"No problem. I thought of that, too."

She turned to face him beneath his light grip. "You did?"

He nodded, grinned, trying to loosen her up. "I knew you'd be nervous."

"I'm not exactly nervous," she said nervously. "Well, maybe I am a little but..."

"You wouldn't be human if you weren't a little tense. I am, too."

"You?" Those luminous blue eyes widened.

He wanted to fold her in his arms and tell her that he loved her, but that would be premature. Instead, he grinned and said, "Me. What I thought was, why don't we take a dip and work off some of these inhibitions? There's a hot spring only about a quarter mile away."

"I wish I'd known. I didn't bring a swimsuit."

He didn't dare laugh. She wouldn't take kindly to that at all. With a mighty effort, he kept a straight face. "Seeing as how we plan to get naked and physical in the foreseeable future, don't you think it'd be all right to try a little skinny-dipping first?"

Her cheeks pinked and now she was the one trying not to laugh. "That was dumb. I'm not good at this," she said.

"The jury's still out on that."

"No, I mean—" He saw it dawn on her that he

knew exactly what she meant and was teasing her. "All right," she said with a sigh. "Let's give it a try—anything to get past this awkwardness." She added self-righteously, "And you shouldn't have done all this—flowers, candy, wine. I'll just have to pretend you didn't."

Which he figured was nothing more than an idle threat, for she snatched a chocolate on her way out the door.

THALIA FELT LIKE Snow White wandering through the woods…like Gretel leading Hansel into danger. The trail was easy to follow through the pines and Luke seemed content to let her plunge ahead on her own. Perhaps he sensed she needed a few minutes to get over the shock of his underhanded… thoughtful…sneaky…delightful disregard for the parameters she'd drawn.

Well, what was done was done. At the moment she felt as if she would explode with nervous tension. A swim was just what she needed. Bursting from the shelter of trees, she nearly ran into Luke's old swimming hole.

The hot spring lay in a rocky cradle, a six-foot-high minicliff on two sides and rocky outcroppings on the other. A faint veil of steam lay over the surface of the water, which couldn't be more than a roughly shaped ten-by-ten.

For a moment her courage faltered, and then she said, "What the hell!" and started pulling off her clothing and tossing it aside willy-nilly. Maybe she

could gain the sanctuary of the water before he even
got here. At least she could try.

Naked, she hurried to the water's edge and stuck
in a toe. "Ahh," she murmured involuntary approval. Heaven—

And then she heard him thrashing through the
forest, suddenly noisy, and jumped in feet first.

FOR JUST A MOMENT, Luke had stood there at the
edge of the trees and watched Thalia strip off her
clothing and dash to the edge of the water. She was
beautiful, as he had known all along, her back
straight and slender and her hips full and womanly.
Her legs were long and shapely and pale. She might
live in California, but she was no sun worshipper.

His mouth was dry; he licked his lips, but didn't
breathe. He didn't want to frighten or embarrass
her, still, he couldn't stand here staring indefinitely
without doing something.

Stepping back into the trees, he whacked a few
limbs aside and stomped his hiking boots in the
collection of pine needles littering the ground. Sure
enough, she jumped in and hunkered down until the
water lapped around her chin.

He halted on the ledge above her. "How's the
water?"

"Fabulous!"

"Mind if I join you?"

"That was the general idea."

Said so seriously, as if determined to do her duty.
But he wouldn't laugh. "Thalia," he said, hauling

his shirt over his head and tossing it aside, "I'm not gonna make you do anything you don't want to do."

"I know that," she said, a bit stiff now. She took a few steps away; the water was only about five feet deep in most places.

He unsnapped his jeans. "Then quit acting like a sacrificial virgin. Unless that's your fantasy? Want me to ravish you in a sylvan glade?"

"I don't want to be ravished at all. I—" He dropped his trousers and those incredible eyes widened. Turning completely around, she said to a boulder "—intend to be adult about this. Just because I'm unaccustomed to...uh...assignations is no reason—"

"Asig—whats?"

"Assignations. You know, trysts."

The splash of his entry into the water cut off the rest of her breathless explanation. He came up right behind her, which wasn't easy considering he didn't want to open his eyes under all that dark water. He found her ankles and skimmed his hands up her sides when he popped to the surface.

Thalia said weakly, "Oh, gosh."

"Yeah." She was naked under there and, although he couldn't see much, he intended to take full advantage.

"Have you ever skinny-dipped here before?"

"Sure. Lots of times." He stroked her shoulder, down to her elbow, the water acting like a lubricant.

"With girls?" she asked sharply.

He did laugh then. "No, although I always wanted to. Just with your brother, with other guys." He slid his hand off her elbow and onto her midriff, then up until he felt the suspended weight of her breast in his palm. She didn't flinch, didn't react at all, until he covered her nipple and pressed it lightly between his fingers.

"Luke." It was a helpless sound, kind of strangled and uncertain.

He said, "Come here," and pulled her gently against him then, because he knew it was time. Her body felt slick and warm and soft and not at all unwilling.

He kissed her, taking his time to savor all the joys of it. After the first few moments, she wrapped her arms around his neck and kissed him back. And then she kind of slowly and casually wrapped her legs around his waist and there was no more need for caution.

THALIA COULDN'T BELIEVE IT. They made love at the pool and then in the bedroom at the cabin and then on the bearskin rug in front of the dead fireplace. She couldn't seem to get enough of him, which wasn't the way it was supposed to be at all.

In between, they ate strawberries and drank champagne, but all she could think about was being in his arms again. After a while, she gave up trying to hold anything back and just went with it.

To her wonder and amazement.

She had never been so mindlessly happy and fulfilled in her life. She must be out of her mind!

She'd be leaving in a matter of days, weeks at the most. Somehow she was able to push that shadow aside until Sunday noon. As they ate the last of the strawberries and drank the final drops of champagne, she realized that their idyll truly was ending.

She'd tried to tell him this before but every time she opened her mouth, he kissed her. This time, she'd managed to get the kitchen table between them so she screwed up her courage and said tentatively, "This has been wonderful, Luke, but—"

"No buts," he said sharply. "You're not gonna mess this up for me, Thalia."

"That's not what I intend to do at all," she protested, although guiltily. "It's just that…well, we've finally finished what we started and—"

"Finished!" He stared at her as if she'd suddenly turned Martian-green. "Nothing's *finished*. Hell, we've only just begun."

"Where in the world did you get that idea?" She stared at him, appalled. "You know that's not what I intended at all. Remember? No strings, no romance, just sex between…well, between friends."

He laughed. He actually had the nerve to look her in the eye and laugh. "Friends my aunt Gertrude," he said. "We're a lot more than that and you damn well know it."

"I don't know it and neither do you. Besides, what's wrong with friendship?"

"Do you sleep with all your male friends?"

"You know I don't," she said with dignity.

"There you go." He looked well satisfied with her answer, as if it proved his case.

Which it didn't. "Luke, it's over now," she insisted. "I've given in to my animal lust and enjoyed it big time. Now I've got to go on."

"I agree."

"As friends," she pressed.

"As lovers."

Frustrated, she glared at him. "Haven't you heard a word I've been saying? We both know this can lead to nothing so why are you—"

"Neither of us know where this will lead," he said, suddenly serious.

She knew where it would lead—to heartache. Hers. "Luke," she said in a warning tone, "it's friendship or nothing. Now back off!"

The expression on his face said he might be listening, but he sure didn't hear her.

# 9

"SO HOW'D IT GO WITH LUKE?"

Thalia stopped short and stared at her mother. "How did you know I was with Luke?"

"Where do you think he bought all those flowers?"

"Honestly, Mother. What do I have to do to have a little privacy?"

Lorraine shrugged. "Go back to California, I guess. You must have plenty of privacy there. The question is, do you like it?"

That jolted Thalia. Of course, she liked it. Privacy was a very big thing with her. On the other hand, privacy could morph into loneliness before you knew what was happening.

"I like it fine," she answered Lorraine belatedly. "As for Luke..."

And she froze. She couldn't think of a thing to say that would make any sense. *As for Luke, he's a fabulous lover and a wonderful man, but I told him to take a hike.*

Wouldn't do at all. Lorraine would think her daughter was a crazy woman. She might be right.

"As for Luke...?" Lorraine nudged.

"Nothing, nothing at all. I refuse to confirm or deny that I spent the weekend with him. Now if you'll excuse me, I have…things…to do."

Thalia marched through the parlor and up the stairs, trying to ignore her mother's voice. "Thalia Renee, you come back here and tell me what you think you're—"

Impossible. Thalia Renee didn't know what she was doing.

All she knew for sure was that she'd told Luke to back off and she knew he wouldn't and then what was she going to do?

MONDAY NOON, Luke saw Emily at the Paper Sack picking up a phone order. He greeted her eagerly.

"Have you talked to Thalia today?" He'd called her already—twice. Neither time had she come to the phone.

"As a matter of fact…" Emily gave him an assessing stare. "Luke, I think we ought to talk."

"About Thalia?"

"That's right."

"Okay, but I don't think I'm gonna like it."

"Probably not." She led the way to one of the two small tables inside what was essentially a take-out business. She looked at him grimly. "What are your intentions where Thalia is concerned?"

He blinked. "Don't you think she should be the first to know?"

"Under normal circumstances, only—" She stopped, chewing on her lip. "Okay, let's try another approach. Have you heard the one about the bird?''

''Emily, you've completely lost me.''

''Set it free and if it's yours, it will come back. Keep it in a cage and it will escape the first chance it gets.''

''That's nutty,'' he said. ''I'm not trying to keep Thalia in a cage.''

''You are trying to manipulate and control her.''

''The hell I am!''

''Think about it, Luke. She says she's going, you say she's staying. She says it's over between the two of you, you just laugh and say she's wrong. She says—''

''All right, all right. I've already heard what she's saying. What are *you* saying?''

''That if you want her to come to you, you'll have to give her room to make up her own mind. That's it.'' She stood, picking up the paper bag. ''Now do what you want and I'll try never to stick my nose in your business again.''

He watched her go, mulling over what she'd said. He couldn't just stand around and wait for Thalia to come to her senses, could he? Time was running out. After that great weekend, he couldn't take a chance on letting her get away from him again.

But what if continued pressure on Thalia pushed her into doing exactly the opposite of what he wanted?

''Ham and cheese on rye,'' the counterman called out.

Luke took his sandwich, paid and turned toward the door. He wasn't sure he could pull back and leave her to figure all this out by herself: that he was in love with her and wanted her to spend the rest of her life here in Shepherd's Pass with him. If he took her at her word and pulled back—

Opening the door, he nearly ran into Thalia coming in while he was going out. She looked as stunned by the encounter as he.

"Luke."

"Thalia." *Say something else; tell her the weekend was great and next weekend could be even better if—*

She stepped around him and headed for the counter. He stood there, wanting to turn around and follow her and point out to her that this was silly, they couldn't go back, they were much more than friends now.

She said, "I called a few minutes ago? One turkey and one veggie pita?"

On that note, Luke walked out of the Paper Sack and closed the door gently behind him.

THE SHEEP FEUD SIMMERED, and so did Thalia— simmered with remorse. She was miserable without Luke, who had pulled back just as she'd asked him to do…insisted he do, actually.

Why did she miss him so much? She still saw him everywhere she turned, just as before in this small town, but now he'd greet her with the same kind of friendly and impersonal nod he'd give to

Emily or Michael or anyone else. No longer did she get the special attention, the special treatment.

Maybe she wasn't all that special to him, after all, she thought gloomily. She'd wanted him to go and he had. Now she regretted the stand she'd taken but wasn't confident enough of his feelings to do anything about it.

Unless she was willing to forgo California so she'd have time to find out, but that would be silly. Talk about pie in the sky! Give up a well-ordered and well-planned life for a blind chance? No way!

Five days before Halloween, she got the telephone call she'd been both dreading and expecting. "Time to hustle your buns back home," her friend Kim in the personnel department said cheerfully. "You start to work the Monday after Halloween."

Thalia said weakly, "Oh." She barely managed to stifle the "no" which would have come next.

Kim laughed. "You sound exhausted. I'll bet you'll be thrilled to get out of all that clean mountain air and start breathing smog again."

"Something like that," Thalia said. "The Monday after Halloween, huh."

"That's right."

"My mother's embroiled in a kind of situation here that may come to a head the day before Halloween. Is there any chance I could come back a week later?"

"None whatsoever," Kim said cheerfully. "The plans have been cast in concrete—be here or be gone for good, if you catch my drift."

Thalia did. Before she had time to talk herself into doing something stupid, she called the Shepherd's Pass travel agency and bought her ticket. Halloween. She was flying back to the coast on Halloween. She'd be able to support her mother this one last time.

And then what?

She longed to talk that question over with Luke, but he was not only the son of the enemy, he was acting like a total stranger. To go to him now would require her to completely humble herself, which she was in no way ready to do.

She did talk to Emily, though—dumped on Emily, more accurately.

"Surely there's something that can be done to head off this range war at the pass," she griped.

"Like what?" Emily wanted to know. "Both sides are way past the talking stage, it appears to me. They're all approaching this like it's already World War III. When's the last time you saw one of them crack a joke or a smile at one of those interminable meetings? It's life or death now. I can't imagine anything you could do to bring about compromise."

"If only everyone would lighten up," Thalia moaned. "Instead, they're peering down a tunnel— from opposite ends."

"Luke might have some ideas."

"Luke and I aren't talking all that much these days."

Emily did not look surprised to hear this. "Really? That's a shame. I guess that's why he's not smiling these days. Neither are you."

"I don't have all that much to smile about," Thalia said.

Emily shrugged. "Laugh, then. People who laugh together can reason together. It's a law of nature."

Maybe so, Thalia thought later while delivering flowers for her mother. Laughing together really was important, even for someone who was as serious as—

She nearly ran into a light pole, so struck was she by a revelation. Like both sides of the Shangri-la controversy, she, Thalia Renee Mitchell, was *too* serious. What she needed was a good laugh, preferably with Lucas Dalton. Maybe then they'd be able to get to the heart of this thing between them.

And maybe if the Shangri-la It Ain't and the Shangri-la It Is folks could share a good laugh, they'd be able to stop vilifying each other and find some way to compromise.

How did you get laughter out of a bunch of turnips?

LUKE SURE AS HELL didn't feel like whooping it up at the Watering Hole, but dammit, he didn't want word getting back to Thalia that he was sulking in his lair, so he went anyway. Emily was there, which looked like a break until Thalia entered and joined her friend.

Now Luke supposed he'd have to act all happy

and sappy so she wouldn't think he was mooning after her. Damn. He hated this with a passion, but if it was his only shot, he was willing to do whatever it took.

His skittering glance snagged on hers and held. He saw a question in her gaze and half rose to go to her before he remembered he was playing it cool. With a casual wave, a half smile, he turned away from the tables where his friends sat. Seeing Michael Forbes sitting alone in a booth, he made a beeline in that direction.

Luke was sweating bullets. This wasn't working. Maybe he should simply tell her that unless she was willing to give a little, he was opting out for real.

Michael looked up in surprise. "What's happening, Luke?"

"Not much. You look like you could use a little company." Luke sat on the opposite bench.

"Yeah?" Michael shrugged. "I just left the office and dropped by for one of those great hamburgers they serve here. I'm used to dining alone."

"That's pitiful." Luke set his beer mug on the scarred plastic surface. "How come you never join the gang?" He gestured toward the rowdy tables across the room.

"I don't like crowds."

"Is that so. I'd have thought it was because you don't like people. Or sheep. Or dogs, for that matter. Or—"

"Actually," Michael cut in, "I'm quite fond of dogs." A waitress appeared and plunked a platter containing a hamburger and fries in front of him. He gave her a brief, impersonal smile and reached for the ketchup. "What can I do for you, Luke?"

"You could help me find a way to nip this sheep war in the bud." Luke took a swallow of beer. "Of course, if you did that it'd cut back considerably on your workload."

"You think I'm only interested in my fees?" Michael didn't look offended or even annoyed.

Luke knew him well enough to realize he was both. "Don't take it personally," he said. "That's what you do—lawyer. But in the interests of the community, I just thought..."

"Go on."

"Ah, forget it." Disgusted, Luke gathered up his beer. "You're on my mom's payroll and you do what you're told. I guess I can't fault you for that."

"The hell you can't." For the first time, a flash of emotion tinged Michael's expression. "I'm as interested in the welfare of this community as you are, Luke. I was born and raised here, just like you. And just like you, I went away for my education and then came back to live and, I hope, prosper. So maybe I don't want to forget it."

Luke sat back down. "That sounded almost human," he said approvingly. "What I'm thinking is, if we could find some way to get everybody talking..."

"Lots of luck." Michael picked up his hamburger. "Everybody's moved way past the talking stage and right on into the screaming stage, especially your mother and Lorraine Myers. Those two women are sweet as pie until you get them together and then they're termagants.''

''Termagants?''

''Impossible,'' Michael translated loosely. ''Naturally, I go with the termagant who writes my checks.''

''Naturally. So you're saying this is an impossible situation.''

''No, I'm saying that I don't know what anyone can do short of catching them at a weak moment and making them see sense before they know what's happening.''

''I'll have to think about that.'' This time Luke really did stand up. ''Thanks for the advice.''

''Such as it was.'' Michael turned back to his dinner.

Catch them at a weak moment, Luke thought as he returned to his friends. Did Lorraine and Sylvia *have* weak moments? Did—

He stopped short. Where was Thalia? She'd been over there right beside Emily and now she was—

At his shoulder, speaking in a low, intense voice. ''Luke, if you have a moment, I'd really like to talk to you. Privately.''

Privately. Jeez.

He nodded wordlessly and followed her to an empty booth, determined to keep his mouth shut.

SHE'D WATCHED HIM talking to Michael and tried not to stew about it. They were probably plotting and scheming on Sylvia's behalf. And here Thalia was thinking about confiding in him her last desperate scheme.

She would; she wouldn't; she—

"Oh, for cryin' out loud!" Emily had given her friend a shove. "Go talk to the man, for heaven's sake!"

So here Thalia was, seated across a table from Luke, fidgeting and trying to find the words to ask for his assistance. Failing to come up with anything brilliant to break the ice, she said, "So how have you been? We haven't seen much of each other since…lately."

"I'm fine," he said calmly. "You?"

"The same." The muscles of her throat constricted, making speech difficult. He wasn't going to help her at all. Apparently he didn't care.

"That's good."

For several minutes they sat there, looking everywhere except at each other. Then she said, "I saw you talking to Michael."

"That's right."

He must think she was an idiot. *Everybody* had seen him talking to Michael. "About the sheep controversy?"

He shrugged.

Did he think she was spying for her mother? She felt her dander rising. "I've been thinking about that," she began carefully. "It seems to me that before I go, I should try—"

"When are you going?" he asked quickly.

Startled, she said, "I have my ticket for Halloween—appropriate, wouldn't you say?" She managed a smile.

He didn't. "You mean this trip home has been a
nightmare for you?"

"No, of course not."

"You got tricks but no treats?"

"Lucas, stop that!"

"You're the one comparing your stay in Shepherd's Pass to Halloween. You met a monster? You
found razor blades in your candy apple? What?"

"It was just a figure of speech. I was trying to
be funny."

"The humor missed me." He stood up, his expression grim. "Thanks for the update and have a
good trip."

Her temper flashed. "I guess that says it all, then,
except 'don't call me I'll call you.'"

"Far be it from me to disagree with the oh-so-
serious Ms. Thalia Mitchell." He looked as if he'd
have tipped his hat in dismissal, had he been wearing one. "Have a good evening."

As if.

Steaming, Thalia stalked back to her seat beside
Emily while Luke disappeared through the crowd,
obviously on his way out.

So much for throwing herself on his mercy.

He obviously had none.


EMILY PURSED HER LIPS. "That didn't seem to go
very well."

"What did you do, plant a bug in the booth?"

"I didn't have to. I just watched the expressions."

Thalia sagged. "Oh, Emily. It was awful. He took everything I said the wrong way."

"You mean about bringing peace to Shepherd's Pass?"

"I didn't get to that part. I was trying to work up to it—you know, ease into it. I said something inane about it being appropriate that I'd be flying west on Halloween and he jumped all over me."

"Maybe he doesn't like to think about you leaving."

"Maybe he just likes to make me miserable."

"Maybe you're being ridiculous."

"Maybe—" Thalia stopped short. "Maybe you're right," she admitted after a moment. "I'm so confused I don't know what I'm doing or saying half the time. Em, I...I miss him so damned much."

"I know you do," Emily said softly. "Why don't you tell him that?"

"And let him stomp all over me again? No, thanks!"

"If he's worth having, he's worth the risk."

"There's only one risk he'd take seriously and that's not a risk I'm ready to take."

Emily raised her brows in question, but Thalia shook her head and changed the subject. She knew what it would take to get Luke's attention, though. She'd have to turn in her ticket and stay in Colorado on no more than a prayer that something might come of it—that she even wanted something to come of it. She'd have to give up her job and her apartment and her life on the glittering golden West Coast.

And for what?

For love?

MICHAEL STOPPED to say hello and goodbye on his way out of the Watering Hole. Emily gave him the cold shoulder, but Thalia had other things on her mind.

"What were you and Luke talking about?" she asked, figuring there was no point trying to out-subtle a lawyer.

"He didn't tell you?"

"C'mon, Michael. If he did, would I be asking?"

He shrugged. "I don't have a clue what you'd do, Thalia, but I guess it's all right to answer your question. As it happens, we were talking about the sheep wars. Luke's got this crazy notion that there might be some way to get both sides to sit down and work out a compromise."

Thalia gasped and her spirits soared. So Luke was as interested as she in working this thing out. Maybe there was still hope if she was willing to take a chance on another put-down.

She gave Michael a dazzling smile. "That's great. Thanks so much for telling me."

"Think nothing of it." But he didn't go, just

stood there beside her chair looking down at her with a puzzled expression.

"What?" she said, once he'd made her sufficiently nervous.

"Something's going on with you and Luke."

"What makes you think—?"

"Reading people is part of what I do. Believe me, it wasn't that hard."

"And your point is?"

"I'm going to win this range war, Thalia, if somebody doesn't step in and broker a compromise. Obviously, this is a job for you and Luke, since you want the same thing, starting but not ending with peace in Shepherd's Pass. How do you expect to get the anti-sheep people to talk to the pro-sheep people when you two can't even talk to each other?"

"I tried. He went off on a tangent and we never did get back to the subject."

"Then try again. If there's one thing I learned from my dear old daddy, it's that when you got nothin' to lose, try anything." With a casual salute, he departed.

Thalia sat there puzzling over his final words. He'd pegged it, all right; at this point, she really didn't have anything left to lose, because she'd already lost everything: her enthusiasm for her job, her eagerness to return to her boring life in California, her...call it *relationship* with Luke Dalton.

Beside her, Emily let out an indignant sniff. "That man makes me so mad!"

"I've noticed. He made a certain kind of sense, though." Thalia sighed. "Honestly, Em, I'm beginning to think I'd have been better off if I'd never come back."

"Don't say that. It's been so wonderful having you here, and I know your mom feels the same way. Then there's Luke—"

"Forget Luke."

"Can you forget Luke?"

Thalia couldn't lie so she said nothing, just clenched her teeth and refused to speak at all. After a minute, Emily nodded knowingly.

"Try again, Thalia."

"I tried and it blew up in my face."

"Then don't try. Give up. Go away and never look back. Chalk it up to experience. Convince yourself that it's better to have loved and lost than never to have loved at all. Life will be sheepless in Shangri-la—so what?"

Thalia burst out laughing at this indignant speech. "Sheepless in Shangri-la?"

"How about a sheepish smile to go with it?" But Emily's smile wasn't sheepish at all, more devilish. "Whatever. I've said my piece and now it's up to you. Just remember, a woman's got to do what a woman's got to do."

Whatever that turned out to be, Thalia thought.

THALIA TOSSED AND TURNED that night, trying to decide on a course of action. How to get both sides to sit down and deal fairly and honestly with each other when everyone was so dead set on having their own way? Dead set...deadly serious...determined...

She sat upright in her bed. *Just like me,* she thought. *I've been way too tunnel-visioned and uptight, too...too serious. What I've always needed was to see the funny side of life, and Luke reminded me of that.*

It *was* possible to be serious without being grim. If only she could make everybody else see that. If she could make them laugh...

She plopped back down on her pillow, her mind racing. How did you make two diametrically opposed groups laugh at a sheepdog and two sheep who'd created such controversy? *Think, Thalia!*

What did she have to work with besides the animals themselves? She ticked off her resources: Luke—she still dared to hope—Emily who was talented in many areas, maybe Michael, a meeting where everyone would be gathered...and Halloween. Halloween...candy, trick or treat, costumes...

There was something here if she could only grasp it, she thought as she drifted off to sleep at last. *All I have to do is figure out what it is—and what I should do about it.*

By the time she woke up the next morning, she had.

THALIA THOUGHT ABOUT calling the Shepherd's Pass Animal Clinic to find out what time Luke would finish work for the day but decided against it. She'd probably be asked why she wanted to know and she didn't want to tip him off. After their brief but unpleasant conversation at the Watering Hole, he'd probably sneak out the back door anyway.

Better to ambush him.

To that end, she parked her mother's old pickup truck behind the clinic next to his Cherokee at five-thirty that afternoon and settled down to wait. Exactly twenty-two minutes later, the door opened and Doc Miller walked out.

He saw Thalia and walked over to her. "What's up?" he asked through the open window. "Lorraine's livestock all right?" His laugh sounded more like a snort.

She gave him a strained smile. "They're fine."

"Good." He cocked his head suspiciously. "What are you doing loitering in our parking lot then?"

She tried not to sound defensive—or guilty. "I'm waiting for Luke. Do you know if he'll be finished soon?"

"He's finished now, just trying to catch up on paperwork. Here, I'll unlock the back door and you can surprise him." The wink he gave her said he thought it would be a good surprise.

That's all *he* knew.

Once inside, Thalia walked to the closed door to Luke's office and hesitated there. Michael's words echoed in her mind: *When you've got nothing to lose, try anything.*

Taking a determined breath, she reached for the doorknob.

THE DOOR CRASHED OPEN and Luke started, his gaze flying to the woman framed there.

The *determined* woman. Then he looked back down at the worksheet on the desk, saw the heavy ink line intersecting all the careful notes and said, "Shi-oot!"

"I'm glad to see you, too," Thalia said, striding into the room. "Luke, I've got to talk to you."

"I thought we talked last night."

"That wasn't talking, that was spitting and hissing."

"Men don't spit and hiss," he said with dignity, but he put down the pen, because he wasn't entirely sure all the surprises were on the table yet. "What can I do for you?"

She marched to the desk and looked down at him. She took a deep, shuddering breath. "Two things," she said, her voice not quite as strong as it had been. "I have a plan to end this sheep war, but I need your help."

"That's doable. I've been thinking along those lines myself but couldn't figure out how to go about it."

"Me neither, until last night. I couldn't sleep...."

Her voice trailed off, but he knew what she left out, or at least, hoped he did: *I couldn't sleep because of our argument.* He cleared his throat. "You said two things I can do for you. What's the other?"

Now her voice faded to a whisper. "You can kiss me?" It ended on an upward squeak. "You can forgive me for sending you away after the best weekend of my life? You can—?"

"Hold it!" He stood, reaching for her. "I can see where this is going, but I think I can handle it."

And he did, right there in his office.

## 10

WITH ONLY TWO DAYS TO GO, the Great Sheep Conspiracy proceeded apace. Both Emily and Michael were easily recruited, although they were coming from completely different places.

Emily shrieked with delight when she heard the plan. "I've got everything you need!" she exclaimed. "I won't have much time to pull it together, but I'll work tonight after the store closes. Of course, I'll have to check out the sheep."

Michael said, "Why not? It's time to end the cacophony of the lambs. I really am more interested in peace on the frontier than in big legal fees." And he sighed, rolled his eyes and added, "It's only money—most of it mine."

Luke and Thalia exchanged amused glances. Both were convinced that with a little help from their friends, this plan, however improbable, could work. Even if it didn't, they'd know they'd tried.

*Now if Thalia would just cash in that airplane ticket,* Luke thought.

*Now if Luke will only ask me to cash in my airplane ticket,* Thalia thought.

But neither said it out loud.

"YOU CAN'T BRING SHEEP IN HERE!"

Harvey Werckle, planning director for the city of Shepherd's Pass planted himself squarely in the path of two skittish sheep and one Border collie with a very strong work ethic. Harvey sounded personally outraged as he glared from Luke to Thalia.

One of the sheep said a soft *baa!* and Harvey looked again. His eyes widened and he struggled against a smile that quickly escalated to a full-fledged grin. "What in the name of—what have you done to those sheep?" he blurted.

Thalia grinned. "These aren't sheep, they're Holstein cows. You can tell by the black spots." She patted the cowhide-patterned robe stitched up by Emily. It fell below the sheep's belly and was held in place by straps. It had been far easier to get the sheep to wear cow costumes than it had been to get Reckless to wear the red cowboy hat perched jauntily atop his head, but they'd managed.

She added, "Bovine animals are on the approved list, you know."

"I know." Harvey's laughter broke through. "Okay, they're cows, but cows aren't allowed in city hall, either. So, I've got to ask—" He shook his head in apparent disbelief. "Where do you think you're taking this livestock?"

"In there." Luke pointed to the council chambers behind closed doors. Over the loudspeaker, Michael's voice picked up the tempo inside.

"...and wouldn't you all like it if there was a way—a fair and equitable way—to end this impasse? I believe there *is* such a way, and a couple of people with vested interests in this situation have come up with it. On this Halloween eve, they believe they've found a way to satisfy everybody.''

Murmurs of disbelief greeted this proclamation; obviously, he'd confused the combatants.

Except Emily, who threw open the double doors and cried, ''Dog, do your stuff.''

Reckless didn't have to be told twice. With a sharp bark and a dramatic lunge, he started his small herd forward. The sheep trotted briskly down the carpeted aisle and one of them let out a distressed bleat as if to say, *Not again!*

People began to turn, those clustered on the right side of the room with the aginners and those on the left side of the room with the proponents. Exclamations of astonishment were quickly followed by shouts of encouragement as Reckless drove the sheep to the edge of the council dais and held them there. Council members stood so they could see while the mayor banged his gavel for order.

Until he got a good look at the cows, formerly sheep, and the cowboy, formerly sheepdog. Dropping the gavel, he burst into disbelieving laughter.

Confused, the sheep stood, trembling, to stare around with dark resignation. Reckless dropped to his belly, tongue lolling and cowboy hat dangerously tilted over one eye and ear. If a dog could smile, that's what he did.

''Order, order!'' the mayor cried. ''Will somebody tell me the meaning of this outrage?'' But the last word was said without conviction.

Michael said into the podium microphone, ''Glad to, Your Honor. If everyone will just quiet down.''

They did, at least slightly, but the smiles remained. Thalia gave Luke a slight nod, which he acknowledged. They had a chance, anyway. Everybody was certainly in a good mood now.

Michael continued, ''I think most of you know Luke Dalton, son of Sylvia Dalton, leader of the Shangri-la It Is faction, and Thalia Mitchell, whose mother Lorraine Myers is leader of the Shangri-la It Ain't group and the owner of these fine animals.'' He indicated the furry trio.

That owner rose indignantly. ''Thalia Renee, what do you think you're—''

''Sit down, Mom.'' Thalia waved her away. ''We're on a roll. Hear us out before you say anything else.''

''That'd be a first,'' Sylvia muttered. ''Luke—''

''Ditto, Mom.'' He grinned at her. ''This is our show.''

''Well, I never!'' But she settled back down to titters from her followers.

Michael cleared his throat. ''With your permission, Your Honor, I'd like to turn these proceedings over to Luke and Thalia. I think everyone will be interested in their explanation.'' He sat down.

Luke and Thalia looked at each other. He held out his hand. She took it. Together they stepped behind the podium.

"When the lawyers outnumber the sheep," Luke said, "it's time to take action."

Michael led the laughter.

"So we did," Thalia chimed in. "We asked ourselves, why are sheep so controversial while cows are held in such high esteem? What have sheep ever done to deserve this? Like cows, they have four legs. Like cows, they're furry and some would say, even cuter. Like cows, they spend most of their time peacefully grazing. Still, sheep don't get no respect."

Luke nodded solemnly. "We decided to do something about that by making them cows for a day."

"We reasoned that it would do wonders for their self-esteem," Thalia picked up the tale, to growing laughter. "We wanted them to feel good about themselves, and what better time for such a transformation than Halloween?"

They were on a roll. Guffaws and chuckles and great bursts of laughter swelled around them. Only the sheep were less than enthralled, but Reckless had that situation well in hand and they quickly settled down again.

"You're all laughing," Luke pointed out. "That's what we wanted. Because this sheep war isn't serious, it's hilarious. Think about it—grown men and women ready to go to war over a few woolly four-legged critters whose only crime is grazing in Shangri-la. Well, folks, it won't be Shangri-la until we sit down together in the spirit of *compromise*.''

"Tomorrow's Halloween. We played a trick on you,'' Thalia admitted. "Now we want our treat—our peaceful, friendly community back. Because if we don't work this out now, we could be looking at *years* of feuding neighbors, escalating discord, and who knows how many broken friendships. Nobody would benefit from that except the lawyers.''

"Easy,'' Michael said to general laughter. "Don't badmouth lawyers. Let's be practical.'' He rose to look around at the rapt audience. "These sheep could turn out to be a cash cow, Mrs. Dalton—Four-Jay, you must see it. Woolly sheep grazing on emerald hills…what could present a better image of Shangri-la? It would be…it would be Ireland all over again.''

Four-Jay saw it at once. "Y'know,'' he drawled, "you could be right. It would—''

"Hold it,'' Sylvia interrupted. "Do we want Shangri-la to be Beverly Hills or Green Acres?''

"Neither,'' Lorraine responded. "We want Shangri-la to be *gone*.''

They were losing the crowd. Thalia clapped for attention. "That's not going to happen, Mother, so what's your next choice? Do you want war or compromise? Be careful how you answer that, because your daughter is listening and expects you to set a good example.''

"I—'' Lorraine stopped short. "I pass,'' she said, and sat back down, glaring at Sylvia.

"That means you're willing to compromise," Thalia pressed.

"No, it means—" Lorraine gritted her teeth. "Well, hell," she said. "Okay, I guess I am willing to compromise. This war wasn't my doing anyway."

"Why, of all the—" Sylvia started up. "If you're suggesting that I—"

"Mother," Luke interrupted, "compromise, remember? You wouldn't let Lorraine Myers be a bigger person than *you* are?"

Sylvia's eyes widened. "That's not the issue, Lucas. The issue is—"

"That is very definitely the issue. Yes or no?"

"But I want to—"

"Yes or no?"

Thalia held her breath along with everyone else. Sylvia's "All right, *yes,*" was grudging, but everyone heard it.

The mayor spoke up. "On that happy note, will somebody get these animals out of this council chamber?" he asked plaintively. "Then maybe we can make some serious progress here."

Thalia looked at Luke and smiled, then at the dog and said, "Reckless, take them out."

The sheepdog sprang to his feet, the sheep pranced up the aisle, and Thalia and Luke dashed after the fleeing trio. Pandemonium erupted; several of the observers in the aisle leaped aside while others joined in the exodus.

Practically everybody was smiling.

WITH THE SHEEP safely corralled by Reckless on the city hall lawn, Thalia and Luke returned to the council chambers in time to hear Four-Jay say, "...be sure I'm gettin' this right. Ms. Myers is willing to withdraw her opposition to Shangri-la number two if Ms. Dalton will agree to placing sheep on the approved list. Plus we're all willin' to talk over other nigglin' little thangs like density and setbacks. Have I got that right?"

Luke looked at Sylvia; Thalia looked at Lorraine. Both targets of attention gave grudging nods of agreement.

Luke and Thalia led the general applause. "This means my mother's sheep will finally be law-abiding citizens," she said.

"Yep. No one will ever have to go sheepless in Shangri-la again," Luke agreed.

And they fell into each other's arms, laughing helplessly.

"So HOW," Lorraine demanded, "did you two get those sheep here, and in costume yet?"

Luke grinned. He felt wonderful, excited and happy but also scared of the step he was about to take, the risk he was about to take. Beside him, Thalia laughed.

"We brought them in your pickup truck, Mom. Once we got Reckless clued in, it wasn't so bad. We set up a makeshift ramp and he drove his little herd right in, then kept them there."

"I'll bet Emily had a hand in those costumes," Lorraine said accusingly.

"She sure did. Michael helped, too."

Lorraine's eyebrows rose. "Don't let Sylvia hear that."

"Don't let Sylvia hear what?" Sylvia herself materialized beside them, her eyes narrow and suspicious.

"Nothing, Syl." Lorraine was the picture of innocence. "Nice of you to let the good guys win."

"We did, didn't we."

Lorraine's eyes flashed. "If you want to think so."

"I don't *think,* I know."

"I don't think you know, either!"

"Ladies, please." Luke held up his hands in an appeal for reason. "You sound like a couple of high school girls."

"Which is how long this has been going on," Lorraine agreed, stepping aside with a smile to let a group of people pass. "To tell you the truth, I'm getting a little tired of it."

"After only thirty-odd years?" Now it was Sylvia's turn to roll her eyes.

"They may have been odd years to you. Mine were great."

"Honestly, Lorraine, sometimes I could just—"

"Hold it." Everyone looked at Thalia, surprised by her tone of command. "Once and for all, will one of you tell us what started this feud—if either one of you remembers?"

"I remember," they said in unison, glaring at each other.

"Then *tell us.*"

"We were always in competition," Sylvia said, "and it wasn't fair. Lorraine was the cutest girl in school."

Lorraine blinked in surprise; that sounded curiously like a compliment. "And Sylvia was the richest girl in school," she retorted promptly.

"Nobody wants to be known as the richest," Sylvia said. "That's insulting."

"Do you think I wanted to be known as the cutest? Nobody ever liked me for my brain."

"I can understand that."

"About my brain or my looks?"

Sylvia laughed. "Both, I guess."

"Okay," Luke said wearily, "we get the picture. But surely it was something more specific than that to start a decades-old vendetta."

"Much more specific," Lorraine agreed. "We were both interested in this guy—"

"The quarterback on the football team," Sylvia inserted. "He was really cute."

"He'd take me to the movies, then take her to the school dance, then take me for a soda, then take her for a ride in his car—"

"Wow," Luke said admiringly. "That guy had it made." Thalia gave him a peeved glance, but he went on as if he hadn't noticed. "Who was this Casanova?"

"John…"

"It wasn't John, it was Gene."

"Are you kidding? I'd never date a guy named Gene. He was John...Hartsell?"

"Hartsell doesn't sound right. It was Gene Hartman...Hartley...Hartwig, that was it. Gene Hartwig."

"Sylvia, you're full of it. His name was John Hartsell, end of discussion."

"Oh, Lorraine Myers, you make me so mad! You always think you know everything!"

"Hold it!" Luke stepped between them. "I'm ashamed of both of you."

"So am I," Thalia agreed. "You're still fighting over some boy you don't even remember clearly."

"No, we're not," Lorraine said unexpectedly.

"We are so!"

"No, we're not, Syl. At the moment, we're fighting over Four-Jay."

Sylvia gasped and took a step back. "No way!"

"Knock it off, girl. I know you. It's been driving you nuts that he's been going out with me after these meetings instead of you."

Thalia waited for Sylvia to deny it. Instead, she stuck out her lower lip and said, "So what's your point?"

"Yes," Thalia agreed, "what?"

"Just this," Lorraine said magnanimously. "I'm going to end this feud once and for all."

"You're leaving town?" Sylvia guessed, her tone dripping acid.

"Ha-ha, it is to laugh. I'll rise above that, but you kids heard what she said, right?"

"Mom, are you just egging her on or do you have a point to make?"

"Oh, my point. Sylvia, Four-Jay is all yours. I give him to you."

"You—" Sylvia's mouth dropped open. "You do?"

Lorraine nodded for emphasis. "I'm supposed to meet him at the Watering Hole for a drink, but I'm willing to give him up. You meet him instead."

"Oh, I couldn't!" But it was obvious Sylvia wanted to.

"No, go ahead," Lorraine urged. "This is your chance. Take it."

"Well...I don't know."

"Jeez, Mom, do it," Luke said. "She's making a goodwill gesture." He looked worried. "You are, aren't you, Mrs. Myers?"

"Absolutely."

Sylvia took a slow step toward the door. "In that case..."

"Go on," Lorraine urged. "You know you want to."

Sylvia took a deep breath. "All right, I will. I'll never forget you for this, Lorraine." She surprised them all by giving her rival an arm's length almost-hug.

"You *bet* you won't," Lorraine said under her breath as she watched her rival sprint for the door.

"I heard that," Thalia said. "Mother, what are you up to?"

"Nothing much," Lorraine said serenely.

"It was a really nice gesture," Luke said, giving Thalia a warning look. "Maybe we ended two feuds here tonight."

"I doubt it," Lorraine said.

"Why is that?" Thalia wanted to know.

"Just that Four-Jay's gay," Lorraine said, "and even Sylvia will probably catch on eventually. Once again, the laugh's on her—the quarterback's name was Jack Hartford." She turned away. "See you later, darlings. I'm off for coffee with Harvey Werckle."

And that was that.

THALIA AND LUKE LEANED against the fence behind Lorraine's house, watching the pseudo-cows settle down for the night. Big fat snowflakes drifted around them, easy to see in the illumination of a string of lights suspended between a tall pine tree and the house. Reckless, sans cowboy hat, lay on his belly between his charges and any danger.

All was right with their world.

All *wasn't* right with Luke's world, at least, not yet. He had high hopes, however.

Thalia turned toward him and he watched in fascination as snowflakes touched her face, then melted away.

"I didn't see Michael and Emily to thank them," she said. "We couldn't have done it without them."

"We sure couldn't."

She smiled and a flake touched her full lower lip beneath his hypnotized gaze. She licked it away and his own mouth went dry.

"That's a dirty trick my mother played on your mother."

He shrugged. "No worse than the one my mother played on yours. She bribed Harvey Werckle to ask you mother out for coffee."

"Bribed him with what?"

"Season tickets to the Bronco games."

"Oh, Luke!" Thalia burst out laughing and, after a moment's hesitation, stepped toward him with a questioning expression.

He took her into his arms and she melted just like the snowflakes. He could barely hear her when she said, "Don't let's ever play those games, Luke."

"No, Thalia. We won't."

She clung to him for a moment. Then she straightened and said in a shaky tone, "I think what we need here is a good laugh."

"I don't."

"You don't?"

He shook his head slowly. "I want to be serious, Thalia."

Her brows shot up. "That's a switch. I'm usually the one who—"

"This time, it's me." He took a deep breath, realizing that what he was about to say could send her back into her shell. Nevertheless, he had to say it: "I don't want you to go back to California."

"You...don't." No inflection, just two words.

"I want you to stay in Shangri-la," he said, "with me. I've bought a house. We can move in as soon as it's built."

"You're asking me to live with you again." It wasn't a question, just a sad statement of something she thought was fact. "This is what you call serious?"

Her tone scraped along already raw nerve endings. "No," he said, more roughly than he intended, "I am *not* asking you to live with me. I'm asking you to marry me. Is a marriage proposal serious enough for you?"

Her eyes opened wide and she stared at him without speaking. When he couldn't take it any more, he took her cold hands in his and said, "Is that your final answer? Thalia, I love you. I just wanted to sleep with you before, but now I want more—lots more. I want to spend the rest of my life with you, settling range wars and shaking up the establishment—even when we're old and gray and a part of the establishment."

Her soft lips parted but no words came out. He was getting frantic, shaken by her apparent inability to speak. "If you insist on flying out of here tomorrow, I'll..." He swallowed hard. "I'll try to understand. It's just that I think I can make you happy. I know you can make me happy. You do, just by being here." He squeezed her hands. "Thalia, speak to me!"

"I—" She withdrew her hands from his and he stood there, separated from her and more uncertain than he'd ever been in his life. She dug one hand into her jeans pocket and pulled something out—paper, a note, something.

Holding out her hand, she let scraps of paper drift down with the more rapidly falling snow. He frowned.

"I don't get it."

"That's my airline ticket," she whispered. "I'd already decided to take the chance of a lifetime, even if it meant throwing away everything I've worked for. Luke, I had to know if we had a future together. I love you, too. If you can be patient with me while I learn the joys of occasionally being less than serious—"

"And here I went and got serious first." He hauled her against his chest, hard, knowing this time he wouldn't have to let her go. "Patient is what I do best," he said, his voice husky. "You should know that by now."

And there, observed only by two sheep and one disinterested dog, he kissed her. She was his and he was hers...forever.

Shangri-la, it was.

# The Purrfect Man

## Ruth Jean Dale

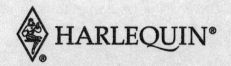

# HARLEQUIN®

TORONTO • NEW YORK • LONDON
AMSTERDAM • PARIS • SYDNEY • HAMBURG
STOCKHOLM • ATHENS • TOKYO • MILAN • MADRID
PRAGUE • WARSAW • BUDAPEST • AUCKLAND

# 1

EMILY STOOD on the sidewalk outside city hall and looked up into the nighttime sky with wonder. She welcomed the gentle kiss of snowflakes on her face. She'd been born and raised in the Colorado Rockies, but snow was still a kind of miracle to her. She loved it, plain and simple.

Turning right, she headed toward home, her mood euphoric. She associated snow with good things: hot cocoa with marshmallows before a roaring fire, long peaceful walks—

"Hey, Emily! Wait up!"

Pulled from her fantasy world by a voice she recognized instantly, she turned with a frown. Michael Forbes hurried toward her, his movements brisk and purposeful, as usual. Common courtesy demanded that she wait for him, but common sense told her to turn and run.

She didn't like Michael Forbes. She had never liked Michael Forbes, not even way back in high school. He'd been several years ahead of her in school, and of course he had nothing to say to a lower classman, probably didn't know she existed. But she knew *he* did.

He'd been president of the student council and had led a revolt that culminated in the complete revamping of school election laws. He'd won the debate championship three years in a row and had bullied the school board into allocating the capital improvement budget the way *he* saw fit—all while he was still a student.

So far as Emily knew, he'd had few friends then and he had few now that he was practicing law in Shepherd's Pass, Colorado. He appeared to be a totally independent man who needed nothing and nobody to be happy.

If he *was* happy.

Emily doubted it. She couldn't imagine it was possible to be happy without other people.

Michael loomed large beside her. He wasn't all that tall, probably no more than five foot ten or eleven, but Emily was only five-two so most people loomed over her.

He brushed flakes off the shoulders of his soft suede jacket. "Damn snow," he muttered. "I thought we were going to get away without the annual Halloween blizzard this year."

"It's not annual," Emily objected. "The Halloween blizzard is more like biannual."

"Biannual means twice a year."

"Oh. Then I don't mean that. I mean every other year. What's the word for that?"

"Biennial."

"Then that's what I mean." She added as an afterthought, "And stop swearing at the weather. Some of us like snow."

"What deluded individual could possibly—" He stopped short and tilted his head to regard her ruefully. "You, huh. Figures."

She strained for a pleasant smile, although her hands clenched into tight fists inside her hand-knitted mittens. "I'm sorry, I don't have time to stand around and be insulted."

"I'd never insult a lady." His grin flashed. He really was quite handsome when he smiled. Fortunately for his shark reputation, he didn't smile often.

"That's reassuring," she said, adding firmly, "Now if you'll excuse me, I—"

"First, tell me, did you see Luke and Thalia leave with the sheep?"

"As a matter of fact, I did."

"Damn! I wanted to talk to him."

"There's always tomorrow, Mr. Counselor." Turning, she walked away.

His voice floated after her. "Where are you going? That's not the way to the parking lot."

"I'm not going to the parking lot."

She heard rapid footsteps behind her and his voice. "Then where the hell *are* you going?"

"Home."

"You're walking?" He sounded astonished at that possibility.

"It isn't far." She kept up her brisk pace, wishing he'd go away and mind his own business. He was definitely intruding upon her formerly mellow state of mind.

"But—a woman can't walk alone at night."

"She can in Shepherd's Pass."

"I wouldn't care if this was never-never land. There could still be a pirate or two lurking about."

"I'll take my chances with pirates."

"Sorry, I can't allow it." He stepped up beside her, taking the side nearest the street. Apparently he did have some modicum of manners. "I'll walk you home," he announced. "Although I've got to say, it's a damned nuisance."

Her temper finally flared. "Then don't do it, Michael," she snapped. "I didn't ask you to and I don't want you to, so *don't*."

"You're just mad because I helped Luke and Thalia end the sheep wars," he countered. "You won't give me credit for anything, will you, Emily."

"Not if I can help it," she admitted grimly. The snow fell faster. The temperature was dropping, which lifted her spirits. Maybe this would turn into a real snowstorm and leave more than a few puny inches behind. She certainly hoped so.

"Surely you must be pleased at the way everything came out," he pressed.

"Of course. Justice—and sheep—triumphed over selfish interests. You, Michael Forbes, represented those selfish interests. You should be ashamed of yourself."

He laughed. He actually laughed, and it sounded as if he were sincerely amused. "It's dirty work, but somebody's got to do it," he said. "Joe John Jeff Jordan and Sylvia Dalton aren't the enemy. They deserve representation just like everyone else."

"I don't care about that," Emily said airily. "That's lawyer talk."

"Which you obviously equate with double-talk. What have you got against lawyers?"

"Plenty, and I'm not going to talk to you about any of it." The last person she'd ever confide in was Michael Forbes. It was none of his business that her father had been a lawyer and had taken her mother to the cleaners in the divorce settlement. If it hadn't been for Grandma—

"What was that?" He stopped short beneath the streetlight in front of the Sew Bee It, Emily's fabric and crafts store on Main Street.

"What's what?"

"I thought I heard a cry."

She frowned. "I don't hear a th—" And then she did, a cross between a howl and a bark, as nearly as she could make it out. It seemed to be coming from the alley between her store and the Paper Sack carryout deli and café. She turned to Michael with a frown.

He listened intently. "It's a dog," he announced.

She shivered and thrust mittened hands deeper into her coat pockets. "I wouldn't be too sure. It could be a wolf or something."

"In a service alley just off the main drag? I don't think so." He started forward.

"Where are you going?" she demanded with alarm. She didn't like the man, but she didn't want to see him ripped asunder by some wild animal.

"To see what that is. You stay here."

He couldn't tell her what to do! "I'll come with you," she declared, and started after him. She was fully prepared for him to forbid it and then there'd be another fight but—

"Okay," he said, and kept walking.

Why, of all the nerve! He didn't even care if he

led her into danger. She'd show him! She remained right on his heels as he plunged into the dark alley.

MUTED WHIMPERS AND YOWLS WERE definitely coming from the big metal Dumpster behind the Sew Bee It Craft and Fabric Shoppe. Cautiously Michael circled the contraption, trying to figure out what was going on.

Emily gave the Dumpster a respectful distance. "Is that a dog?" she asked.

"Sounds like it."

She caught her breath in outraged reaction. "Do you suppose someone threw away a dog like a sack of trash?" she demanded. "I'm not crazy about dogs, but that's *awful*."

The animal, if dog it be, punctuated this deduction with increased yowling. Michael supposed it had heard voices and was hoping for rescue.

"Yeah," he agreed, "it is awful. If people would only spay and neuter their pets this kind of thing wouldn't happen nearly so often."

"Now that it has," she said indignantly, "we've got to do something."

"You're right." He checked the latch holding the heavy bar in place. The opening was a good five feet off the ground.

"I think we should call the fire department and let them handle it," she announced, her tone anxious. "Come on, we can call from my place."

"Uh-uh."

"Uh-uh? What do you mean, uh-uh?"

"I've got my cell phone if I want to call, which

I don't. They'd just haul it off to the pound. I'll handle this myself.''

"Handle it how?"

"There's only one way. I'll have to crawl in and boost the dog out.''

"Michael, don't be crazy.'' She edged a little closer and the light at the rear of her shop revealed her wide-eyed concern. ''That could be a wild dog in there, or a mad dog—rabid, anything. It could be—''

"—scared to death,'' Michael interrupted impatiently. ''Calm down, Em. I know what I'm doing.''

He always knew what he was doing, even when what he was doing didn't make a whole lot of sense to everyone else. For example, he knew that taking on the Shangri-la case wouldn't make him any too popular in many circles, but that didn't even factor into his decision. Public opinion never influenced Michael Forbes.

Not even the public opinion of a beautiful woman with long black hair and big blue eyes.

He unlatched the bar and threw open the door to the Dumpster. Inside, the animal launched himself toward freedom but fell short and crashed back down again. Michael had only a glimpse of the furry form, but that was enough to see there was no way the dog was going to make it out on his own.

Michael really *really* didn't want to climb inside that dark hole with a strange dog. But sometimes the thing you dreaded most was the thing you most needed to do, he reminded himself. Like root canals and writing checks to the IRS and—

Behind him, Emily said a single distressed word. *"Don't."*

"Got to." He braced his hands on the opening and hoisted himself up. "If I'm not back in fifteen minutes, call animal control. Or maybe the paramedics."

"Don't joke about it! Look, I don't *want* you to do this. It's too dangerous. You could be—"

But it was too late; he swung his legs over and dropped down inside the pit, hoping he didn't land on the dog.

He landed on the dog.

THE CREATURE INSIDE the Dumpster let out a yowl and Michael began to swear. This was followed by sounds of thrashing and tumbling about.

Emily ran to the Dumpster door and tried to peer inside, but it was dark as a tomb in there.

"Michael," she cried. "Are you all right? Speak to me!"

His only response was an exclamation that sounded strangely like *"Aargh!"*

"Oh, my God! Are you hurt? What's going on?"

"He's licking me. Get away! Yuck! Stop it—"

More sounds of scuffling and then he began to laugh. "Enough of this gratitude! If I can just get hold of him—"

Emily gave up and backed away cautiously. Just because the dog hadn't attacked with bared fangs didn't mean he wouldn't. Michael was crazy to take such a chance.

She frowned. This was totally unlike the Michael Forbes she knew, both personally and by reputation.

That Michael Forbes was a hardheaded, no-nonsense individual who was always playing the angles.

What possible angle could he have now?

From the Dumpster came a muffled exclamation. "I think I've got him—hold still, dog! Dammit! I'm trying to save your miserable life." He grunted, and his voice grew louder, as if he were standing near the door.

"Here he comes! I'm just gonna boost him through."

The front end of the dog emerged into the light. Mouth open, tongue lolling out, vicious teeth shining—

Emily stumbled backward, her mouth dry with alarm. Before she could take more defensive action, Michael apparently gave a hearty shove, because the dog shot out of the Dumpster and fell to the ground with all the grace of a rock.

MICHAEL HOISTED HIMSELF up to the high threshold and swung out of the Dumpster. He was none the worse for wear, although his suede jacket might not be able to make the same claim. Fortunately, the Dumpster was no more than a third full of trash.

Emily screamed, a high, frightened sound that pierced him like a bolt of lightning. Leaping to the ground, he started forward, only to stop short.

She cowered against the back wall of her shop while a middle-sized dog leaped and jumped around, leaving dark smudges on her coat. With every touch, the creature yipped joyfully.

Poor little mutt was showing his gratitude, but it

definitely wasn't appreciated. Michael knelt and snapped his fingers, stifling his smile.

"Here boy, here! I don't think the lady appreciates your gratitude."

As if sensing rescue, Emily cried, "Get it away from me! Please, Michael, do something!"

"I'm trying. Here, boy!"

The dog turned, its head tilted questioningly. Seeing Michael, it galloped forward and plowed right into him, knocking him over backward in the snow.

Again Michael got the full treatment: wet tongue slurping at the side of his face. Laughing, he tried to wrestle the dog aside so he could get up. Apparently thinking this was a swell new game, the dog darted in for another sloppy kiss.

Finally Michael got hold of the animal and held him off long enough to rise. His hands felt bony ribs through the rough coat, and he realized this dog must be starving. Anger rose in his throat, nearly choking him. Whoever had dumped the dog didn't deserve to live.

The dog plunked down his rear end and looked from the man to the woman and back again. The eager expression on his canine face clearly announced his availability.

"That," Emily said in a faintly disbelieving voice, "is the ugliest dog I have ever seen."

In his heart, Michael had to agree. The creature was medium-sized, scruffy and filthy. One ear flopped over while the other stood upright, its paws were much too big for the rest of it, promising further growth. A scraggly tail, much too long for its body, waved uncertainly.

It was ugly as sin, all right, but also painfully skinny and painfully eager to please. Even dog-lover Michael couldn't believe how strongly he was responding to this mutt. Whether it was the animal's friendliness or his friendlessness, *something* was coming through with a vengeance.

Emily said, "Ug!" and straightened away from the wall where she'd been cowering. "Use your cell phone and call the pound this minute. Do you suppose it's open at this time of night?"

Michael stared at her as if she'd lost her mind. Already he was feeling proprietary about this dog. "Are you crazy?" he demanded. "That would be like signing his death warrant."

"You're being melodramatic," she scoffed. "They find homes for the animals who go there and—"

"Not a chance. Who in their right mind would adopt a sad-sack dog like this one, when the world is full of roly-poly puppies and fluffy little kittens?" he demanded.

"Exactly. He's not cute, he's not trained, he's certainly not charming. Why should we make him our problem?"

"Because we happened to be walking past when he called for help." Michael thrust out his chin at an aggressive angle. "And what do you mean, he's not charming? I think he's *damned* charming."

"Just because he *kissed* you?" She brushed ineffectually at the dark stains on her coat. "Me, he just wiped his dirty feet all over. I *hate* dogs that jump all over me.''

"I suspect you hate all dogs, period.''

She glared at him through the falling snow. "Not at all. I like *good* dogs, like...like Lorraine's Reckless.''

"That's hardly fair. Jack Reckless is old, and he's a Border collie to boot. Everybody knows they're smart, serious, no-nonsense working dogs.''

"So?''

"So this is a mutt, and young to boot.'' He indicated the dog, which squirmed under the attention and let out a plaintive combination groan and growl, obviously meant with friendly intent. "It's like comparing apples and oranges.''

"I still say he belongs in the pound,'' she said stubbornly.

"And I say he doesn't.''

"Then are you going to take him?'' she countered. "We've *got* to call the pound. We can't just go off and leave a stray dog roaming the streets, can we?''

"We certainly can't do that.''

"Then you've got yourself a dog. Good. That settles that.'' She looked at him with dread, as if sensing it wasn't settled at all.

"We'll get to that in a minute,'' he hedged. "First tell me why you dislike dogs so much.''

"I'm a cat person.''

As if that explained anything. "Lots of people like lots of different animals, dogs and cats included. One doesn't cancel out the other.''

Her soft face took on the stubborn expression he

was beginning to know. "I'm not lots of people, I'm me. Besides, I've gotten along just fine for twenty-seven years without getting cozy with dogs, so why should I change now?"

"Because this dog needs you."

"Forget it. No way, no how, will I have anything further to do with that animal." Chin up, she turned toward the street, dismissing both man and beast.

The dog immediately leaped to his feet and galloped after her. With a squeak of alarm, she whirled away from him.

"Do something! Make him stay away from me!"

"He's not vicious, Em. He just wants to be friends."

"Good for him. Tell him to find somebody who needs a friend, which isn't me."

"What's with you and this dog? Everybody likes dogs unless…were you bitten by a dog or something?"

"Yes!" She glared at him, her hands pressed flat against the building behind her. "It was a stray, just like this one. When they couldn't find it, I had to take those awful shots." She shuddered. "And I had to get stitches. I've still got the scar on my leg."

"Poor Emily. But that doesn't mean all dogs are bad," he coaxed. "Look at this one. All he wants is to be friends."

"I don't want to be his friend!" She appealed to Michael. "What difference does it make, how I feel about dogs? You're the one who intends to keep him."

"Well, actually…"

She groaned. "Don't even go there. I will *not* get involved with that animal. You do it, if you're so determined."

"I would, only there's a little problem with that."

"Such as?"

"I live in an apartment—no pets allowed. I'd take him in a minute if I had someplace to put him. You, on the other hand, have a nice little yard and—"

"And nothing!" Her fighting spirit had returned. "It's completely out of the question." She waved one mittened hand dismissively. "If you'll just call your dog, I'd really like to go home now."

"Our dog."

"*Your* dog."

"Be reasonable, Emily. You can't just turn your back on this poor, pathetic creature."

She looked at the poor, pathetic creature, and Michael's description was no exaggeration. She closed her eyes for a moment as if to steel herself.

She opened her eyes. "You aren't going to sway me with pity," she said grimly. "I'm going home and I never want to see that creature again."

She took a cautious step. When the dog didn't follow, she took off for the sidewalk again, walking fast.

Michael called after her. "Can't we work out a compromise?"

Her voice floated back. "No way! I'm out of here. Good luck with your new dog and do not, I repeat, do *not,* bring him to visit."

The dog looked at Michael and whined. Calling

it to him, he bent to scratch an ear, the floppy one. The dog flinched but held firm.

This animal had been abused. Someone had mistreated him and then thrown him away like so much garbage.

Maybe Michael couldn't take him home, but there were other things he *could* do.

That is, if he could successfully butter up Ms. Emily Patton.

"Hey, Emily! Wait up!"

Michael took off after her at a trot, his new best friend gamboling around him.

# 2

EMILY LOWERED HER HEAD against the blowing snow and trudged toward home, trying to ignore the unwelcome pursuit of man and dog. If Michael Forbes thought he was going to trick or shame her into taking that animal, he had another think coming. She liked her dog-free life; she loved her cats. Not for a single moment would she consider turning her world upside down for a really ugly dog.

Maybe he'd get lost in the snow and find some other chump. She could hope so, anyway.

"Look." Michael touched her arm and pointed. "He's following us."

"Was there a doubt in your mind he would?" she shouted back. "He knows a sucker when he sees one."

"You're not a sucker."

"No, but you are. I told you, I want no part of this—period."

"I know that's what you said, but I'm betting that's just a knee-jerk reaction."

"Don't bet the farm." She turned off the main sidewalk and pushed through the swinging gate in the picket fence around her small white house. It had been her grandmother's before her and it suited Emily's modest needs perfectly. Even the gingerbread curlicues decorating the porch and roofline delighted her.

Pausing beneath the porch light, she fumbled in her pocket for her key. "Thanks for walking me home," she said insincerely. "Don't let me keep you and your dog any longer."

"No problem." He made no move to go. "You know, that was a long and stressful meeting. I didn't have time for dinner and I'm kind of hungry."

The door swung open beneath her hand. "I think the Watering Hole will still be open. You could get a hamburger."

"I was thinking of something a little different."

"Well, good lu—"

"Like one of your cookies."

She frowned, her gaze going to the dog sitting at the foot of her step with his tongue lolling out and that goofy grin on his face. "What do you know about my cookies?" she asked finally.

"I used to watch you eat lunch at good old Shepherd's Pass High School. You always had the best-looking cookies—great big and squishy looking."

"Yes, well—"

"Sometimes with chocolate chips. I love chocolate chips." She'd never seen such a blissful expression on a human face. "And a nice hot cup of chocolate...mmm." He licked his lips. "I sure could use one of those cookies. But if you don't have any around..."

She could lie to him and say she didn't have any cookies, that the thought of a hot cup of chocolate didn't appeal to her in the least. She could, but not convincingly.

She rolled her eyes and grimaced in frustration. "Oh, all right, come on in if you insist."

"Gosh, thanks." He started forward and so did the dog. Michael blocked the animal with a leg. "Hold on, sport. You can't go in there."

"Ever." Emily slipped inside and held the door open just a crack. "Hurry up, before that mutt—"

Michael slipped inside and slammed the door in the dog's face. The animal promptly let out a howl. For a moment, Emily feared the man would open the door again.

Turning, she marched with determination through the house toward the kitchen in back. She felt sorry for the dog, she really did. He'd apparently had a rough life but that wasn't her problem.

She couldn't let it *be* her problem. A long-haired black cat skittered awkwardly beneath her feet and she bent to pick it up. Rosie had not recovered her former grace following a mugging by another stray dog. Now the cat snuggled in Emily's arms and began to purr.

Emily rubbed her cheek against the soft fur. She owed it to her own pets to stand firm.

The dog was Michael's problem. Let him solve it.

MICHAEL SAT at the small table in Emily's kitchen and watched her moving around to prepare the hot chocolate and pile big fat chocolate chip cookies on a saucer. His mouth watered at the sights and smells.

He couldn't even kid himself by thinking that the homey scene reminded him of his childhood, because it didn't. His mother had been an attorney whose time was much too valuable to spend any of it in a kitchen. She'd been a barely adequate cook who refused to hire someone better qualified because then someone might think she couldn't handle it all.

Something had to suffer and it wasn't her work. Michael's father, a stoic rancher, had endured bad food and late meals with a stolid acceptance that eventually convinced the boy that this was the way it was supposed to be.

Sitting at Emily's table in the cheery yellow kitchen suggested that both he and his father had been dead wrong.

Emily pulled a plastic container of whipped topping from a refrigerator that looked like it must be fifteen years old. She piled big spoonfuls on top of the steaming cups of chocolate before setting both on the table next to the overflowing plate of cookies.

"Dig in," she invited. "I need to feed my cats before I join you."

With ambrosia in his mouth, he watched her open a small can and spoon the contents into two dishes set on some kind of mat in a corner of the room. The big black cat wrapped itself around her ankles, purring. She stroked its soft fur and smiled. A smaller calico scooted around the corner and made straight for the food without a glance toward anyone or anything else.

Emily washed and dried her hands before sitting

across from him. She picked up her cup and sipped. She seemed more relaxed now, and marginally friendlier.

He finished his first cookie and reached for another. "Great cookies," he said enthusiastically. "Where'd you get them?"

"I made them, what else?"

"Really?"

She laughed. "It's not that big a deal."

"It is if you grew up with a mother who didn't know how to turn on an oven."

"You mean your—" She stopped short, as if catching herself being interested. "About that dog—"

As if on cue, the back door shook; Michael knew without a doubt that it was the dog jumping up on it. A howl followed.

Emily looked alarmed. The two cats looked annoyed but kept on eating.

They had warm, safe homes while that stray dog could be starving to death. It set Michael's teeth on edge to think about it.

"What?" Emily sounded annoyed.

"Did you get a good look at that dog?"

"As good as I wanted," she said with distaste.

"Emily, he's starving."

She jerked back in her chair. "I don't think it's very nice of you to try to shame me into—"

"I'm not trying to shame you," he said impatiently. "I felt his ribs when I tossed him out of the Dumpster. He's skin and bones. I don't suppose you've got anything around you could feed him?"

"No! I refuse to feed him. If I do, I'll never get rid of him."

"That's harsh."

"Stop it!" She shot to her feet, her blue eyes blazing. "That's not fair. I simply won't have a stray hanging around here looking for a handout all the time."

"That won't happen," he declared confidently, without the least idea how he'd keep his word. "He'd welcome anything—milk, bread, moldy cheese, old bones—"

"I'm fresh out of moldy cheese."

"Does that mean you do have milk and bones?"

She gave an exasperated grunt. "I had steak for dinner and I haven't carried out the garbage yet. But I still don't think it's a good idea to—"

He was on his feet heading for the door, behind which the dog yowled. "You get the food and I'll let him in just long enough to eat it. Don't worry, I'll watch him. I promise."

"Michael, don't open that door until I get the cats out of—"

He opened the door and the dog rushed in. The animal took one quick look around the room and apparently decided to follow his nose, for he headed like a disheveled streak for the cat dishes.

The calico shot straight up in the air and took off like a multicolored rocket. The black cat stood her ground, arching her back and hissing. When the dog got close enough, she took an angry swipe with a paw, curved claws gleaming.

The dog yelped. Rosie must have connected, but he wasn't after the cat anyway, he was after the cat food. While Rosie stalked haughtily from the room, the dog swallowed the remaining cat food in about two gulps, then looked around for more.

By then, an obviously unhappy Emily had poured milk into a plastic bowl. The dog thrust his muzzle into the dish almost before she could set it on the floor. Muttering under her breath, she retrieved a meaty steak bone from a covered dish beside the sink, put it on a pie plate and more or less tossed it in the dog's direction.

Nevertheless, Michael could tell she wasn't as cool about all this as she let on. She was watching the dog devour the milk and pretending she wasn't. The animal was obviously famished. She must feel like Cruella deVille to have even *thought* of not feeding him.

Michael said tentatively, "Pitiful, isn't it."

She gave him a sharp glance. "I never said I approved of people being cruel to animals. I just said I wasn't getting involved."

"I can understand that." He took his time with his third cookie, savoring it. She was a helluva baker.

"Really. I mean it." Her composed air slipped and she almost pleaded. "I just can't, Michael. Please don't ask me again."

"Well, okay, but, it's just that we found him together. I'd think you might feel a little bit responsible."

"Not in the least." She glared at him.

"Okay, okay." He didn't want to antagonize her unduly. "Suffice it to say that I do. But Em, I don't live in a nice house with a fenced yard like you do. I live in that miserable little apartment.''

"Michael Forbes, you live in one of the nicest apartment complexes in Shepherd's Pass," she objected.

"A nice apartment is an oxymoron," he improvised. "I've actually been looking for a bigger place for some time now. I'll speed up the search if you'll just, you know, help me out a little."

"I asked you not to ask me that."

"I'm trying not to." *Shame on me,* he thought. *Poor girl's on the ropes now.* "Look, it'll be a piece of cake."

"Are you kidding? You saw how my cats reacted to that dog."

"I saw one cat take off and the other smack the dog a good one."

"That was Rosie." She looked almost proud of the unprovoked assault. "But poor Patches was scared to death."

A gusty sigh from the dog brought them both swinging around. The animal grinned at them over the empty milk dish—or at least it looked like a grin. Picking up the steak bone, he ambled over to the table where he lowered himself to the floor. Stretching out, he rested his chin across Emily's instep. He still held the bone in his mouth.

She glared down at her unwelcome guest but didn't pull away. After a few moments, she transferred the glare to Michael.

"Okay," she snapped, "out with it. What are you trying to do, get me to adopt this dog? Because I'm not going to, and that's final."

"Not adopt," he said quickly. "More like…like foster. Foster this dog until I can move to a place where I can take him."

*"Foster a dog?"*

"Sure." He was warming to his own idea. "Just temporary, see? I'll be happy to pay pet support. In fact, I'll draw up legal papers so you'll have proof that he's my responsibility, not yours."

She said weakly and disbelieving, "Oh, good grief."

"You'll have physical custody, but I'll have liberal visitation rights. For example, I'll take the dog every weekend and all holidays."

"I thought you said dogs aren't allowed at your apartment."

"They're not, but for just a few days at a time, I think I can sneak him in."

"What if you get caught?"

"I'll cross that bridge when I get to it," he said cheerfully.

"I don't know, Michael. As a lawyer, aren't you supposed to uphold the law? If dogs are illegal—"

"Whose side are you on, anyway? 'No dogs' is a rule, not a law." He softened it with a smile. "I'll buy all his food, pay his vet bills."

"And replace everything he destroys?"

"Oh, sure," he agreed dismissively. "I don't think he's destructive, though." He frowned. "Do you?"

"How would I know? What I know about dogs you can write on the head of a pin."

"I'll buy you a how-to book."

"I won't have time to read it."

"Then I'll read it and tell you what it says."

"What will you do if he harasses my cats?"

"I'll—" She had him there, so he just grinned. "I suppose I could give him a good talking to."

She smiled reluctantly. "Okay, I guess that was unreasonable. But I'm just so leery about this. It's *not* going to work. I feel disaster hovering over my head."

"Self-fulfilling prophecy," he warned. "We could use a little positive thinking here."

"I'm positively certain this isn't a good idea."

"But he loves you. Look at that face."

They both did. The dog still lay with his head across her foot. When he realized he had their attention, he rolled his big brown eyes and banged his long tail against the floor.

She groaned. "I'm being hustled here."

"Not at all." He could afford to be magnanimous. He had her now. Time to move in for the kill. "What shall we name him?"

"Name him?" She looked at Michael with wide blue eyes. "You name him. I don't want any part of that."

"Okay. Let me think. How about Killer?"

"Are you kidding?"

"Spot's a good name."

"Not for a dog without a spot on his body." She sounded completely disgusted.

"Fang, then. I've always wanted a dog named Fang."

"Great. Can you hear me standing in the back yard screaming, 'Fang! Come home, Fang!' at the top of my lungs?"

Oh, yes, he had her. "That would be a bit of a problem," he conceded. "You come up with something."

She grimaced. "How about Lad?"

"Sissy name. This is a tough dog."

"Then I don't suppose you'd go for Snoopy, either."

He laughed. "Not a chance."

"Let me think." She chewed on her lower lip. "Blacky?"

He shook his head. "You're not very good at this, are you?"

"I haven't had much practice naming dogs," she said, taking offense. "So what do we do now, just keep referring to 'the dog'?"

"No, we'll *name* him Dog—with a capital *D*. How about that?"

She considered. "Well," she said grudgingly, "it doesn't sparkle, but I guess I could live with it."

"Then it's a deal." He held out his right hand.

She looked at it, considering. Chewing her lip. Grimacing. Then she ever so slowly extended her own hand and slipped it into his.

At her light touch, he felt the most curious thrill pass up his arm. It was such an innocent gesture on her part, combined with a clear-eyed look that said she was going to trust him on this one. He didn't want to let her go. He wanted to simply sit there holding her hand and staring into her eyes like some smitten fool.

Which was laughable, really. He was a grown man, a *cynical* grown man. She was not at all the kind of woman he favored. Oh, she was pretty enough—beautiful, really, with the contrast of black hair and blue eyes, creamy translucent skin and high cheekbones.

But she was also old-fashioned, what his mother would call "backward." He'd bet she had no interest whatsoever in feminism or any of the other great issues of the day. She stayed home with her cats and baked cookies; she used her sewing machines for more than running up curtains, although he was confident she did that, too.

Even her work was old-fashioned; she ran her grandmother's fabric and craft store.

The last woman Michael had dated with any degree of serious intent had been a pediatrician on the fast track. She'd been busier than he and a hell of a lot more ambitious.

His mother, who still practiced law in Albuquerque where she had moved after his father's death, had openly hoped something would come of that relationship. It hadn't, and Michael wasn't quite sure why.

Looking down now at that soft little hand, he had a glimmer of an idea. There was something disturbingly appealing about a woman who was happy simply being a woman, without anything to prove to anyone.

Except maybe to herself: that she could stand having a dog around without losing her cool.

THERE WAS SOMETHING curiously comforting about sitting there with her hand engulfed by his. He had nice hands, really, although she'd never noticed before: long and square tipped, the nails nicely tended.

Just what you'd expect from a lawyer. Clearing her throat, she slowly withdrew her hand and sat upright, at the same time sliding her foot from beneath Dog's chin.

"In all seriousness, Michael…"

He waited for her to go on, his expression serene. She supposed he must feel pretty satisfied with himself at this point. He was, after all, getting his own way.

"I'm not at all convinced this will work," she announced.

"I know you're not," he said without a trace of regret. "I want you to know how much I appreciate the fact that you're willing to give it a shot."

"I don't guess I want him sent to the pound," she admitted. "If we can prevent it, anyway."

"I knew you didn't mean that, about the pound."

Her eyebrows shot up but it was time to move on. So she said, "The next problem is, where should he sleep? I wouldn't worry about putting him in the yard if it wasn't snowing."

"Oh, yeah. That's right." He frowned. "Do you have a basement?"

"A little one. I use it mostly for storage."

"Can we put him down there for the time being? All he'd need is an old blanket or rug to sleep on."

"I suppose." Her sigh conveyed defeat.

"I'll walk him before I go," Michael offered. "Then if you let him out first thing tomorrow, he should be okay."

"I hope so," she said grimly. "If he's not…"

She gave Michael a pointed look that she hoped said *it's your responsibility*.

"I don't suppose you have a rope or a dog collar laying around?"

She laughed. "I have a couple of cat collars, but I don't think they'd fit him."

"Right." He rose, as did Dog. "Well, he won't run away and we'll close the basement door, so it should be all right." He crossed to the back door. "Come on, boy. Let's go." He snapped his fingers.

Instantly Dog began to hop and prance around. Opening the back door, Michael stood aside to let the animal rush out first. Then he turned up the collar of his jacket, hunched his shoulders and followed.

Emily sat there alone for a few moments, wondering what she'd gotten herself into. Rosie ambled into the kitchen, looked around with disdain, then sprang upon her favorite lap and snuggled down.

Emily rubbed the cat's small pointed ears and immediately felt vibrations as the purring began. "Well, Rosie," she said softly, "I may be making an awful mistake, but what can I do?"

Rosie sighed and snuggled deeper. Her golden eyes closed.

"I don't think Dog is mean, exactly," Emily went on, stroking the cat's back. Rosie was obviously having a bad hair day. Baby-fine hair stuck out in every direction and static electricity made it worse. "I'll keep him away from you and Patches, I promise."

Rosie opened those yellow eyes and her expression said she'd believe it when she saw it.

"I don't think it will be for long." Emily wondered if lying to a cat was the same as lying to anyone else. "We'll be all right. Trust me."

The door banged open and a black whirlwind entered, flinging snow all over the clean kitchen floor.

And over the black cat, Rosie, who shot to her feet with an arching back. Cat claws shot out to twist into her owner's jeans.

"Ow! OHH! EEE!" Emily tried to pry the cat's nails out of her jeans—and her leg. Dog stopped short and stared with interest.

Michael made a dive for the animal, who side-stepped neatly. Apparently thinking this a wonderful new game, Dog lunged at Emily or the cat or both. Spitting and hissing, the black cat leaped onto a kitchen counter and darted right on up until it reached the top of the cabinets. Baring its teeth, it spit fury at the dog capering around below.

Emily lifted denim from her thigh and winced. Several red lines crisscrossed the back of her hand, filling Michael with guilt. Kneeling, he caught her hand so he could examine it.

"That damned cat scratched you," he declared, all righteous indignation on her behalf.

"Only because that damned dog scared her." Emily glared at Dog, who wiggled all over in rapture at any attention, however negative. "Let go!" She wrenched her hand away. "When you live with cats, you get scratched. It's a law of nature."

"Oh." He sat back on his heels. "I never had a cat. For that matter, I never had a dog."

"Until now," she corrected sharply. Then she

frowned. "In that case, why are you so determined to have *this* dog? It's not only inconvenient for someone living in an apartment, it's goofy."

His brows rose. "Goofy?"

"Sure, when you could have a *nice* dog. Huskies are very gentle and popular, and they do real well in our climate. Or a Border collie like Lorraine's— there's a smart animal."

"I don't want a nice dog, I want this dog." Michael draped an arm over Dog's neck and then had to dodge the slurping tongue. "Look, I know this is a real inconvenience to you."

"Oh, do you really?" He hadn't thought her capable of such sarcasm.

He would rise above it. "I want you to know I'll make it as easy as possible," he promised. "I'll be over bright and early tomorrow to help out, and I'll buy all the stuff he needs just as soon as the stores open."

"Stuff."

"Like a doghouse and a bed. Then he'll need a collar and a leash, plus some kind of rope in case he gets loose. He needs dishes and food and toys. I'll also have to make an appointment for Luke to take a look at him. Dog will need his shots and a license and…what am I forgetting?"

"Nothing, I devoutly hope." She slumped back in her chair, her beautiful blue eyes widening. "I don't deserve this."

He patted her knee. "Don't worry. Everything's going to work out just fine."

She lifted his hand away distastefully. "Maybe,

if you'll start looking for a place with a yard to-morrow.''

"Absolutely." He stood up. "It's getting late. Let's take Dog down to the basement and get him fixed up for the night. Then everyone can get some rest."

"Michael," she said, "I have a feeling it will be *weeks* before I get any rest."

But she stood up obediently and led him to the stairs.

DOG HOWLED AND YOWLED until Emily dragged herself from a warm bed and went to check on him. He met her at the basement door, his entire body wagging.

"What's your problem, Dog?" She glared at him, hands on her hips and disgust in her heart. "You've got a nice place to sleep—see, an old blanket between those two boxes. Michael says that will make you feel secure."

Damn dog. The basement was warm and cozy. What possible reason could this mutt have for his lousy attitude?

Dog whined and licked her hand, looking up at her with adoring brown eyes.

"Are you hungry?"

Dog wagged the lower half of his body.

"Maybe you want to go outside?"

In the snow—ugh. Emily looked down at her fluffy slippers and sighed. If Dog wanted out, she'd have to put him out.

He galumphed around her to the kitchen door. She opened it and he skipped through happily. Only a few inches of snow had stuck; according to the big outdoor thermometer, the temperature was in the high twenties.

Emily closed the door and leaned against it, stifling a yawn. A glance at the clock on the stove told her it was only a little past one in the morning.

Damn dog!

Patches wandered into the room, the very carriage of her little calico body conveying her disgust. She looked at Emily with disapproval, then pitterpattered to the water dish with her light-footed gait.

Why couldn't a dog be more like a cat? Emily wondered. Cats were so independent, so selfsufficient. Dogs, on the other hand, weren't even smart enough to come in out of the snow.

Yawning, she opened the back door—and her mouth—in preparation for summoning her unwelcome guest. She might have saved her energy, for Dog hit the opening with such timing and force that he nearly knocked her down.

Then he headed straight for Patches, who froze, a horrified expression on her furry face. The cat took off for the living room, the dog took off after the cat, and the woman took off after both of them.

It was shaping up to be a long…long…night.

# 3

MICHAEL KNOCKED on Emily's front door at seven-thirty sharp the next morning. Waiting for her to respond, he looked around with satisfaction.

A light mantle of snow covered the house and yard, making it look like an old-fashioned Christmas card. The weather forecast called for highs in the low fifties today, so all the white stuff would soon melt away.

He'd have arrived earlier, but he hadn't thought she'd appreciate it. He knew he'd manipulated and shoved her into something she didn't want to do but figured the end justified the means. They'd saved that dog. They were therefore responsible for it. He couldn't let her ignore her part in the rescue, could he?

It finally occurred to him that he'd been standing there on her porch for several minutes. Where was she? Surely she wasn't still asleep. He knocked again.

He didn't know Emily well, but now it looked as if that would be rectified. She wasn't his kind of woman; that much was obvious. But then, he wasn't her kind of man, either.

She was old-fashioned and he was new fashioned. She was traditional and he was cutting edge.

She liked old houses—obviously—and for him, the newer and more modern the better. She—

Some slight sound inside caught his attention. He frowned and strained to hear. What was going on in there?

Tentatively he reached out to give the door a little shove—just a little one. It promptly swung wide to reveal a sight he wouldn't soon forget.

There stood Emily, wearing a long white nightgown, her hair a dark cloud around her shoulders. She clutched a black cat in her arms, or maybe the cat clutched her. She was kicking a small bare foot at the grungy dog cavorting around her.

"Dog!" Michael spoke sternly. "Get over here!" He pointed to a spot on the flowered carpet right in front of him.

With a joyous yelp, Dog dashed to Michael and right on out the door. Unfortunately, Michael had failed to close the front gate and Dog didn't even slow down.

"Good riddance!" Emily's voice was full of fire. "If I never see that animal again, it'll be too soon!"

Right away, Michael recognized a couple of things: she'd had a bad night and her morning was worse. "Not to worry!" he exclaimed, starting after Dog. "Go get yourself a cup of coffee and pour me one, too, because I'll be right back." He stepped onto the porch.

"Don't hurry!"

And Emily slammed the door behind him with a little more vigor than necessary.

EMILY WAS TAKING A PAN of cinnamon rolls out of the oven when Michael barged through the kitchen door, a wiggling Dog clutched under his arm. He looked flushed and disheveled, which pleased her more than a little.

"Well, hell," she said. "You caught him."

"Or he caught me," Michael grunted, putting the animal on the kitchen floor. "He's a speedy little devil."

"You must be, too, or he'd still be at large." She eyed the dog with disapproval. "I wish."

"At the risk of leaping to conclusions—" he pulled out a chair and plopped into it "—did you have a bad morning?"

"And night. That blasted mongrel got me up at least a half-dozen times. I don't know what his problem was. I let him out, I let him in, I fed him every slice of bologna in my refrigerator, I gave him water, I—" Her frustration burst its bounds. "I sang to him. I sang *lullabies* to that miserable beast and he just howled." Her shoulders slumped. "At least now I know why someone dumped his miserable carcass in a Dumpster."

"Emily Patton, you don't mean that."

"I certainly—" all the air went out of her attack "—don't." She glared at the man. "But I wish I did. That dog is a spawn of hell, sent to punish me for every rotten thing I've ever done."

"Which would amount to what? Fudging an inch off a yard of fabric?" But his smile was sympathetic. "You know, I'm perfectly willing to listen to you rant and rave just as long as you want me to, but I would appreciate a cup of coffee while I'm doing it. And maybe one of those cinnamon rolls? My mouth is already watering.''

"Of course. I'm sorry. When it became obvious I wasn't going to get any sleep, I figured I might as well accomplish something." She poured his coffee, topped off her own cup and brought the pan of rolls to the table along with saucers and forks.

The rolls did look good, she thought: huge circles dark with cinnamon and frosted with thick white icing that reminded her of snow. One just about filled a saucer.

Michael dug in with his fork. At the first taste, his eyes closed in ecstasy. "This has got to be the best thing I ever ate," he breathed, his tone respectful. "How do you do it, Emily?"

He was obviously trying to butter her up by changing the subject. "Surely that's a rhetorical question," she said haughtily. "I do it with a recipe and an oven."

He sighed blissfully. "And a lot of talent. You could make a whole lot of money by selling these."

"I sell fabric and crafts. That's plenty." But she did feel somewhat mollified, now that Dog had settled down at Michael's feet and closed his eyes. Then she remembered something he'd said the previous night, something that had come back to her during those long dark hours of dog-duty. "Why didn't you have a dog when you were a kid?" she asked. "If you had, you probably wouldn't be all worked up about this miserable animal now."

"That's entirely possible." He gave her his most charming smile, the one he regularly pulled out for judges and jurors. "May I have another roll?"

She shoved the pan toward him. "Take all you want. If you'll answer my question, that is."

He took another bite and chewed thoughtfully. "My mother didn't like animals as pets," he said then. "In fact, she didn't like animals much, period."

"That must have been tough, considering that your father was a rancher."

"It *was* tough." He stopped eating finally, half a cinnamon roll remaining on his saucer. "My mother moved me into town with her when I was five. Dad worked the ranch while she practiced law. Since we lived in an apartment, there was no room for a pet."

"But you wanted one." Her feelings toward him at that moment softened almost imperceptibly. She could see the little boy he was, begging his mother for a pet. She could imagine his mother, the sleek counselor-at-law, refusing with a lecture about why he should be grateful to be denied.

Everybody in town knew Liz Forbes was a shark, a cold potato. Up until this very moment, Emily had thought Michael was a chip off that old block.

His father was something else.

John Forbes's life had ended when his son was in his early twenties. A well-respected man of strong character, the senior Forbes had remained married to a woman who apparently valued him considerably less than her career until the day he died.

Less than a year later, Liz Forbes had moved away. Emily had never known where.

Michael picked up his cup. "I suppose all kids

want pets," he said in a more detached manner. "I hadn't thought about that in years until…"

She reheated his coffee. "Until what?"

"Finding old Dog in the Dumpster was kind of a wake-up call for me," he said. "I've been needing something or someone to think about beside myself and my career." He grimaced. "I hate to admit I've been leading a very self-centered life but—I have been leading a very self-centered life."

"Then I guess you need this dog." He was getting to her. She didn't like the softness she heard in her voice and added more briskly, "I, on the other hand, *don't*."

"You're a goddess for helping me out this way." He sought to soothe her. "You won't be sorry, Em. You'll see. Look at him. He's not really such a bad dog, is he?"

She didn't want to look at Dog, but she couldn't help it. He lay on the floor under the table, his chin on his paws and those big soulful eyes peering up at them. When he had their attention, his tail began flopping against the floor.

Emily groaned. "It's not going to be that easy," she said. "After the night he put me through—"

"Tonight will be different," Michael promised. "He'll have a doghouse and a bed all his own. He'll—"

"Tell it to Rosie and Patches. He's scared them both out of ten years' growth."

He walked to the counter to refill his coffee cup. "For some reason, I thought you had more than two cats."

"You're probably thinking of Tom. Nobody

owns Tom. He's a stray who deigns to drop by the shop when he's in the neighborhood. He's never come home with me and it's a darn good thing. He's half as big as Dog and twice as tough.''

"I don't know about that. I think Dog's plenty tough.'' Putting the cup on the table, Michael leaned over to ruffle the dog's head affectionately.

"Whatever. I just want to be perfectly clear about one thing. I will *not* go through another night like that.''

"You won't have to. I promise.''

"You can't promise that,'' she snapped.

"Yeah, I can. I'll make sure he's settled for the night before I leave.''

"Before you——?''

The wall phone rang and she rose. "Before you leave? I don't recall inviting— Hello?''

"Emily!''

"Hi, Thalia. Wow, you sure sound happy.''

"I am! Can we get together for lunch today? I'll bring something from the Paper Sack, if it's okay.''

"Sure.'' Emily couldn't help the grin spreading over her face. "You wouldn't have any news for me, would you?''

"Me? Whatever are you suggesting?'' Thalia clicked off on a happy trill of laughter.

Emily hung up the phone. "I have a feeling Thalia won't be going back to California anytime soon,'' she predicted.

"How so?'' He sounded only mildly interested.

"I think she and Luke have reached an understanding.''

"What understanding? You mean...like...?''

"You got it, Sherlock. As in marriage. I strongly suspect he proposed last night."

"Poor sap." But he said it cheerfully. "Can I have another of those cinnamon rolls for the road?"

"Be my guest." Grabbing a paper towel from the roll mounted over the sink, she placed it before him, then lifted the last of the rolls off the baking sheet and plopped them down on the paper. "Now if you don't mind, I have to get ready for work."

"I don't mind." He rose, taking the paper-wrapped parcel with him. "I'll put Dog out in the yard."

"Good."

"And I'll come back and feed him just as soon as the pet store opens."

"Good."

"And I'll come back tonight and make sure he settles down in his new home."

"Okay, but how you think you can do that is beyond me."

"Trust me." He lingered at the door. "Thanks for everything, Emily."

"I'd say it was nothing but I'd be lying."

A broad grin lit up his face and she found herself thinking that he really should smile more often.

"See you later, then." he said. Tsk-tsking to Dog, he let them both out into the backyard and closed the door.

Only then did she let out the breath she'd been holding.

"WE'RE ENGAGED!"

Emily had already guessed that. In case she

hadn't, Thalia's sparking smile would have been a tip-off.

"I'm so happy for you!" They hugged, and Emily added, "But not surprised."

"I am." Thalia set the sandwiches from the Paper Sack on the table of the small lounge area at the Sew Bee It. "I really, really didn't expect it, but I took a chance anyway. I tore up my airplane ticket!"

"You didn't!"

Thalia nodded. "Even if he hadn't proposed, I was prepared to hang around and see what developed. Because—" a faint pink tinged her cheeks "—I think I've loved him always."

Emily melted. "Thalia, that's beautiful."

Thalia sighed blissfully. "It's true. You know how it was when I was sixteen."

"I remember it well."

"I never got over that first crush. Somewhere along the line, it changed into love. I'm so happy I can hardly stand it!"

"I see that." Emily couldn't look at her friend without smiling. Until she yawned.

"You're bored?" Thalia inquired, tongue in cheek.

"I'm sorry. I didn't get much sleep last night."

"Me, neither. What's *your* excuse?"

How to begin? Emily pondered for a moment, then said, "I've got temporary custody of this dog."

Thalia's eyes widened. "*You? A dog?*" She opened the brown bag and began pulling out sandwiches.

"I'm a victim of circumstances. See, Michael and I were walking home after the meeting last night—"

"Michael *Forbes?*" Thalia took a bite of ham and cheese.

Emily nodded. "—and we heard—"

"Why was he walking you home? Where was your car? Where was his car?"

"My car was home where I left it," Emily said impatiently. "I just felt like walking to the meeting last night. Is there a problem with that?"

"Oh, you're really testy. I'm *sorry.*"

"No, I'm sorry." Emily let out a dejected breath. She was not only sorry, she was exhausted. "Anyway, Michael saw me leave and came after me to see if I knew where you and Luke had disappeared to. When he found out I was walking home, he insisted on going along."

"That was nice of him."

"I thought it was presumptuous of him." Emily glared at her tuna on wheat. "Anyway, I'm making a short story long. As we were passing the Sew Bee It, we heard noise coming from the Dumpster in the back alley. It turned out to be a dog."

"How awful." Thalia frowned. "But how lucky for the dog that two such compassionate souls happened to be passing by."

"I suppose." Emily put the sandwich back on the table. "The thing is, Michael is completely smitten with this dog."

"Is it cute?"

"Lord, no!"

"Lovable?"

"I wish."

"Well trained?"

"That dog doesn't know sic 'em."

"Does this dog like cats?"

"Only for breakfast, lunch and dinner."

"Then I guess it's the old underdog syndrome," Thalia said. "Who'd have expected that from *Michael?*"

"Who, indeed. The thing is, he's conned me into putting up that dog until he can move to a place that allows pets."

Thalia frowned. "That sounds a bit open-ended."

Emily felt panic rise. "You're right." She shivered. "Look, I'm sorry I dumped on you about this. Let's forget my troubles and turn to more pleasant things. Like when do you and Luke plan to get married?"

"We haven't set a date. He's in a hurry, though."

"And you're not?"

Thalia laughed. "I guess I am," she admitted. "But I want to do it right this time. Last time was just a justice-of-the-peace thing. I want to marry Luke in a church in front of God and everybody."

"I have visions of a white wedding gown," Emily began.

"Not the second time around!"

"Why not? I could do something really special for you in an off-white or even in a peach."

"You mean make it yourself? You'd do that for me?"

"Oh, Thalia, I'd do that and more! Let's go through the pattern books and see what you like."

And so they did, without a thought to lunch or dogs or conniving men.

EMILY HAD ACTUALLY FORGOTTEN that this was Halloween until one of her customers mentioned it. Thus reminded, she stopped off at the grocery store on her way home and picked up several bags of candy—her own favorite kinds in case any was left over after the trick-or-treaters came around.

Carol, one of her clerks, always locked up on Thursdays, leaving Emily free to enjoy the junior goblins and ghosts who were sure to drop by. She always looked forward to seeing the children, but tonight she was so tired she just wanted it over with as quickly as possible.

Dog met her at the front gate, jumping up and down in a frenzy of excitement. A sharp word sent him slinking away, which only made her feel guilty. Once inside the house, she checked on the cats' food and water, then passed through to the backyard to make sure Michael had done everything he'd promised.

He had.

An imposing doghouse shaped like an Eskimo igloo graced one corner of the small yard. Before it rested two shiny stainless steel bowls, one filled with water and the other with a few nibbles of dog food. The ground around this arrangement looked as if it had been trampled by a herd of wild horses, all trace of snow wiped away by the patter of great big dog feet.

The owner of those dog feet came galloping up, flinging droplets of mud in every direction. Drooling, he leaned down to lick her boots.

"Stop that, Dog!" She batted at him and tried to slip back inside the house. He was too quick for her, unfortunately, and managed to slide inside while almost knocking her down in the process.

"Dog! Come back here!" She took off after him, swearing under her breath. This was *not* starting out to be her best Halloween.

"TRICK OR TREAT!"

Emily looked down at the little masked figure before her, noting his broad grin. She grinned back.

"Davy Robinson, is that you?"

"It's a monster!"

Karen Robinson, standing behind her five-year-old son, patted his shoulder fondly. "I don't know where this monster came from," she said, "but he insisted we come to your house first, Emily."

"I'm honored." She reached inside the orange plastic pumpkin and pulled out a big handful of candy. "Is this what you want, Davy—I mean, Mr. Monster?"

Davy shook his head a firm no and stepped back. "I want to know if I can play with your new dog," he announced.

"That might not be a good idea. You see, he isn't really mine. He's just...he's just visiting."

Davy frowned beneath the paint. "But I like dogs. Please, Ms. Patton? Please? Can I play with your dog?"

"Don't whine, Davy," his mother said reprovingly. "Take the candy and say thank-you."

Davy thrust out his lower lip but did as directed. "I still want to play with that dog," he said, his mouth quivering.

Karen looked around. "Where is the dog, by the way?"

"I tied him to the doghouse so he wouldn't wipe out all my trick-or-treaters," Emily explained. "He's a nice dog, I guess, but he's got no manners at all."

"I don't care," Davy piped up. "I just want to *play* with him." He walked away muttering under his breath.

"I'm sorry," Emily said to Karen. "I don't know that dog well enough to vouch for him."

"Don't worry about it," Karen advised, steering her child back to the sidewalk. "Davy just loves all dogs."

Like someone else I could name, Emily thought, watching the approach of the next batch of costumed kids. Maybe when she got to know Dog better she'd like him herself.

Or maybe not.

"Trick or treat!"

And she was off again, dispensing sugar.

IT DIDN'T TAKE MICHAEL LONG to realize he'd made a tactical error.

He'd timed the departure from his office to coincide with what he guessed would be dinnertime at Emily's house. Surely she'd take the hint and feed him, since he was willing to skip his own dinnertime to take care of Dog.

But as he drove through the streets of Shepherd's Pass, he realized that they were much busier than usual—busier with ghosts and goblins and all kinds of costumed children.

Halloween.

Jeez, he didn't even like Halloween. His mother had never let him have a costume or go trick-or-treating, anyway, calling it legalized extortion. As an adult, he usually locked himself in his office until it was over, because there was no way he was going to be responsible for all that tooth rot.

He pulled up to the curb in front of Emily's house just as a gaggle of kids rang her doorbell. Walking up behind them, he heard the giggles and the repartee and wondered what the heck could possess a grown woman to lower herself this way.

Candy in hand, the trick-or-treaters parted to flow around him like water around a rock. They were happy, he saw, out of all proportion with what they were doing.

He looked up to find Emily glaring at him.

"Oh, it's you," she said

"I told you I'd be here."

"Apparently I forgot."

The hell she had. "I promised to take care of Dog," he reminded her. "The only thing is, I forgot it's Halloween."

That admission seemed to soften her. "I did, too. Someone had to remind me." She stepped aside to let him enter the house. "Look," she said, handing him the bowl of candy, "I've got a chicken on the stove. Will you handle the door while I check it?"

He was torn. He had no interest in paying off

pint-sized desperados but on the other hand, he *did* have an interest in anything she might have on the stove.

Maybe he'd get lucky and nobody would ring the bell.

"Okay," he agreed without enthusiasm. "But—"

A bell pealed, followed by a pounding on the door.

"Get that, will you?" Turning, she walked away, leaving him in charge.

It was going to be a bumpy night.

EMILY DID IT ON PURPOSE.

One look at Michael told her he was not a "Halloween person," and he *should* be. Everyone should be. It was fun to joke around with the kids in their costumes, some extravagant and some cobbled together at the last minute.

Plus, she really did have a chicken on the stove. Later, when the crowd thinned out, she'd whip up a batch of dumplings, add a salad and fresh broccoli, and...

Feed him. Darn it, she felt almost obligated to give him dinner, although she shouldn't. With Dog barking and howling in the backyard, kind thoughts were misplaced. Bustling around her kitchen, she reminded herself that this was all Michael's doing. Why should she feel any obligation toward him at all? She could always change her mind, she reminded herself. She didn't *have* to invite him to eat with her.

Especially if he was in there being surly to the children of Shepherd's Pass. Stopping stock-still with a long wooden spoon in her hand, she suddenly realized she might have made a mistake.

Dropping the spoon, she hurried back to the living room just in time to find Michael opening the door.

He peered at the trio of kids on the front step. "What's going on here?" he demanded with apparent seriousness.

"Trick or treat!" the kids chorused, holding out their goodie bags.

"I've got the treats, all right," Michael admitted. "Let me see your tricks first. If they're any good—"

"Tricks?" The cowboy frowned at the pirate. "What kinda trick?"

"I don't know what you can do," Michael said reasonably. "Can you sing or dance?"

The kids looked flummoxed; from the shadows behind them, a giggle emerged—a mother enjoying the exchange, no doubt.

"I can sing," the cowboy said at last.

"Then let's hear you."

"'Home, home on the range...'"

"Hey," Michael said when the song came to a conclusion. "That was great. You guys get the special stuff." Digging into the bowl, he pulled out great handfuls of candy to drop into the proffered bags. He added, "Happy Halloween," a wish echoed from the shadows by the watchful mother, then closed the door.

Turning, he looked surprised to find Emily standing there. "I didn't hear you come in," he said.

"You were busy. Where did that stuff about tricks come in?"

"It's half of trick-or-treat, isn't it?"

"But the idea is, if you don't give them treats they'll do tricks you won't like."

He looked skeptical. "Like what?"

She frowned. "I don't know. I always *do* give them treats and so does everyone else. I guess it would be stuff like throwing eggs or draping toilet paper around the yard."

"Anyone tries that and they'll find their little butts in big trouble."

She had to laugh at his intensity. "Michael, I'm getting very strong vibes that you somehow managed to miss out on many of the joys of childhood."

"Yeah, maybe I did."

His answer surprised her. It also made it even harder to remain detached. She couldn't resist saying, "Not so bad, handing out the treats, is it?"

"No." He cocked his head and grinned ruefully. "Especially if I can have a few of your leftovers. Like these—" He held up a miniature candy bar. "This happens to be my favorite, so I kinda pulled them over to one side to hand out last."

She laughed. "Strangely enough, that's my favorite, too, which is why there are so many of them. But I'll share."

"I'll bet you always do," he said with what sounded like approval. "In that case—" He pulled the outer wrapper off the small bar of chocolate and nuts.

"Don't eat that now," she said quickly. "You'll spoil your—"

Damn! She wasn't going to do that.

Too late. He brightened. "Are you inviting me to dinner?"

She sighed. "I guess I am."

"In that case—"

The doorbell rang. He shrugged and turned away. "Don't start eating without me." He opened the door to a princess and a bumblebee, who shouted "trick or treat!" in unison.

# 4

IT WAS ALMOST EIGHT-THIRTY before they sat down to dinner. Michael looked at the spread before him and his mouth dropped open.

"You cooked all this?"

"Do you see anyone else lurking around? Of course, I cooked it." Emily shook out her napkin and dropped it on her lap, but she was pleased by his response nonetheless. The man was obviously impressed.

"Wow! Do I have to eat the salad first or can I go straight to the good stuff?"

"You can begin anywhere you please."

"I'll do that." He helped himself from the big bowl of fluffy dumplings and tender pieces of chicken, all smothered in savory gravy. "I'm starving."

"Handing out all that candy can give you an appetite, all right." Stifling a grin, she picked up her salad fork.

"Mmm." He lifted the first bite to his mouth and chewed thoughtfully, his eyes closed as if to more completely savor the experience. He sighed. "I don't think I've ever tasted anything so good," he declared.

"Don't go overboard," she said dryly. "It's only chicken and dumplings."

"No, it's not. It's ambrosia."

"Am I safe in adding cooking to the growing list of things your mother didn't do?"

"Yeah." He stopped eating for a momentary frown. "Don't get me wrong. My mother's a real dynamo. She's probably the best lawyer I ever saw or heard tell of. She just didn't waste time on what she considered to be nonessentials."

"Like cooking? People have to eat to live."

"But they don't have to eat *well*. I'm living proof of that. Uh, mind if I have seconds?"

"I don't mind at all. There's plenty."

As he ate, she slowly became aware of the warm glow spreading through her. It was good to share her table with a man so completely complimentary about her efforts.

But it wasn't good to look upon him so favorably. He was only here because of the dog sprawled beneath the table—the *quiet* dog, not the noisy wretch who'd barked and howled at every passing kid.

Michael ate with utter concentration. Only when he'd had his fill did he sigh and lean back in his chair.

"I'm sorry," he said. "I'm not usually so single-minded about food, but that's the best meal I've had in—maybe ever."

She laughed. "And it's not even over."

"It's not?" Fresh interest widened his eyes.

"I have dessert and coffee, if you're interested."

"I'm interested."

"Sight unseen?" She carried their plates to the sink.

"Em, if you cooked it, I'll eat it."

"It looks as if I have a fan." She transferred big wedges of apple pie onto dessert plates and carried them to the table, to be joined by steaming cups of coffee. "Dig in," she invited.

"I've died and gone to heaven," he announced. He sampled the pie and groaned in apparent ecstasy. "Emily, will you marry me?"

"No, and I won't board your dog indefinitely, either," she responded tartly. "You don't want a wife, you want a cook."

"I don't actually want either," he admitted, "but if that's the only way I can eat this well every day, I'm ready to make a few sacrifices."

"Not with me, you're not. I've got a life."

"Yeah, and am I ever glad." He picked up the final crumbs of piecrust on the tines of his fork and ate those, too. "That was great. I can't thank you enough."

"You already have. More coffee?"

"If I do, I won't sleep a wink tonight."

"Yes, you will. It's decaf." She poured from a steaming carafe.

"You think of everything."

"I appreciate a good night's sleep."

"So do I, but I don't often get one." He picked up his cup. "I wouldn't say I have insomnia, but I'm not the world's greatest sleeper."

"I am." She added a teaspoon of sugar to her cup and stirred. "So tell me, what should I know about Dog before you go?"

"Is that a hint I should be hitting the road?" He grinned, not the least offended. "Where Dog's concerned, I think everything's under control. It'll be okay to leave him in the yard tonight. He should eventually find his doghouse. I've already put a few dog biscuits in there to tempt him."

"Okay. Did you make an appointment for Luke to see him?"

He nodded. "Tomorrow at two. I'll come by and pick Dog up. You won't be bothered at all."

She eyed him askance, thinking that some way, somehow, she *would* be bothered. "I guess that's all, then. You'll also pick him up Friday night for the weekend, right?"

"Right. I don't know what I'll do with him, but I'll think of something." He finished his coffee, dropped his napkin onto the table and rose. "I'll go ahead and put him out for you."

"Thanks."

"Do you notice how calm he is? He just got a little excited earlier because of all the people coming and going."

"I suppose."

"If we give him a chance, I'm sure—"

At that moment, Patches wandered through the kitchen door. She zeroed in on Dog, arched her back and went up on her tiptoes.

Dog leaped to the challenge. For an animal who looked more than half-asleep, he moved with lightning speed, launching himself like a spear at the discombobulated cat.

"Stop him!" Emily jumped up, knocking over her chair in the process. "Don't let him—"

"I'll handle this!" Michael threw himself at the dark streak, his arms closing around the furry body. His momentum sent them both rolling across the kitchen floor—right into the cat dishes in the corner.

Patches gave them a sneering glance and walked serenely back out the door through which she'd entered.

Emily should have been so calm.


"HOW'S MY DOG, DOC?"

Luke stroked his hand down the back of the shaggy dog sitting alertly on the metal examining table at the Shepherd's Pass Animal Clinic and Hospital. Dog had an eager expression on his face, made comical by one floppy ear and one alert ear. His tail hadn't stopped thumping the table since he'd been placed there.

Michael rephrased his question: "Is Dog okay?"

Luke looked thoughtful. "He's not in bad shape, actually, overlooking the fact that he's painfully thin."

"Yeah, I thought so, too."

"You say you pulled him out of a trash bin?"

"That's right. Jeez, who could do a thing like that?"

"You'd be surprised what people can do." Luke looked grim. "Or maybe not. In your business, I expect you see a lot."

"Too much, sometimes, but not usually in a canine sense."

"If this was a person instead of a dog, we'd be calling the police right about now. He's been pretty badly abused.'' Luke gave Dog a final pat on the head and stepped back to strip off his gloves. "It's a wonder he's still so affable after what he's been through.''

Michael felt his temper rise. "To think of anyone beating on a helpless puppy,'' he said through clenched teeth. "But he'll be all right now that he's got a home,'' he added hopefully.

"More than likely. I'll have to see the results of the blood test, but all things being equal, you've got yourself a good dog.'' Luke cocked his head, his eyes narrowing. "What are you planning to do with him?''

"Keep him, naturally.''

"At Emily's? I doubt she'll go for that on any extended basis.''

"Well, yeah, but...'' Michael stumbled around, looking for an answer. "I'm going to try to find another place to live,'' he said finally. "Then Dog can move in with me full-time.''

"It might be hard to find an apartment that allows pets.''

"Hey, I don't need any more roadblocks here,'' Michael said sharply. "I'll do what I have to do.''

"Are you interested in a house? I think Thalia and I are going to buy a place in Shangri-la number two. You might look there.''

Michael grimaced. "What would I do with one of those big places? I need room for a dog, not a wife and kids.'' He added as an afterthought, "And congratulations, by the way. Emily told me about the engagement.''

"Thanks." Luke grinned broadly. "We're happy about it."

The smile was infectious. "Whatever works," Michael said.

"How about you?"

"How about me what?"

"You said you're not interested in a wife and kids, but I doubt it."

"You think I'm lying?" Michael demanded sharply.

"I think you're deceiving yourself. At your age—"

"How old is thirty-one these days? Over the hill?"

"It is in some circles. It's just that hearing about the further adventures of you and Emily—" Luke shrugged "—I have to wonder if there might be something there."

"There's something there all right. I gotta admit, I'm seeing her in a whole new light. I used to think she was just a fussy prig but now…"

"She's *not* a fussy prig?"

"Oh, she is. But there are extenuating circumstances. She's really been a good sport about all this, especially considering how she feels about dogs."

"Yeah, she's a cat person all the way."

"It's more than that. She was bitten by a dog when she was a kid and it traumatized her."

"I didn't know that." Luke's expression was assessing. "Apparently she's taken you into her confidence."

"Something more important than her confidence.

She's taken me into her kitchen. Can that woman cook! I'm not kidding—I'll bet she could make a gourmet meal out of earthworms.''

Luke laughed and Dog jumped to his feet, looking from one man to the other. When Michael snapped his fingers, Dog leaped off the table and bounced over to his master.

''Anything else?'' Michael wanted to know, snapping the lead on Dog's brand-new red collar.

''I'll give you complete written instructions, but the most important thing is to feed him properly and give him plenty of love and attention.'' Luke scribbled on a sheet of paper. ''I'm always here if you need me.''

''Thanks.'' Michael accepted the sheet and stuffed it into the pocket of his blazer. ''We appreciate it.''

''Give Emily my best,'' Luke called as the pair retreated through the office door.

''Will do.'' Michael waved a hand, thinking that Luke seemed determined to make a lot out of nothing. Little did he know that Michael's taste in women ran to something tall and blond and sophisticated, not something short and brunette with a spatula in her hand.

THE BELL ABOVE the shop door tinkled, and Emily looked up from the cash register just in time to see Dog lunge forward, yank the lead out of Michael's hand and make a beeline for Tom, sprawled on his carpeted window ledge. But this time Dog was trying to bite off more than he could chew.

Tom lunged to his feet and met the panting dog

with a dangerous growl and a swipe of one long-clawed paw. Dog yelped and changed direction with lightning speed. Tom bared his teeth and let loose with a veritable symphony of outraged cat noises.

"Ye gods!" Mrs. Weller picked up her plastic shopping bag with the Sew Bee It logo outside and nearly a hundred dollars' worth of fabric and notions inside. "How did that crazy dog get in here?"

Michael stepped on the trailing end of the leash, halting Dog in his tracks. "I'm afraid I'm responsible, Mrs. Weller. He got away from me." He gave her a charming smile.

Mrs. Weller stared at Dog. "He's certainly an ugly one," she observed. "Is he yours?"

"Mostly," Michael said. "About ninety percent of him is mine and the other ten percent—"

Emily interrupted quickly, not wanting her name attached to this project. "That's okay, Michael. No harm done." And if it had been, Dog would very likely have been the recipient, not the other way around. She handed a copy of the charge slip to Mrs. Weller. "Thanks so much. I'll call as soon as that quilting book comes in."

"Thank you, dear." Package clutched in both arms, Mrs. Weller started for the door. When she got even with man and dog she stopped short, looked them both over, burst into laughter and continued on her way out of the store.

Emily glared at Michael. "Doesn't it bother you to own the ugliest dog in the world?"

"He's not *that* ugly." He looked offended. "But

even if he was, I love him for his character, not his looks.''

"His character. I see." She came out from behind the counter. "Can I do something for you, or did you just drop by to harass the cat?"

Michael cast an oblique glance at Tom, still growling softly under his breath. "Who harassed who?" He softened it with a grin. "I thought you'd be happy to know Luke's given Dog a clean bill of health. Mostly."

Internal alarm bells went off. "Mostly?"

He knelt to stroke the dog's back and got licked in the face for his trouble. "He's been abused, Emily. Luke found evidence of broken bones and...other stuff."

"Oh." Emily felt the blood rush from her face, leaving her cold and constricted. "Poor Dog."

Dog looked at her and perked up his ears. He apparently recognized compassion when he heard it and took a jump in her direction.

She retreated back behind the counter. "I'm sorry he had a hard life," she said. "But now he's got you—or will, as soon as you find a new place to live. Have you started looking?"

"Are you kidding?" He looked greatly offended by her nagging. "I haven't had a minute since I got into the office this morning. I had to avoid an appointment with Mrs. Dalton and Four-Jay to take this dog to the vet. And you want to know if I'm looking for a new place to live?"

"It was an innocent question," she said—innocently. "Well, I know you're in a hurry, so if you want to take Dog home and stick him in the backyard, you can get back to work.''

"I'll do that.''

She could tell by his set face that he was mad. She hadn't meant to hurt his feelings. She just wanted to remind him that she wasn't in this for the long haul.

Two minutes after the duo exited, the doorbell announced Thalia. "Was that your new dog I just saw Michael trying to drag into his car?" she inquired.

"Puh-leeze don't call him *my* new dog," Emily pleaded. "He's all Michael's. I'm just the dog sitter."

"Sorry. I didn't mean to set you off." Thalia looked at her friend through narrow eyes. "You seem a little jumpy today. Is everything all right?"

Emily stifled a yawn. "Everything's great."

"I don't think so. You've got bags under your eyes. Aren't you sleeping?"

"Who could sleep with a dog yowling in the backyard?"

"All night? I'm surprised the neighbors aren't complaining."

"Well, maybe not all night, but most of it," Emily said defensively. "It's all that dog's fault, regardless. I mean, I'm a world-class sleeper. What else could it be?"

"It could be the man, not the dog."

"Michael?" Emily stared at Thalia in astonishment. "I don't think so."

"Why not?"

"Because I've known him forever and have never even liked him."

"Maybe you didn't *really* know him until now."

Emily considered this. "Yeah, maybe," she finally conceded ungraciously. "At least he's nicer than I thought. I mean, he's nuts about that dog."

"Be careful," Thalia said.

"About what?"

"About Michael. I've never thought he was a bad guy, just hard to get to know. He never let people get real close."

"That's a fair assessment."

"But through unforeseen circumstances, you're seeing a side of him not visible to many people. Just be careful. You and Michael are about as different as any two people I've ever known. I wouldn't want to see you get hurt."

"Hurt?" Emily laughed contemptuously. "No chance!" She came out from behind the counter. "You didn't drop by just to harass me, did you? Tell me, Thalia, to what do I owe this unexpected pleasure? Are you by any chance ready to talk wedding gowns?"

Thalia's brilliant smile and happy nod conveyed the hoped-for answer.

MICHAEL CAME OVER to Emily's Friday night, loaded Dog into his long, shiny car and drove happily away. She watched them go with relief.

Once again, peace and quiet descended on her little house on Pine Avenue. Patches and Rosie came out of hiding, crawling all over her and purring with satisfaction. Being cats, they probably figured Dog was out of their lives for good.

They should be so lucky.

Emily went into the shop Saturday morning in high spirits. Few traces of the recent snow remained. Judging by the brightness of the sun, even that would be gone soon.

Her best clerk, Carol Cleary, arrived shortly afterward. Together the two handled customers, stocked shelves and answered a hundred and one questions and telephone calls. By closing time at five, Emily was tired but happy. Now she could go home, fix a light dinner and spend the evening with her cats and a novel she'd been trying to get to for weeks.

Driving home, she spared a quick thought to Michael and Dog but pushed such ruminations aside. Maybe now he'd have some idea of what she'd been going through. Why, he might even decide pet ownership was not for him and—

She slammed on the brakes.

Michael's car stood at the curb before her house and she could clearly see Dog jumping up against an already rickety front fence. What in the world was going on?

Parking in the driveway in front of the garage, she climbed out of her car reluctantly. She didn't need any more problems. She was too tired, too fed up with her unwelcome boarder. Yet, there was Michael, climbing out of his car and walking toward her with a downright guilty expression on his face.

She stopped short. "Now what?" she demanded.

He grimaced. "Take a guess."

"Dog chewed up your suede jacket."

"Yes, but that's not what brings me here."

"Dog barked all night and kept the entire apartment complex awake."

"Yeah, he did, but that's not it, either. I could cope with that."

"Maybe, but why should your neighbors?"

"Exactly what the complex manager said when he banged on my door at seven this morning."

"What did you do with Dog all day?"

"Took him to the office with me."

Emily laughed incredulously. "I can just see it now. Did he run amok?"

"Mostly." He essayed a tentative grin. "Do you suppose we could go inside to discuss this?"

"Because...?"

"I've been waiting here for over an hour and I'm beginning to feel conspicuous."

"I get your point." Opening the front gate, she sidestepped Dog's enthusiastic leap and walked to the front door. Inserting the key, she swung the door open, realized Dog was making a move to slither inside and hastily pulled it closed again.

Dog smacked headfirst into the solid wooden surface and bounced back with a yelp of surprise. Michael glared at him.

"Serves you right," he said, but nevertheless bent down to rub the mutt's forehead. "Go away, will you? I need to talk to the lady."

Dog gave his master a big doggy kiss in response.

But apparently he'd learned that lesson, because they entered the house without further incident. She walked through the living room and into the kitchen, dropping her coat onto the sofa in passing.

"I could use a cup of tea," she said, turning on the gas burner beneath the teakettle.

"Yeah, me, too." Michael sat at the small break-fast table with a sigh.

Emily glanced his way, ashamed of herself because his dejected posture made her smile. "As you were saying, your landlord dropped by for a little visit."

"Yeah. He said it was me or the dog, or maybe both. He waved my lease in my face."

"You're a lawyer. Did you tell him he couldn't *do* that to you?"

"Because I'm a lawyer, I went over the lease with a fine-tooth comb before I ever signed it. He *can* do that to me."

She recoiled. "Are you trying to tell me I get stuck with that animal full-time?"

"I'm trying *not* to tell you that." He leaned forward earnestly. "I'm going to step up my search for someplace else to live," he promised. "I'll come over every day to check on Dog, I'll—I'll pay you rent for the use of your yard, I'll—"

"Don't insult me." She glared at him. "I'm not going to rent my backyard to you, for heaven's sake."

"Then what else can I do to make this easier for you? Because I'm riddled with guilt about the whole thing, Em. I never intended to maneuver you into anything—"

"Don't you mean manipulate?"

"Manipulate, maneuver, whatever you want to

call it. The thing is, the more I get to know that dog, the better I like him. All he needs is a little training and he'll be a great companion."

"A little training." She pulled down cups, flipped in teabags, poured in boiling water and served the tea. "This is getting way out of hand, Michael."

"Not really. It won't be for long, I promise. If there's anything I can do to make it easier on you in the meantime…"

"Hurry. All you can do is hurry."

He frowned. "Somehow that doesn't seem like enough." He took a tentative sip of tea. He brightened. "I know."

"I'm afraid to hear this."

"I can take you out to dinner."

"Bribery?" She raised her brows to let him know she was kidding. "Is that your way of finagling an invitation to stay for dinner?"

"You cut me to the quick." He gave her a sorrowful glance. "It's my way of thanking you for all you've done for me and Dog. Please let me take you to dinner."

"I don't know." But she was weakening. She'd planned to open a can of tomato soup and grill a cheese sandwich, but this sounded like a better idea.

"No big deal," he nudged her. "We could go get hamburgers at the Watering Hole or spaghetti at Luigi's or—"

"A hamburger does sound good," she said to cut off a recitation of every restaurant in Shepherd's Pass. Besides, it was early—not quite six—and there wouldn't be anybody there to link her name with Michael's. *That* she didn't want. "But it will have to be quick," she added.

"Why? Do you've have a late date?" He looked annoyed at that prospect.

"No, but I—" Too late she realized she'd just confirmed her wallflower status. "I have plans, that's all."

"No problem." He seemed considerably more cheerful. He glanced at his heavy gold wristwatch. "Can we go now, or is it too early for you?"

"Now is fine. Just let me feed my cats first."

"Great. While you do that, I'll make sure Dog's got everything he needs."

She nodded, already thinking that she could be making a gigantic mistake here. And when had she actually agreed to take on Dog full-time, anyway?

She sighed, recognizing a fait accompli when she saw one.

MICHAEL WAS SURPRISED to find the Watering Hole jumping this early in the evening. Everywhere he turned, he saw someone he knew.

Apparently, Emily did, too. She didn't look happy about it, either.

The minute the hamburgers were delivered, she grabbed hers and said, "Let's eat and get out of here."

"What's your hurry?" He cocked his head, teasing her.

"I told you, I have plans."

"Why, Emily Patton, I do believe you're ashamed to be seen in public with me."

The telltale flush on her cheeks belied her words, which were, "Of course not. Don't be ridiculous."

He popped a French fry into his mouth and chewed thoughtfully. "I don't think I'm being ridiculous at all. You never did like me."

"I never said such a thing."

"Actions speak louder than words. You've never wanted to be my friend."

He could tell she wasn't joking around when she said, "I never knew you had any friends, Michael. You always seemed like a real lone wolf."

That shocked him more than he wanted her to know. He'd never seen *himself* that way. He'd thought he was…self-contained. He knew everyone but kept his own counsel. He depended upon himself, just as his mother had taught him to do.

Until now. Now he seemed to be depending upon Emily Patton, the most unlikely accomplice he could imagine.

And maybe the prettiest. He frowned. She really was a knockout. He'd been blind to her physical attraction, although it was difficult to imagine how he'd overlooked her all these years.

She shifted uneasily. "Say something. Have I offended you? I didn't mean to."

"I'm not offended, just surprised."

"No kidding." Those beautiful long-lashed blue eyes opened wider. "How do you see yourself, then?"

"As a very lucky man."

"Because?"

"You were with me when I found Dog."

She squirmed. "Oh, I don't know about that."

Her lips tightened as if she were making a determined effort to ignore the growing intimacy of the conversation. "Whatever. Can you just eat so I can go home?"

He could almost hear the part she left out: *before I have to explain what I'm doing here with you.*

That hope was blasted when Thalia's voice interrupted them. "My goodness, Emily, what are you doing here with *Michael?*"

# 5

"I—WHY, I—MICHAEL—?"

Emily looked helplessly at Michael, willing him to provide an answer to Thalia's astonished question.

He smiled that easy lawyer smile, the one nobody in their right mind would trust. "We're here to discuss custody," he said smoothly.

Luke gave a snort of laughter. Thalia was puzzled. "Custody?"

"Of Dog." Emily picked up the fiction. "Michael ran into a little pothole on his road to dog ownership. We've got a few issues to work out."

Michael added insincerely, "Care to join us?"

Thalia and Luke looked at each other and smiled. For the first time, Emily realized they were holding hands, and her romantic heart melted.

"Don't feel you have to," she said. "I'll bet you want to be alone."

"We wouldn't mind it," Luke admitted. "Before we go, how's that dog doing, anyway?"

"Fine," they said in unison.

"I got back the test results and planned to call Monday. But I can tell you both now, he's basically a healthy animal."

Michael's grin was so broad Thalia seemed surprised by it. "That's good to know," he said.

Emily felt a grudging relief, too. Dog's life *had* been a hard one. Besides, she'd never wish any animal ill.

Even one she didn't particularly like.

Luke lifted a hand in farewell. "On that happy note, we'll run along. Talk to you in more detail Monday, Michael." The couple moved away, walking so close together that their shoulders touched.

Emily sighed. "I'm so happy for those two."

"Yeah." But Michael didn't *look* happy. He muttered, almost under his breath, "I hope they know what they're getting into."

"Aha!"

"What aha?"

"You don't believe in marriage." That conclusion now seemed crystal clear.

"Not much." He picked up his hamburger. "Let's finish eating and get out of here, okay? I just remembered something I have to do."

Yeah, right, she thought, but she obediently returned to her dinner.

"THANKS FOR A NICE EVENING," Emily said, loitering just inside her front door. It had begun to snow lightly on the way to her house, and now she wrapped her arms around her waist and shivered. "You said you had something to do, so if you have to go—"

"Yeah, I do." So why didn't he? Michael tried to convince himself that he didn't have the foggiest idea why he lingered.

He did, though. Seeing Luke and Thalia had

shaken him up. Regardless of what the future held, they were happy in the here and now.

As Michael was. The past few days shuttling between his real life and Emily's, sharing his concerns for Dog with her, had filled a void he hadn't even realized he had.

So he said, "I'll bring the custody papers over tomorrow."

"On Sunday?"

"Sure, why not? How about early afternoon?" That would give him time to prepare the document, which he hadn't done to date.

"I guess that will be all right." She leaned harder on the half-open door.

He cupped her chin and tilted her face up. "Good night, then, Emily. Thanks for everything."

He intended a quick peck on the mouth, or maybe even on the cheek, but the instant he leaned toward her, he seemed to lose his compass. His lips touched hers, lightly at first. He wasn't as strong as he'd thought, though. An urge he'd ruthlessly tamped down ever since they'd hauled Dog out of the trash bin grabbed him and wouldn't let go.

The kiss heated up in a flash. He couldn't be sure if she was actively participating or simply being swept along by his intensity. Whichever it was, the kiss was definitely worth waiting for.

Even when she shoved herself out of his light embrace, glared at him and shouted, "Goodbye!" in no uncertain terms.

SHE SLAMMED THE DOOR almost in his face.

She was ashamed of herself for doing it, but her

temper had simply gotten the best of her. How dare he kiss her! How dare he presume so much!

How dare he make her like it?

Stamping around, she got the cats as stirred up as she was. By the time she flung herself into bed, she was seething.

She didn't want her relationship with Michael Forbes to go any deeper. He was not the kind of man she enjoyed being around. He was too cynical and tricky, for starters.

At least, he *had* been, up until he found Dog. Now he seemed to be changing right before her eyes. But she'd never believed a leopard could change its spots, and she didn't believe Michael could change sufficiently to satisfy her. He was what he was, and they'd been on opposite sides of every fence for far too long.

She just wished he hadn't kissed her.

Tossing and turning, she finally looked at the glowing dial of the bedside clock. Two o'clock. She groaned and fumbled for the pillow to pull it over her head. What had happened to her ability to fall asleep in a nanosecond? She wasn't accustomed to this insomnia. She couldn't stand it!

Neither, apparently, could Rosie and Patches. Rising in unison from the foot of her bed where they usually slept, they walked over her legs a couple of times to register their strong objections, then jumped to the floor and disappeared into the dark.

It was all Michael's fault.

She'd been thrashing around for another half hour before she realized that Dog hadn't made a sound all night. Maybe there was hope for him after all.

Was there hope for *her*?

"SIGN RIGHT THERE." Michael pointed. "And then again here."

She hesitated, strangely reluctant to formalize their arrangement. On the other hand, what did she have to lose?

She signed.

He folded the papers, looking well satisfied with himself. "That's that," he announced. "We now share joint custody of Dog."

"I suppose." A yawn sneaked up on her and she covered her mouth with her hand. "I'm sorry," she exclaimed. "I didn't mean to do that, but—" Another yawn overtook her.

A slight smile hovered around his mouth. "Am I to deduce you didn't sleep well last night?"

"You could jump to that conclusion, if you want."

"I'm sorry. I'm sure once Dog gets used to his doghouse he'll stop keeping you up."

"Oh, he didn't keep me up." She caught her lower lip between her teeth. "That is…"

He waited. Finally he said, "If it wasn't Dog's fault, was it mine?"

"Yours?" She stared at him in consternation. "Why would you think that?"

"Because I kissed you," he said blithely. "I couldn't help myself, Emily. You looked so darn cute, and you've been so helpful—with Dog, I mean. I lost my head."

She laughed incredulously. "You? Lawyer Forbes? I don't believe you've ever lost your head in your entire life."

"Is that a compliment or an insult?"

"You decide."

"I'll take it as a compliment, then, although I don't believe that's how you meant it."

"Just don't do it again."

"What? Take what you say as compliments?"

"No, kiss me."

"Glad to." He reached for her.

She hopped back in alarm. "Stop that!"

"But—"

"Have you lost your mind?"

"But you said, kiss me."

"I said, don't do it again, period. Kiss me, I meant."

"If I had you on the witness stand, I think I could break down that story."

"But I'm not, so don't try."

"Even if—"

A banging on the front door interrupted them and she started. "Good heavens, now what?" she wondered aloud, hurrying to answer what sounded like an urgent summons.

Little Davy Robinson stood there, his cheeks flushed and his eyes wide. "Come quick!" he cried, pointing to the open gate. "Your dog got loose and I think he's running away or something!"

"DAMN DOG," Michael muttered under his breath as he trotted down the snowy street, looking right and left for his missing canine. "Just when things were getting good."

"Dog!" Emily cried. "Here, Dog! Where are you? Please—"

"I'll help!" Davy joined in the chase.

Emily stopped running and caught the boy's hand. "Thanks, but you'd better go back home. I'll bet your mom's looking for you."

"Ah, Emily—"

"I'm sorry, Davy, but I don't want your mom to worry. I'll come let you know when we get Dog back." She smiled encouragingly. "Thanks for letting us know. Uh, do you know how he got loose?"

Davy nodded eagerly. "He busted a board. I saw him. He was chasing a cat."

Emily groaned. Just what she needed in her backyard: an escape artist. "Thanks, Davy. You go on home, now. I'll talk to you later."

The boy turned back, muttering under his breath. Emily looked around just in time to see Dog come dancing out of the small park a block ahead. The animal dashed up to Michael, then shied away. Tail wagging, he took off again, glancing back over his shoulder as if to tease the man into following.

Michael took off running and Emily hurried after him. Dog and man disappeared into the trees in the park and she slowed her pace. The sun blasted down on her, warm out of all proportion to the actual temperature, which must be in the fifties. Patches of snow still lay about, with considerably more in the shadows of the trees. Over to one side, several kids tossed a Frisbee around and a number of adults strolled the paved walkways.

"Stop him!"

Emily whirled to find Dog hurtling toward her, Michael in hot pursuit. She flung out her arms and stepped into the dog's path.

Dog neatly sidestepped without losing either balance or speed.

Michael didn't.

Hurtling into her, he wrapped his arms around her and took her to the ground with him. They landed on a mound of snow, Emily on top. She struggled to free herself.

"What do you think you're doing?" she cried. "Michael!"

Belatedly she realized he was gasping for breath. "Michael? Speak to me!"

"Let me catch my breath," he gasped. "That damn dog!"

For some reason, that struck her as funny. Here they were, two mature adults outwitted by a lone stray and wrestling around in a snowbank. Her grin turned to laughter.

At that moment, Dog pranced up. Bending forward, he licked the side of Michael's face. Emily lunged for the animal, who darted nimbly back out of reach.

"Ow!" Michael dragged her back down. "Those elbows hurt."

"Sorry. I thought I had him that time. If you'll just let me up—"

"Why? I kinda like you right here." He wiggled beneath her, reminding her that they remained in intimate contact with her body sprawled on top of his, virtually from head to toe.

"I *don't* like it," she said, although she did. "Don't forget why we came here."

"To fool around in a snowbank?"

"To catch a runaway mutt!"

Dog darted in for another teasing feint. Michael grabbed, in the process tossing Emily off into the snow. She let out a screech of protest. Dog jumped over Michael, shoved his cold nose in Emily's face, then took off again with head and tail high.

Michael sat back disgustedly on his heels. "Well, hell," he said. "So this won't be a total loss—" Looking into her face, laughing, he leaned over and kissed her.

Emily couldn't believe it. Kissing her at her front door was bad enough, but kissing her in public was unforgivable. There were people around. They'd be seen. She didn't want to be the subject of gossip.

While she debated her options, she might as well kiss him back. But before she could figure it all out, she felt the wet slurp of Dog's tongue on her cold cheek. *Go away,* she thought. *Not now. I'm busy!*

"Got you!"

Michael was talking to Dog, not to Emily. She opened dazed eyes to find the man sitting up beside her prone body, his arm around the animal's neck. He grinned.

"Fooled him, didn't I." He roughed the dog around affectionately. "Dumb dog doesn't think I can walk and chew gum, I guess."

Or kiss and spring dog traps.

Emily sat up in disgust. "You fooled him, all right."

"Damn straight." Michael looked very pleased with himself. "About what happened…"

She raised her brows. Was he going to apologize for using her as dog bait?

"I didn't mean to knock you down like that. When I ran into you, I just automatically grabbed hold."

She gave him a sweet smile. "Luckily, I landed on something soft—you."

He said, "Ouch!" and gave her a rueful grin. "You aren't hurt, are you?"

She wanted to say, *My ego's bruised,* but instead simply shook her head.

"You're a good sport, lady."

"Among other things." She climbed to her feet. Brushing snow off the seat of her pants, she regarded man and dog. "Davy said Dog broke a board. I'm taking that to mean the fence."

"I'll fix it." Hanging on to Dog's collar with one hand, he unbuckled his belt with the other and dragged it free of the belt loops. Slipping it under the collar, he fashioned a makeshift leash.

"Great. Fix it. There'll always be something else." And she was getting darned tired of it, too.

As if sensing her mood, Dog edged toward her. Before she could stalk away, the miserable mutt licked her hand. Then she compounded the situation by looking down into those big brown beseeching eyes.

"See?" Michael said. "He's sorry, and so am I."

Then she made the mistake of looking into the second set of big beseeching eyes.

For the first time, she felt real stirrings of affection—for the dog, not the man. She cleared her throat. "Whatever. Let's get him back home and see how much damage he's done this time."

She marched out of the park, back straight.

"THE FENCE IS FIXED."

Emily looked up from the stove and the pot she was stirring. "Do you think it will hold him this time?"

"Oh, sure." He looked down at his muddy hands. Dog had knocked down the board and then chewed on it for a while before taking off. "Mind if I wash up before I go?"

"Be my guest."

Cool, he thought. She was real cool about that little encounter in the park. One of these days he was going to have to get her to admit she wasn't any more indifferent to him than he was to her.

But what the hell. The chase was his favorite part.

On the way back to the kitchen, the black cat crossed his path. Completely without superstition, he scooped her up and carried her along—Rosie, he thought the name was. He walked into the kitchen holding the cat against his chest and stroking the fluffy fur.

Emily's eyes widened. "I can't believe she let you do that."

He grinned. "I have a way with females."

She rolled her eyes. "Apparently. Rosie doesn't normally like to be handled by strangers."

"I'm not a stranger. She's seen me around." He

set the black cat on the floor; she twined around his legs a few times before heading for the cat food dish in the corner.

He looked around the cozy kitchen then, taking in the pot simmering on the stove, the luscious aromas of tomatoes and onions and other good things wafting through the air. His mouth watered for another of her home-cooked meals, but would it be prudent to start hinting around? He'd already tried her patience.

Still, he wasn't sure he could force his feet toward the door and leave all these attractions behind.

"Uh—" he licked his lips "—is there anything else I can do for you?"

She gave him a slanting glance. "Can't think of a thing."

He sighed. "Nothing at all?"

She paused with her hand on a cabinet pull. "One thing, maybe."

He brightened. "Name it."

"You could eat a bowl of this vegetable beef soup I've been working on all day. If you don't have other plans, of course."

"You're joking, right? Your homemade meals are worth any number of other plans."

She laughed and he could see the stiff set of her shoulders relax. "Michael, you're such a fraud. You were just waiting for me to invite you."

"That's true." He watched her carry two large soup bowls to the stove. "Can I set the table?"

"Silver is in that drawer." She pointed with her chin, both hands busy serving the soup. "Crackers are in that cupboard. Glasses are on that shelf."

"And all's right with my world," he said, and started pulling out utensils. He owed Dog a nice big steak bone for this one.

IT WAS NEARLY EIGHT O'CLOCK before Michael left.

It was nearly eleven o'clock before Emily went to bed.

It was nearly one o'clock before she gave in and got up. Sitting on the side of her bed with her head in her hands, she wondered what in the world was causing this unfamiliar insomnia.

It couldn't be Michael.

Why would she lie awake thinking about a man she'd known most of her life and disliked the entire time? No, it had to be something else.

It was her crummy social life, that's what it was. She was getting tired of her own company. She hadn't been dating anyone special for at least six months. She spent too much time alone with her cats—make that pets, since the temporary addition of Dog.

She felt restless and unfocused because she needed a social outlet, she decided. The next guy who asked her for a date would get a resounding yes!

Unless that guy was Michael Forbes, which seemed unlikely. He might cozy up to her to get a good meal but he wasn't really interested in *her*.

Any more than she was interested in him.

THALIA DROPPED BY Sew Bee It on Monday. Emily was just unloading fabrics, including the beautiful pale pink satin specially ordered for Thalia's wedding dress, and was delighted to see her friend.

She spread the luscious fabric across one of the cutting tables. "Isn't it gorgeous?" she demanded.

"Wow!" Thalia's eyes were wide and she looked impressed. "I'll say it is."

"It will make up beautifully in that pattern you liked." Emily refolded the fabric and rerolled the bolt.

For the first time, Thalia looked doubtful. "I don't really know, Em. Luke's getting impatient. I'm not sure there'll be time for you to make it before—"

"Oh, yes I will! I'm determined to do this for you, and Luke, too. I'll get started right away."

Thalia still looked uneasy. "I love the idea of the dress, truly I do, but I hate to rush you. It doesn't seem right."

"Of course, it does." Emily waved away all objections. "This is something I really want to do."

"Okay." Thalia's expression turned sly. "Although I'm surprised you have time."

"I've got the same amount of time I've always had."

"But a lot of it these days is being taken up by Michael—and Dog, of course."

Emily stifled a groan. "Okay, what are you getting at?"

Thalia gave an elaborate shrug. "Nothing, except three people have dropped into Mom's flower shop this morning and mentioned that they saw you kissing Michael at the park yesterday."

"I didn't kiss Michael!" Emily glared at her friend.

Thalia looked confused. "But weren't you rolling around in the snow kissing—"

"Absolutely not!" Emily turned away, determined to cut off this turn in the conversation.

Behind her, she heard Thalia's incredulous gasp and then she said, "I get it. He was kissing you. Is it a matter of semantics, Em?"

Emily's shoulders slumped. "Can we talk about something more interesting?"

"There *is* nothing more interesting. Honestly, this is all over town—kissing in the park in broad daylight!"

At last Emily turned around, feeling sheepish and off balance. "Okay, you caught me. But it was nothing, really. We were chasing that darn dog. When we ended up in that snowbank, things just sort of happened."

"Things."

"Don't tease, Thalia."

Thalia seemed to realize that she'd reached the outer limits of Emily's patience because she pulled up immediately. "I'm sorry," she apologized. "It's just that you and Michael are such an unlikely pair."

"More unlikely than you know."

"You do have a dog in common."

"But not for long. Michael swears he'll find another place just as fast as he can."

"As a matter of fact, I might know of a possibility for him. I can give you a name and number. In the meantime, maybe the two of you can get better acquainted," Thalia suggested. "You know, I never disliked Michael. I just never felt he cared to be my friend."

Emily nodded her understanding. "He still seems that way, but I think it might be partly because he doesn't like people getting too close."

"Knowing his mother, I can understand why."

Emily looked at her friend in surprise. "Why would you say that?"

"Because I *do* know his mother—or did. She represented my parents in a few legal matters. She's apparently an excellent lawyer but so cold. Mom said she almost had a case of frostbite by the time everything was straightened out."

Emily felt a sudden sympathy for the little boy growing up with such a parent. No wonder Michael wasn't all touchy-feely.

But that didn't make her like him any more.

Again she changed the subject. "Come look at the evening shoes I got on my lunch hour," she said, leading the way behind the counter. "They were on sale at Clark's and I just love them."

BY THE TIME EMILY REACHED home that night, the temperature had dropped to a chilly thirty-two degrees. After she'd fed all the animals, checked the mail and prepared dinner, it had plummeted to twenty.

It's going to snow, she thought happily, peering out the window. It didn't usually snow much in November. By the glow of the porch light, she watched Dog walk across the yard to the food and water dishes in front of his doghouse.

She felt an unwelcome sympathy for him. The water was probably already frozen, and the food, too. She really should let him in to eat in the warmth of the kitchen.

No, darn it! She'd refill the dishes later, but she wasn't going to let him in. Every time she did he got into trouble.

By eight-thirty, the thermometer registered a mere fifteen degrees. She really had to do *something*.

What she did was open a can of dog food and spoon it into a foil pie pan, which she placed near the back door, along with another dish of water. She'd let Dog in just long enough to eat and she'd watch him every single minute. But that was *all* she'd do.

Dog was there almost before she could get the door open. As if drawn by a magnet, he skidded up to the food and water and pounced. The whole lower half of him wagged in time with his tail; this dog was one happy camper.

She sat on a chair to watch, not trusting him as far as she could see him. He really was a loveable doofus who obviously meant well, even if he did goof up a—

The telephone rang. It was Michael.

"I'm just checking up on our dog," he said cheerfully.

"What do you want to know?"

"Has he been in any more trouble today?"

"None that I know of, but the day isn't over."

"Hey, that's no way to talk. He's not a *bad* dog."

"He's trying to be."

"I hear affection in your tone. Emily, you're softening."

"I am not!"

"You are. I'm a trained observer of the human scene and I recognize these things."

"Well, recognize this—I've got a lead on a house for you."

"You do?"

"It's on the north side of town, a small single-family home with a fenced yard. Thalia told me about it."

"Who owns it?"

"Someone I don't know. I wrote everything down, though. Hang on a minute, will you?"

Putting the phone on the counter, she scooted into the living room where she'd left her purse. Digging into it, she extracted the scrap of paper upon which she'd written a name and phone number.

Anything she could do to get him into a place with a yard, she was more than willing to do. She dashed back into the kitchen and stopped short, her mouth open in horror.

Dog sat in the middle of the room, bright-eyed and happy, a silver slipper dangling from his mouth.

# 6

EMILY'S SHRIEK FLASHED across the telephone wires and into Michael's ear, where it exploded along every nerve ending. His own roar overwhelmed hers. "What's wrong? What in the name of God is going on?"

All he heard was lots of heavy breathing; she was apparently having trouble getting herself together. Then in a voice more like a croak she said, "Nothing! Forget it."

The line went dead.

Michael stood there in the middle of his sleek and modern apartment feeling as if the rug had just been snatched out from under him. Something awful had happened at Emily's and he had a horrible suspicion that Dog was at the root of it.

He glanced at his watch and groaned. He was due at Sylvia Dalton's mansion in five minutes for a meeting. The time was, of course, ridiculous, but Four-Jay had just returned from an out-of-town trip and was eager to be brought up-to-date by his attorney.

Four-Jay and Sylvia Dalton were Michael's biggest clients. No way could he stand them up.

At least not for anything less than a full-blown emergency, which Emily was obviously having.

Michael hit the programmed cell phone number on his way to the parking garage. The Dalton family butler answered and accepted the terse message: *"Emergency…hope I'll only be a few minutes late…let you know as soon as I can…sorry…"*

And he turned the car toward the little house on Pine Avenue.

EMILY JUST SAT DOWN on a kitchen chair and bawled.

Holding the shredded shoe in one hand, she threw back her head and howled. It wasn't even the shoe, not actually; it was the impossibility of her situation.

Here she was, baby-sitting an animal she didn't even like while he destroyed her life. It wasn't fair! She cried harder.

Dog responded by whimpering and creeping up to her with his tail between his legs. He rested his muzzle on her lap and looked up to her with those big brown eyes begging for forgiveness.

Choking back sobs, she pushed him aside, stood up and walked away from the source of her grief. She would *not* forgive him that easily. She wouldn't! She opened the back door, then turned to glare at him.

Dog slunk outdoors, a mere shadow of his usual bouncy self. That made her feel even worse, and she sobbed all the way to the bathroom. Once there, she washed her face with cold water, took a deep breath, glared at her reflection in the medicine chest mirror and told herself to *get a grip*.

No one would be coming to her rescue. Michael

had his big important meeting to worry about and wouldn't have time for her petty problems. Well, she'd had enough! Dog should be *Michael's* petty problem, not hers. If he couldn't find a place to stash the animal, he could just find another patsy because Emily—

—was startled by the sudden and incessant pealing of the doorbell, followed by a rough male voice calling her name.

Michael had arrived.

"OPEN THIS DOOR or I'll break it in!"

He meant it, too. His fears had grown with every inch he'd driven to reach her. No way would a locked door deter him.

The door flew open in his face and there she stood, backlit so he couldn't see her expression. "You!" she said, as if it were an accusation. "What are *you* doing here?"

He barged inside. "I'm here to find out why you screamed and hung up on me."

"That's n-not exactly how it happened."

The little catch in her voice did not escape his notice. And once inside the room, he saw that her eyes were red. She'd obviously been crying. It was all he could do not to clench his hands into fists and hit something.

Only what would he hit? Dog?

"Tell me," he demanded, his tone grim.

She swallowed hard and licked her lips. "While I was getting that name and number for you, D-Dog chewed up a new pair of shoes."

"Is that all?" He stared at her, baffled.

He'd roused her ire and her blue eyes flashed. "Isn't that enough? It was the last straw, Michael! Don't you get it? *It was the last straw!* I'm sick and tired of being harassed by that creature."

She looked so alone when she said it. He had the strangest feeling that this was not the time for reason, certainly not the time to point out that shoes could be replaced and he'd be glad to do so.

Now was the time to offer a little sympathy and support, two things with which he had very little experience either getting or giving, except in a professional capacity. Nevertheless, he opened his arms awkwardly; equally awkward, she walked into them, put her head on his shoulder and sobbed.

Something welled up in his chest, some emotion more tender than he'd before encountered. He patted her shoulder, murmured meaningless but heartfelt words of support and understanding, and wondered why he felt such possessiveness toward this completely mystifying woman.

AFTER A WHILE, Emily straightened, sniffled, forced a tremulous smile and said, "Can I offer you a brownie and a glass of milk?"

He frowned. "That's all you've got to say?"

She managed an anxious smile. "I'm willing to tell you what set me off," she hedged, "but if you're going to have to listen to me make a fool out of myself, you at least deserve a reward." She added as an afterthought, "That is, unless you've got to rush off for that meeting you mentioned."

"I've got plenty of time." His grin was welcome. "Plus, I never turn down food at your house."

"I've noticed." She led the way to the kitchen and indicated that he should sit while she rounded up the snacks. When she'd served him, she sat across from him with a sigh. "I lost it," she said mournfully. "When I walked in here and saw him with my new shoe in his mouth—" Her glance strayed to the remnants of a silver slipper on the floor at their feet.

His gaze followed hers. "I'll replace the shoes," he said.

"I can't let you do that."

"Why not? I said I'd cover all Dog's expenses."

"That means food and collars, not my personal items."

"Be reasonable, Em." He popped the last bite of chocolate brownie into his mouth and reached for a second. "You shouldn't have any out-of-pocket expenses related to our deal."

She shook her head stubbornly. "I shouldn't have left him alone in here. It was my fault and I accept responsibility. It's just that..." She chewed her lower lip. "It hit me wrong, that's all. I'm all right now."

"Are you?" He stopped eating to stare at her with an appraising gaze. "Because you don't look all right to me."

"Thanks for nothing."

"Now, don't get mad. I'm on your side, remember?" He licked crumbs from his fingertips. "Emily," he said suddenly, "have you ever thought of hiring out as a cook?"

Caught off guard, she frowned. "No. Never."

"If you ever do, I want first dibs."

She couldn't doubt his sincerity. "It's a deal," she said, secure in the knowledge that there was no way she would ever cook for anyone for money. Plucking a tissue from the small packet in her pocket, she patted her face, took a deep breath and said, "There. I'm fine again, see?"

She gave him a bright smile, which he didn't return. "If you say so." He rose. "Is there anything I can do for you before I go?"

"I can't think of a thing."

"In that case…" He reached out unexpectedly and touched her cheek with gentle fingers. "I'm sorry, Em. I'll look into an obedience class for Dog, I promise."

"Thank you." She should move away from his touch, but it warmed her inside and out.

"Good night."

"G-good night."

He left and she sat there for a long time, wondering how he'd managed to calm her so fast and so completely.

Which got her all worked up again.

MICHAEL DROVE QUICKLY to the Dalton place, pulling up just behind Luke's car. They met halfway to the house and walked inside together.

The butler met them in the front hall. Luke asked, "Is my mother in?"

"No, sir. She and Mr. Jordan went out a few minutes ago."

"Thanks, James." Luke turned to Michael. "Sorry."

"I'm late," Michael admitted. "Something came up. Damn!"

"Join me in a drink and tell me all about it." Luke turned toward the library and its massive oak bar.

Michael followed with some reluctance. "I'm not sure I want to tell you about it."

"Why not?" Luke considered the rows of bottles behind the bar.

"Because it's dumber than hell." Michael was just beginning to realize how dumb.

"Sounds intriguing." Luke offered a brandy.

Michael sipped. "I was on my way out for this meeting when Emily called. In the middle of it, she screamed and hung up on me."

Luke raised a skeptical brow. "Whatever you said, I hope you apologized."

"It wasn't what I said, it was what Dog did. Naturally, I had to drive over there to find that out."

"And?"

"He chewed up a new pair of shoes."

Luke considered. "Yep, that would upset a woman."

"She said it was the last straw. I believed her." Michael stared into his glass moodily. "She hates dogs anyway, and this one is particularly trying."

"Then why's she doing this?"

"I sort of finagled her into it." Michael tossed off the rest of his drink. "I've got to get Dog out of there as fast as I can, because she's close to the breaking point."

"You really like that animal, don't you."

"Yeah, I do. She would, too, if she'd give him a chance." Michael set the glass on the bar. "Thanks for the drink. Tell your mother I'll call tomorrow and apologize. Grovel, actually, if that's what it takes."

"It will, if you tell her the truth." Luke rolled his eyes. "Tell her you had a flat tire or got hit by lightning on the way over. Just don't tell her that she wasn't as important as some dog."

"Good advice. I'll take it," Michael said, relieved that Luke had apparently missed the point: it was the woman who'd caused the delay, not the dog.

The woman.

THE FRONT DOOR BELL at the Sew Bee It tinkled. Emily looked up with a quick smile which slipped when she saw Michael.

"Oh," she said, "it's you."

"Who did you expect, the Lone Ranger?" He crossed the room and slapped a package on the counter.

She eyed it warily. "What's that?"

"Open it."

She took a quick step back. "No, thanks."

"Then I will." Reaching inside, he slid out a box.

A shoe box.

"You didn't!"

"I sure did."

"But—" She flipped open the box and stared at the shoes inside. Right style, right size. "How did you pull this off? You didn't even see these shoes, at least, not in the original version minus the tooth marks.''

"Simple. I went from shoe store to shoe store asking for a pair exactly like the pair you bought yesterday."

Her stomach lurched. "You told everyone in town you were buying me shoes?"

"Not everyone in town, just everyone in town who sells shoes." He looked quite pleased with himself. "I got it right, didn't I?"

"The shoes are right, but the method is all wrong. People were already talking and you had to go and—"

"Who's talking?"

"Everybody!"

"About?"

"Us!" She bit her lip.

He looked genuinely puzzled. "What about us?"

She let out an exasperated sigh. "About us kissing in the park the other day. That's what about!"

He laughed. "Really?"

"Don't look so proud of yourself. I'm not eager to have my name linked with yours."

"Why not? I'm single, a contributing member of society, an all-around great guy."

"That's *your* opinion."

His brows rose. "And your opinion is…?"

"I don't want to talk about it. Just take those shoes back." She pushed the box toward him.

"No way. What would be the point? Everybody already knows I bought them, but nobody would know I returned them. Don't cut off your nose to spite your face."

Gritting her teeth, she considered that and finally had to admit he was right. "All right," she said ungraciously. "Just don't do anything like this again."

"I'm not promising a thing."

"Why am I not surprised?" Reaching into her pocket, she pulled out a slip of paper and thrust it toward him. "Here's the information about the house I thought might work for you."

"Thanks." Without looking at it, he thrust it into his pocket.

When he didn't immediately leave, she asked peevishly, "Was there something else?"

"Yes. I found out about obedience lessons."

"For you or for Dog?" She laughed: Ah, to have him properly trained to respond appropriately to her concerns.

"Both," he said. "Actually, more than both—all."

"All who?"

"All of us—you, me and Dog. According to Natalie—"

"Natalie?"

"Natalie Colson. She raises and trains Dobermans. She also teaches obedience classes. The current class started last week, but she says we can catch up if we show up tonight and work hard."

She frowned. "Why do I have to go? Dog is your dog."

"But he's living with you. You want him to obey you, don't you?"

"Yes, but I don't want to have to put in a lot of effort in that direction," she said pettishly.

He laughed. "That's what I like about you, Emily. You don't have any problem being unreasonable."

"I'm not being unre—" But she was and she knew it. She gave him a sheepish smile. "Okay, I guess I see your point."

"Good, because Natalie said it's as important to train the people as it is the dog. You can't expect him to respond properly if you're not consistent and don't know what you're doing."

"I suppose I can see that," she said grudgingly.

"I knew you would." He flipped her a quick salute. "I'll pick you and Dog up at a quarter of seven, then. The classes are held at Colson Kennels just outside town. There's an indoor training area in case of inclement weather, but that shouldn't be a problem tonight. See you later, Em."

"Later."

She watched him leave, thoroughly annoyed by his pushiness. Did the man always get his way?

Shivering, she took the shoe box off the counter and stowed it below, just so she wouldn't have to do any explaining.

THALIA DROPPED BY mid-afternoon for an update on the wedding gown. Emily showed off her progress proudly: The pieces were cut out and marked, the findings and trim collected.

"That's wonderful," Thalia said enthusiastically. "Under the circumstances, I thought—"

"What circumstances?" Emily asked quickly.

"You know. Your problems with Dog."

Emily frowned. "How do you know about my problems with Dog?"

"Luke told me."

"Who told Luke?"

"Michael, of course, when he went to the Dalton place for that meeting last night."

"He had a meeting with Luke?"

"No, silly, with Luke's mother and Four-Jay. Only he was late—"

"Four-Jay?"

"No, Michael. He was late and they hadn't waited for him, so Luke gave him a drink and they talked."

"About Dog."

"And you. Too bad about your shoes."

"My shoes! Michael even blabbed about my shoes?"

"Oh, no. I heard that at Clark's. They got quite a kick about Michael coming in and asking if they had sold you anything yesterday."

Emily sat down hard on the wicker chair. "I don't believe this."

"Neither did I, at first—you and Michael as a couple, I mean. But the more I hear—"

"I don't want to be the topic of conversation around here," Emily wailed.

"Well," Thalia said reassuringly, "you are, so get used to it. As I was saying, the more I hear, the more I'm beginning to think you two would be a great match. You're different, but as they say, opposites attract. And I think you're having a good influence on him already."

"You do?"

"He missed a really important meeting for you, didn't he?"

Emily's lips tightened. "If he did, he didn't tell me about it. He said it was no big deal."

Thalia laughed. "See? He put you ahead of his best clients."

"Or his favorite Dog."

But later, while she was cutting ten yards of bright blue sailcloth for Karen Robinson to use in redecorating little Davy's room, Emily thought about what Thalia had said...and wondered.

EMILY AND DOG WERE WAITING when Michael drove up. It was a pleasant evening, not too cold and without wind, so only light jackets were required.

Emily opened the gate, keeping a tight grip on Dog's leash. The animal darted forward, dragging her behind him. Michael cut off escape, however, and took the leash from her.

His grin warmed her. "You're ready. That's good."

"You said—"

"Yes, but not all women pay attention to times."

"I do," she said airily, watching him open the car door. "How are we going to keep him from running all over the car? If you think I'm going to sit back there and hold him down—"

"No need." Stepping back, he made a clicking sound. Dog jumped into the back seat without hesitation. Michael climbed in after him and shut the door.

Emily opened the passenger door. "Well, if you think I'm going to drive your car—"

"I don't." Grunting, Michael slid an arm around Dog's neck and pressed him to a sitting position. He fumbled with a variety of straps and buckles while restraining the wiggling dog.

Emily frowned. "Would you like to explain what you're doing?"

"I'm buckling Dog into his seat belt."

"A seat belt for dogs? Now I've heard everything."

"That's entirely possible."

Snapping the last strap into place, Michael twisted to open the car door. Dog's dive was brought up short by the harness secured to the regular seat belt. He blinked, looked confused, then settled down to a sitting position.

"My gosh," Emily said when Michael had climbed behind the wheel, "I think it's going to work."

"Yeah." He gave her a broad grin. "Nice, huh?"

Nodding, she settled back in her own seat. Michael was obviously ready to do what had to be done, spend what had to be spent, to keep this dog.

And heaven help anyone who got in his way!

IT TOOK MICHAEL about two minutes to realize that dotty old Natalie Colson had forgotten more about dogs than he or Emily would ever know. The same could doubtless be said for the other seven dogs and assorted owners clustered outside the graveled training ring.

Natalie clapped her hands for attention. "People," she announced, "we have a new member in our little class. Say hello to Mr. and Mrs. Forbes and their dog, Dog."

Emily's face flushed. "Wait, I'm not—"

"All in good time," Natalie interrupted. "Pay attention and you'll soon catch up with the class. Everybody, let's have those dogs sitting on your left side—remember? Shorten up on the lead and lift it as you press down on your dog's rear end—that's right. Keep his head up, Mrs. Wilson—don't let her tangle you up in that lead, Angela! Uh-huh…uh-huh…good."

Slowly she walked between and around the ragged line of dogs and their amateur handlers. Occasionally she'd offer a private word, or reach down to position a dog or scratch its ears. All seemed calmer after her passing.

She came to a halt in front of the newest class members.

Michael held the leash and vainly tried to keep Dog still while Emily watched with disapproval written all over her face. Natalie took one look and shook her head in disgust.

"Sit!" she boomed, bending to press Dog's hindquarters down while simultaneously grabbing the collar and lifting. Dog sat with alacrity, then glanced around in confusion. Natalie praised him effusively and he licked her face, acting like the perfect dog.

The minute she turned her back, he jumped up and darted between Michael's legs, nearly knocking him over.

Natalie didn't notice. She was opening the gate to the training field. "Tell your dog to heel and enter in an orderly manner," she instructed. "Mr. and Mrs. Forbes—"

"I'm not—"

"Either one of you can begin and change off later. Bill, keep that dog under control! Don't let him snap at the other dogs. Laura—"

Michael and Emily exchanged glances. She looked so frustrated that he nearly laughed.

"I'll go first," he offered, hanging on to Dog's leash.

"Fine. I'll sit and watch."

"Great. You'll get your chance later."

"I can hardly wait."

He didn't think she meant that. Taking an extra wrap around his wrist, he led...or maybe dragged...Dog into the parade of dogs.

He feared it was going to be an evening he would long remember, and not fondly.

THE CLASS ONLY LASTED for an hour, but to Emily, it seemed to go on forever. She didn't know which was worse, watching Michael wrestle with Dog or wrestling with him herself.

Not that he was stupid—the dog, not Michael. Whenever Natalie approached, he snapped to attention and behaved like a perfect student. The minute she turned her back, Dog was prancing and dancing and pulling and panting. Making matters worse, he was incredibly strong for a dog his size.

Not that he was the only lousy canine student in class. There was a woman with a German shepherd that seemed determined to kill every dog that came within striking distance, plus a teenager with a yippy little terrier that spent the entire hour trying to jump up into her arms. The best student in the class, not too surprisingly, was a Border collie.

That darned dog did everything with a determined perfectionism that soon set Emily's teeth on edge. How could the dog's owner stand an animal smarter than she was? Emily had to wonder.

By the time the class ended, her arms ached and her frustration level was several notches higher than when they'd arrived. Michael didn't look any too pleased, either.

As the other students and dogs filed out, Natalie approached, frowning.

Michael spoke with a combination of dread and eagerness. "So how'd he do, teach? Does old Dog have a future competing in obedience classes?"

He held his breath waiting for the answer.

Surprisingly enough, so did Emily.

# 7

NATALIE PURSED HER LIPS. She walked around Dog and Michael, frowning, nodding, grunting.

Michael fidgeted, but Dog behaved perfectly, craning his neck to watch her while remaining planted where he sat. He looked, Emily thought, alert and intelligent.

And why would she even think such a thing? For some reason, she felt like a parent waiting for the verdict on her child: would he pass or fail?

"How old is this dog?" Natalie asked suddenly.

Emily and Michael looked at each other. He shrugged.

"We're not sure. We just got him."

"A stray?"

"Yes. How did you know?"

"He acts like one." Natalie squatted in front of the dog and raised his muzzle, peering straight into his eyes. "Had a hard time of it, eh, youngster? Well, you'll be all right now."

Michael's smile revealed vast relief. "Does that mean he's made the grade?"

Natalie rose. "Not really. Folks, if you want my advice—"

"We do," Emily declared. "Don't we, Michael?"

"Absolutely."

"Then take this dog home and give him a lot of love and affection," Natalie said briskly. "Bring him back in four or five months. He's too immature and insecure to be tossed in with all these other animals and expected to concentrate."

Emily breathed an exasperated sigh. "What are we supposed to do with him in the meantime? Let him run wild?"

Natalie chuckled. "Hardly." With a final pat for the dog, she rose. "Play with him. Work with him as we were trying to do here tonight. Work on *heel* and *sit*—easy stuff like that. Hug him a lot and tell him he's a good dog."

"Even when he's not?" Emily snapped. "Which is most of the time."

"When he makes a mistake, scold him," Natalie said evenly. "But never, ever hit him. He's been hit enough already."

"I would never hit him," Emily protested.

Natalie cocked her head toward Michael. "How about you? Can you be patient with him?"

"Patience is my middle name," he said blandly. "Don't worry, we'll do exactly as you say. Once we have his confidence and he's calmed down, we'll be back."

Natalie nodded and gave Emily an oblique glance. "Your husband's got the right idea. Just watch him and do what he does. Now if you'll excuse me, I've got another appointment."

"But Michael's not—"

"Sure he is," Natalie said, turning away. "I

know patience when I see it, and that man is *patient*.''

Emily looked at Michael, her frustration about to spill over. She'd counted on this class to make Dog easier to live with, if live with him she must. She wanted a *good* dog—actually, she wanted *no* dog, but if she had to deal with one anyway, he better be good!

Michael patted her arm. ''It's all right, honey,'' he said soothingly. ''We'll work it out.''

''Don't you call me honey,'' she snapped. ''I—''

Natalie paused and Emily realized the conversation was being overheard. Since Natalie apparently thought Michael was a saint, she must now consider Emily a shrew.

Dog wasn't the only one who'd failed to pass muster here tonight.

Gritting her teeth, Emily said to a grinning Michael, ''You're right, of course. We'll work it out.''

Then she stomped away in high dudgeon.

LIFE, OF COURSE, WENT ON, even when you shared your abode with an obedience school drop-out. At least Emily and Dog had achieved a kind of cool mutual truce. She would care to his physical needs if he would respect her turf. He could go to Michael for his emotional needs.

And did.

Michael visited Dog every day. They'd roughhouse in the backyard, go for walks, practice Dog's limited bag of tricks.

*Sit* and *heel* remained pretty much beyond his

abilities, but of all things, he quickly learned to sit up and *beg*. It was disgusting.

The first time it happened, Michael called her into the yard with such excitement that she feared another catastrophe. Rushing outside, she found him holding a dog biscuit just above Dog's head. "Beg!" he ordered in a strong voice, and Dog did!

"Good dog, good dog." Michael tossed the animal a treat, then threw his arms around the wiggling animal's neck. They fell over together on the dead grass and the sight made Emily smile until she caught herself. Since she had no intention of softening toward either man or beast, it would behoove her to remain aloof from their hijinks.

Despite her best intentions, she was thinking about that scene when Miss Pauline walked into Sew Bee It the next day, which was the Tuesday before Thanksgiving. The pleasant little lady was a favorite of Emily's and everybody else.

But she was neither a sewer nor a crafter. Emily had no idea why she was here.

"May I help you, Miss Pauline?"

"I hope so, dear." The elderly lady smiled. "I need to do some mending."

"What kind of mending?"

"Well—" Miss Pauline shook out one of the squares of cloth in her hands—a napkin, Emily saw. Leaning over to examine the item, she realized that this was indeed an antique with hand-tatted lace fluttering loosely from the edges, the fabric itself fragile and yellow with age.

"How beautiful!" she exclaimed. "Are these family heirlooms?"

"You could say that. I believe they belonged to my great-grandmother. I take them out from time to time because they make me feel closer to my family, now that everyone's gone."

"They're exquisite." Emily touched the fabric with reverent fingers. "All your family's gone, then?"

"I'm afraid so."

"Moved away gone or...?"

Miss Pauline sighed and refolded the napkin. "They've all passed on, I'm afraid. I'm the last of my line."

"Oh, dear." Emily thought fast.

Thanksgiving was the day after tomorrow and she had no plans, although she'd been invited to join Thalia and her mother. But Luke would doubtless be there, too, and Emily didn't want to intrude on family. At the moment, she had no plans whatsoever.

In that case, why not invite Miss Pauline to join her for Thanksgiving dinner? A wonderful idea, but Emily didn't want the invitation to seem like an afterthought. How to make this work?

"I don't have any family nearby, either," she said. "Since I'm going to be all alone for Thanksgiving, I wonder if you'd care to join me for dinner at my house?"

"Now, dear, you needn't feel obligated just because I came in asking for help."

"No, no, it's not an obligation," Emily said quickly. "I would be ever so grateful if you'd join me Thursday for a holiday dinner. If you'll bring the rest of your napkins, I'll be glad to repair them for you while our dinner cooks."

Miss Pauline lifted her chin. "I wouldn't want to impose."

"It's no imposition, neither the dinner nor the mending. I love doing both, but since I live alone I have only myself to look out for. You'd be doing me a favor."

"No young man?" Miss Pauline asked archly.

A vision of Michael flashed across Emily's mind, but still she shook her head emphatically. "None whatsoever," she said firmly. "I do have two cats, and there's a dog visiting."

Miss Pauline's pale brows rose, but she didn't ask the obvious. "In that case," she said, "I would be most pleased to join you, dear. Thank you for your thoughtfulness."

Emily's smile blossomed. She hadn't realized it, but she must have been dreading spending the holiday alone all along. In fact, she felt absolutely relieved.

MICHAEL'S TUESDAY business lunch with Sylvia Dalton and Four-Jay did not go well. Although the Texan seemed all right with Michael's lame excuse for missing the previous meeting, Sylvia didn't.

At all.

Her patrician features cool, she concluded their business before fixing her attorney with a gimlet eye and inquiring too sweetly, "So tell me, Michael, have you solved your time-management problems yet? At least, you were on time today."

"Now, Mrs. Dalton—" he squirmed "—you

know I was late because of car trouble." Actually, he'd claimed two flat tires, which now seemed to him to be an excessive number.

"That's right." She tapped tapered fingernails on the linen cloth covering the best table at Luigi's. "And how is Emily?"

Michael blinked in surprise and Four-Jay let out a guffaw.

"She's got your number, partner," he bellowed. "The whole town's talkin' about all the time you been spending with that little gal."

Sylvia's expression hardened. "Don't ever do that to me again, Michael. I won't be stood up by the people I employ, not for any reason. I'm overlooking it this time because you've done a good job for me so far—for us." She nodded toward Four-Jay. "Once, however, is quite enough. Do I make myself clear?"

Michael's ire had risen with every word, but he contained himself. "Perfectly clear," he said. "Since I doubt that particular circumstance will ever pop up again, I think it's safe to say—"

He saw Thalia and Luke enter and grasped at that straw.

"Excuse me, there's your son and his girl. It's critical that I speak to him. Again, I offer my most profound apologies."

"But—"

"Fine," Four-Jay said heartily, "fine. You run along, boy. Me 'n' this pretty lady have to talk to our architect anyway. You won't believe what he's fixin' to do to one a' them houses in Shangri-la number two." He shook his head mournfully.

With a nod, Michael made a hasty escape. Then, because he'd said he was going to, he had to stop by Luke and Thalia's table. They greeted him with smiles and Luke pointed to an empty chair.

"Thanks." Michael sat. "Since I just used you two as an excuse to flee the inquisition, I'll take you up on it for a minute, anyway."

Luke's brows rose. "Mom giving you a hard time?"

Michael nodded. "She's still mad because I stood her up the other night. Can't say I blame her."

Thalia shook her head reproachfully. "You could try the truth. She likes Emily. She'd understand."

"I won't use my private life to bail out my professional life."

"Then I guess you'll just have to take your medicine." She glanced at her fiancé, then added, "By the way, do you have plans for Thanksgiving?"

Michael brightened. He sensed an invitation in the offing and he knew that they'd already invited Emily to join them at Thalia's mother's house. He didn't mind being an afterthought if it got him what he wanted.

What he really wanted was to finagle an invitation to Emily's. As wonderful as all her meals were, he could barely imagine the splendors of Thanksgiving. But when he'd heard from Luke that she had an invitation, he had to admit he'd felt left out.

"No plans," he said.

"Would you like to come to Mother's, then?" Thalia asked. "We wanted to invite you all along but we've got a lot of out-of-town cousins and aunts coming, too. With Emily, we had the max at the table, but now that Em's turned us down—''

"Emily's not going to be there?" That put a new twist on the holiday.

"She's cooking dinner at home. She's invited Miss Pauline and apparently it'll be just the two of them."

*Maybe not,* Michael thought.

"Well?" Thalia urged. "Would you care to join us?"

"I…don't think so. Thanks anyway, but I'll probably just stay home, eat a TV dinner and work." He gave an exaggerated sigh of regret and rose to make his farewells. Thalia's news threw an entirely different light on Thanksgiving. He could barely keep from rubbing his hands together in glee.

MICHAEL HUNG ON to Dog's leash with both hands and tried to carry on a conversation at the same time. Emily found the sight amusing to say the least.

Davy wasn't helping matters any by hunkering down just out of Dog's reach and calling to him in a loud voice. The five-year-old loved the dog and spent all the time he could in his neighbor's yard. His mother approved, since the boy had stopped begging for a dog of his own.

"Quiet!"

At Michael's roar, Davy stopped talking, Dog stopped barking, and Emily stopped laughing. When all were quiet, he went on.

"We have a trick to show you, Emily. Will you come outside and watch?"

She didn't want to. She didn't want to soften toward dog or man. But with no clear way to refuse graciously, she sighed and nodded. Pulling her cardigan sweater closed, she walked outside and closed the door behind her.

Davy jumped up and down in excitement. "Watch this!" he shouted, taking off across the yard at a dead run.

Dog leaped after him, hit the end of the leash and bounced around to face the other direction. It took Michael several minutes to calm everyone down, but he did it with the patience Natalie the dog trainer had sensed in him.

When everyone was straightened out again, Michael glanced at Emily to make sure she was watching, then said firmly, "Sit!"

To her surprise, Dog did, then looked up at his master with his doggy grin.

Michael turned to Davy. "Are you ready?"

The boy nodded. For the first time, Emily saw three plastic bowls which had once held whipped topping, turned upside down in front of him. Michael explained his intentions.

"This is a canine version of the old shell game," he said. "Davy's put a dog biscuit under one of the bowls and Dog will go straight to the correct one."

Davy pointed a rigid finger. "That one!"

"Don't tell!" Emily cried.

Davy grinned. "Dogs don't speak people, they speak dog. Michael said."

"Oh, that's right." Davy was an adorable child and really into this. She couldn't help teasing him.

"Okay," she said, "I guess you didn't tip him off. But I still think this is goofy."

"No, he can do it!" Davy clapped his hands. "Turn him loose, Michael!"

"Okay, here he comes!"

Michael released the leash and Dog leaped forward, dashing straight for the three bowls—and Davy. Leaping over the former, he plowed into the later, knocking the boy over and jumping on top of him to lick his face and wrestle with him.

Davy laughed so hard he could barely fend the dog off. "No, no, find the treat!" Davy pleaded.

It took Michael, laughing almost as hard as Davy, to pull the animal away. He gave Emily a plaintive glance. "This isn't the way it's supposed to go," he declared, looking down at the tumbled bowls and the dog biscuit lying on the grass at his feet.

Dog saw the biscuit, too, and leaped on it. The bone-shaped treat disappeared in a twinkling.

"But he can do it," Davy insisted, climbing to his feet. "Can't he, Michael?"

"Uh, yeah, sometimes. I guess we need to work on his consistency."

"His con…consis-telly?"

"Close enough for government work, partner. That's consistency. It means…"

While the man enlightened the boy, Emily slipped back into the house. She wasn't the slightest bit surprised that Dog had let them down.

That's a truly useless animal, she thought, picking up the delicate silk blouse draped over a kitchen chair. She'd been sewing on buttons while making out her shopping list for Thanksgiving dinner. She'd stop at the grocery story on the way home tomorrow, the day before the holiday, and pick up what she needed, including the turkey.

It would be a lovely meal and she'd have a lovely time, if she could just get over her guilt at refusing to invite Michael to share it with her and Miss Pauline. Heaven knows, he'd hinted broadly enough. But she'd clenched her teeth stubbornly and refused to do what her upbringing and good manners insisted she should.

She was already feeding him a couple of nights a week. Wasn't that enough? Not that she minded the expense. It was the mental wear and tear that got to her. He spent too much time singing Dog's praises, for one thing. For another, the way he looked at her made her downright...*nervous* was too mild a word for what he made her.

There was a quick knock on the door, which opened to admit Michael and his canine companion. "Heel!" Michael ordered, and Dog promptly planted his rear end on the kitchen tile.

Michael looked up triumphantly. "See that?"

"You said heel and he sat down. What happens when you say sit?"

"Usually nothing. At least it's progress." He grinned. "Of a sort."

"Of a sort," she agreed.

"I'll come back tomorrow, but it'll be later," he said, leaning down to pat the dog on the head. "Is eight all right?"

"Yes." She folded the bit of wispy pink silk over the back of the chair again.

"And then Thursday—"

"Surely you don't intend to visit Dog on Thanksgiving."

"I thought I should."

"That's not at all necessary. I can take care of him one day."

"I didn't mean to imply you couldn't. It's just…" His face grew long. "I don't have any other plans so…"

"Something will come up," she said, pretending a denseness she didn't have. "You can come by Friday, if you like."

"I guess I can do that."

She turned toward the door to the living room because if she kept looking at him, she'd break down and invite him and she didn't want to do that. He was putting on an act to get her to do something she didn't intend to do. She knew he was.

And it was working, darn it.

He followed. "I'm meeting a few friends for a drink at the Watering Hole tomorrow evening," he said. "I promised I'd ask you to join us. Just Luke and Thalia and Juan and Bill—"

"I don't think I'll have time." She opened the front door and faced him squarely.

"Hey, it's the day before a holiday. Surely you'll have time."

He was doing it again: teasing, coaxing, charming. She hardened her heart against him. "Thanks for the invitation. Do I have to decide now?" Her answer would be the same whenever she decided, but he wouldn't necessarily know that.

Or maybe he did, because he sighed and said,

"Whatever. Just drop by about seven if you have time."

"Okay." But don't count on it.

He moved to the open door. "Have a good evening, Emily. If you change your mind about... anything, give me a call."

"I'll do that, Michael."

She closed the door behind him and leaned on it for a moment, wondering if he was talking about drinks or Thanksgiving dinner or both.

Fat chance.

Turning, she walked into the spare bedroom, which she'd converted into a sewing and crafts studio. She needed another spool of pink thread to finish sewing on the buttons. Selecting the appropriate shade from the spool holder nailed to the wall, she paused to replace the scissors in the holder and plunge several loose pins into the pincushion.

She really should bring Thalia's wedding dress home from the shop and finish it here, she thought. It was getting down to details now, and she'd do better work at home.

She only hoped it turned out as well as the dress draped over the dressmaker's dummy in the corner. She'd decorated the baby-blue cotton with free-motion machine embroidery and beads. It was her masterpiece.

And her distraction.

THUS IT WAS that Emily didn't reenter her kitchen for nearly twenty minutes, and when she did it was in a warm glow of accomplishment. She loved her sewing studio, loved touching and manipulating beautiful fabrics and threads and making something uniquely her own out of—

She stopped short.

The kitchen tile was littered with bits and pieces of pink silk, shreds and threads and—

"Oh, my God!"

Stopping short, she stared at the remains of her new silk blouse. Inevitably, her gaze skimmed across the floor to zoom in on the dog lying next to the back door, pink fabric hanging out of his mouth and stuck between his paws. His tail was flapping and his ears cocked forward as if to say, *Look at me! Look what I've done!*

Emily screamed. Dropping to her knees, she gathered fabric remnants toward her. This couldn't be happening again! Could this dog do nothing right?

Including sensing when people hated him? The stupid animal just kept grinning at her and thumping his tail against the floor. Giving up on the blouse, Emily settled back on her folded legs, trying to calm herself. Even so, she felt the slide of tears down her cheeks.

When was enough enough? How much did she have to go through before she faced the inevitable fact that this wasn't working? That Dog was a disaster, plain and simple. Either Michael was going to take him away—now, tonight!—or Emily was calling the pound.

There, she'd made up her mind. Rising, she stamped to the phone and checked his number on the write-on wipe-off board on the wall. Punching it in, she waited impatiently.

When he answered, she said, "It's me. Can you come back?"

"To your house?" He sounded astonished by her request.

She spoke forcefully because if she didn't, she'd cry. "Yes. Right now, please."

"Is something wrong?"

"I'll explain when you get here."

Explain that this dog had chewed up her clothing and chased her cats for the last time. Shoulders shaking, she sat on a kitchen chair, head bowed.

She simply couldn't do this any longer. She wasn't cut out for dog duty. She didn't understand dogs or like them.

It was the pound for Dog. Good riddance.

Propping her elbows on her thighs, she rested her face in her hands and closed her eyes. She didn't like what she had to do, but she'd reached her limit. Besides, it wasn't her fault, it was Michael's. He—

A soft whimper beside her was followed by the swish of a wet tongue across her equally wet cheek. She stiffened, opened her eyes, turned to look at the source of all her grief.

Dog sat there and he wasn't smiling. In fact, she'd never seen such an expression of sympathy on an animal's face. He whined and leaned forward to "kiss" her again.

It was too much. Everything tumbled out.

"Oh, Dog!" Flinging her arms around his neck, she buried her face in his soft fur. "Why are you so obnoxious? Why don't you ever get any better? Why don't you know sic 'em?"

He wiggled in her embrace and slipped away.

Yipping and dancing around, he tried to entice her into a game.

"Stupid mutt," she murmured, but she was smiling. Drying her eyes with the palms of her hands, she rose. "So what's the big deal? It was just a stupid blouse I didn't need, right?"

Dog jumped up and down, whining.

"And you'll never do it again, right?"

Dog practically broke himself in two with the force of his wagging.

"And if I throw you out at this late date, Michael will think I'm a complete and total wimp, right?"

Dog barked; apparently he agreed with that statement big time.

"Okay," she said, "you can stay. But if you ever, ever do such a thing again, I swear I'll—"

The doorbell rang; it rang again, urgently.

"Oh, my God!" She met Dog's gaze. "It's Michael. Now what do I do to keep him from knowing what just happened here?"

Dog's expression plainly said, *Whatever it takes.*

THE MOMENT THE DOOR SWUNG OPEN, Michael rushed inside. He fully expected to find the same scene that had kept him from that important meeting last week: Emily in tears and Dog in disgrace.

"What is it? What's wrong?"

She stood before him, tense but calm. She swallowed hard, licked her lips and said, "Uh..."

"For God's sake, Emily, what is it? I broke every speed limit in the books to get here." He grabbed her by the upper arms and stared into her eyes: Had she been crying?

"I...just..." She drew in a shuddering breath and said, "Would you like to come to Thanksgiving dinner? No big deal—it'll just be Miss Pauline and me. B-but after you left, I got to thinking maybe you were hinting that you'd like an invitation?"

Hinting? He'd all but shouted it in her face: *Invite me!* Now here she was, doing that very thing.

Out of the clear blue, but this was what he wanted.

Confused but pleased, he smiled a bit uncertainly. "I'd love to join you and Miss Pauline for Thanksgiving dinner, but couldn't you have asked me this on the telephone?"

"I suppose I could have, but I wanted to do it in person." She turned away, head down as if caught in a lie.

"You're sure this is why you called?"

Her head snapped up. "Of course."

He decided to push his luck. "And you'll join me for drinks tomorrow night."

"I suppose I could do that."

Man, this was working out just fine. He finally let his hands fall away from her arms, although he didn't want to. "What can I bring to dinner Thursday?"

"Nothing, nothing at all. I'll do everything."

"Wine, then. I'll bring champagne."

"That would be nice." She took an anxious step away. "I guess that's it, then. Good night, Michael, and th-thanks for coming."

It felt kinda like a brush-off, but that was all right. He had what he wanted. "I'll pick you up a few minutes before seven tomorrow."

"I can drive," she said quickly. "I'll meet you there."

"Okay." He took another step and said, "Dog's not in any trouble, is he?"

"What makes you ask that?"

"I dunno. Maybe all those pink threads caught on the sole of your shoe."

She looked down, looked back up. "I was sewing. I'm messy. See you tomorrow, Michael."

"Tomorrow." And the next day. Things were looking up.

# 8

"YOU'RE LATE," MICHAEL SAID.

Emily glared at him. His smile slipped. He hadn't meant it as a criticism, more like a statement of fact. Now she was mad at him.

She slid into the seat next to his at the big table at the Watering Hole and said, "Don't ask."

Might as well wave a red flag in front of a bull. Now he *had* to ask. "Sorry," he said cheerfully, "but now you've made me curious. What's going on?"

Her jaws tightened. "Dog's going on."

He suppressed a groan, having spent most of the day praying that, just this once, Dog would behave. So much for heavenly intervention. "Okay, out with it," he said with a dispirited sigh.

"It's just more of the same." She signaled to a passing waiter. "Vodka and tonic," she said firmly.

Not her usual white wine. This was getting serious. He waited with professional patience.

Finally she said in a grumpy tone, "I made the stupid mistake of checking Dog's food and water before I left. He not only jumped up on me and tore my stockings, he got tangled up in the lace on my skirt and ripped most of it off trying to get loose.

Then when I bent to pick it up—oh, forget it! I don't even want to go there.''

She didn't have to. He could see her bending over, see Dog rushing up to make amends, see the animal plow into her and knock her—

"You've got a smudge of dirt on your cheek," he said kindly, reaching out to brush it away.

She smacked his hand aside. "Thanks *so* much for pointing that out. If you'll excuse me, I'll go wash my face—*again.*"

Rising, she stalked toward the ladies' room in the back.

This, the closest they'd ever come to a date, was not off to a good start. He was going to have to do something about that.

Assuming she came back.

"EMILY! What on earth is going on?"

Emily looked in the mirror above the sink in the ladies' room where she was scrubbing at her cheek with a wet paper towel and saw Thalia approaching. "Nothing," she said shortly.

Thalia blinked in surprise. "Come on. This is me, remember? And don't blame it all on Michael. You were already mad as a wet hen when you came in."

Emily let out all the anger in a resigned sigh. "You're right. It's that miserable animal. He's a walking disaster and I don't know what to do about it."

"Encourage Michael to find another place soon?"

"I'm doing that. But I think he likes it just fine

the way it is, with me doing all the dirty work. I don't even think he's looking.''

''You're wrong.'' Thalia peered at herself in the mirror and then fumbled in her handbag. ''I happen to know he's looked at a half-dozen places at least,'' she said, pulling out a tube of lipstick.

''Really?'' That was encouraging. ''In that case, maybe I should cut him some slack.''

''Under the circumstances, I'd say that's a good idea.'' Thalia applied lipstick, recapped the tube and dropped it back into her purse.

''Under what circumstances?'' Emily, ever attuned to the nuances, asked quickly. Dropping the paper towel into the trash, she turned toward the door.

Thalia followed. ''Under the circumstances that you and Michael are dating. If there's anything there—''

Emily stopped just beyond the door, so suddenly that Thalia stepped on her heels. ''We're not dating! Where did you ever get that idea?''

''Why...'' Thalia frowned. ''What do you call this?'' She gestured toward the table they'd so recently left.

''I call this having a drink with friends,'' Emily said indignantly.

''Everybody else calls it dating.''

''*Everybody?*'' Emily groaned. ''Are people talking about me?''

Thalia shrugged. ''Not in an objectionable way. We all just assumed you and Michael were a couple. You do spend a lot of time together, plus you're putting up his dog. What would your interpretation be?"

"That I was in the wrong place at the wrong time and apparently I'll have to pay for it the rest of my life!" How to make the point? "Look, Thalia, I'm just trying to get along until he takes that darn dog out of my place."

"Oh, oh, sounds like Dog's done something else to annoy you."

"You mean besides chewing up my new shoes and a silk blouse? And ripping my stockings and skirt as I was leaving tonight? You mean something else besides that?"

"That pretty silk blouse you made?" Thalia wailed. "The pink one?"

"That's the one," Emily agreed grimly. "Idiot animal couldn't chew up something I hate, oh, no, not him."

"I'm surprised Michael didn't offer to make it right."

"I didn't tell him about the blouse. He'd just think I was a wimp, to get all emotionally involved with an article of clothing. In fact—" she chewed on her lower lip "—I was ready to tell him—to scream at him about it, actually. When I realized how shrewish I was starting to sound, I ended up inviting him for Thanksgiving dinner instead and now I'm stuck with *that*, too."

"*Stuck* may not be the right word. You have to admit, Michael can be terribly charming when he wants to."

"Yes, and that's when he's the most dangerous," Emily agreed. "What I hate above all is, he seems to believe that he can buy or talk his way out of anything. Instead, all he does is embarrass me.''

''You're talking about the shoes,'' Thalia said wisely.

''That's right. The shoes.''

Thalia looked down pointedly. ''But you're wearing the shoes.''

''What was I supposed to do? Let them sit in my closet? The damage was already done once Michael went from store to store looking for the darned things.'' With an annoyed shrug, Emily led the way back to the table.

Michael wasn't there.

She felt a moment's alarm and then lifted her chin in defiance. Good. She certainly didn't need him to have a good time.

Which she didn't expect to do anyway, since she'd been hustled into coming in the first place.

By him. He had his nerve, practically forcing her to come here and then abandoning her.

MICHAEL WAITED until Thalia and Emily were seated before coming out from behind the potted palms. He hadn't intended to eavesdrop but figured it was better to stop where he was when he heard their low voices, rather than charge out and embarrass them.

Or maybe he had intended to eavesdrop. Hell, that was apparently the only way he'd know what was going on with Emily.

Disgusted, he returned to his seat. She gave him a tentative, if impersonal, smile and he realized she was trying to put her complaints aside for the moment.

That was okay with him, but he wasn't going to forget. He was just trying to do the right thing. If she didn't tell him of Dog's misdeeds, what was he supposed to do? Read her mind?

*Now* who was grumpy?

MICHAEL DIDN'T ARGUE when Emily said she had to be going. In fact, he seemed almost eager to be rid of her, which simultaneously pleased and infuriated her.

The night was clear and pleasant and bright. At her car, she turned to him, more than halfway expecting him to reach for her. If he did, she would give him such a tongue-lashing! All that kissing stuff had to end and this was as good a time as any to announce her resolve.

Instead, he reached past to open the car door for her. In shadows cast by street lamps, his face looked set and distant. His voice was calm and impersonal. "What time should I come Thursday?"

"Thursday?" It took her a moment to remember that Thursday was Thanksgiving. That's how much he'd surprised her. "We'll eat about five, I guess."

"I won't be late." He turned away.

She called after him, almost in a panic. "We'll have munchies earlier—Miss Pauline and me, I mean. If you'd like to come around three…"

He lifted a hand in a dismissive wave but didn't look around. "I'll see how it's going when the time comes," he called back.

Of all the nerve! Annoyed all over again, Emily got in her car and drove away.

EMILY DIDN'T SLEEP worth beans that night.

It wasn't that she spent the long dark hours thinking of Michael...not entirely, anyway. She also thought about Dog, which got her all upset, and of her Thanksgiving menu, which soothed her. Until she thought of Michael again, at which point her blood pressure soared.

Patches rose, too, from the foot of the bed. The calico cat walked over Emily's legs and then jumped off the bed. At least Rosie still loves me, Emily thought—until the black cat followed her feline friend into the darkness.

Great, just great. Good and mad at the entire animal world, Emily rolled over, punched her pillow and implored herself to *go to sleep*.

THANKSGIVING HAD NEVER BEEN special to Michael.

Neither had Christmas or Halloween or even his birthday. Holidays were more or less ignored in his family, and that was his mother's doing, he'd realized early on. She'd considered holidays frivolous. There were presents, when appropriate, but they were given almost as an afterthought.

Holidays weren't even noted for good food, he realized as he watched the minutes drag past. Although not a vegetarian, his mother was very into healthful eating and eschewed desserts and elaborate dishes and even the traditions surrounding, in particular, Thanksgiving.

No pumpkin pie, no cranberry sauce, and certainly no turkey stuffing. Looking out the window of his apartment, Michael sighed and let the drapes fall back. Check that: When he was fifteen, his mother had brought home frozen TV dinners that featured all the above in horrible versions.

He'd eaten it anyway and was glad to get it.

Now after all these years, he was beginning to feel the loss of those traditions. He could almost see Emily moving happily around her kitchen, could imagine the wonderful smells wafting from the oven, see the beautiful dishes of food—

The telephone rang and his heart skipped a beat. Was she calling to tell him she'd changed her mind, that he shouldn't bother to come?

His hello was testy.

"Darling! It's your beloved mother."

Relief swept through him, quickly followed by surprise. "Hi, Mom. Anything wrong?"

"Does something have to be wrong for a mother to call her favorite son and wish him a happy Thanksgiving?"

That stopped him cold. He didn't recall his mother ever wishing him a happy anything. He said suspiciously, "All...right. Happy Thanksgiving to you, too."

"Thank you, darling." Her voice literally bubbled with cheer. Was she sick? "So what are your plans for the holiday?"

This was getting weirder and weirder. "I've got an invitation to dine with...friends."

"That's wonderful. I wouldn't want you to be alone on Thanksgiving."

This was getting too sticky. Time to stop beating about the bush. "Mom," he said, "what's going on? Is someone holding a gun on you? You don't sound like yourself at all."

The sudden silence lengthened and he felt his tension growing.

Finally she said, "Was I an awful mother, Michael?"

It shocked him to think she could have doubts at this late date. Yet her tone told him she was sincere. "You were okay," he said defensively. "Why do you ask?"

"Because something's happened and I...I'm rethinking a lot of things. About my life, I mean. And about you and how I brought you up."

"Uh-oh. Now you *are* making me nervous."

She laughed uneasily. "I don't mean to do that. It's just that..." He heard her take a quick breath. "I'm beginning to take a different view of a lot of things."

His stomach clenched. "Different how?"

"Michael, I've found someone." She laughed nervously. "Or maybe I should say someone found me."

Astonished, he said, "You mean...?"

"I mean I'm in love." Her voice strengthened. "Gloriously, completely in love. He owns a nursery."

"He provides day care for kids?"

"Not that kind of nursery! A plant nursery. And he does landscaping, that kind of thing. I defended him in a civil suit and we got to know each other. He's completely unlike anyone I've ever known, darling. He's laid-back and easy to be with and he likes all the traditional things."

"Like Thanksgiving."

"Yes, and Christmas and every other holiday, even a few he makes up himself. He'll be picking me up in a few minutes to take me to his daughter's for Thanksgiving. In the meantime, I was struck with an irresistible desire to talk to my favorite son."

"Jeez, I don't know what to say." Except maybe that he was stunned.

"I wanted to put off talking to you about this until I saw where this new relationship is headed—I mean, why get you all excited if there's no point?"

"You lost me. All excited?"

"You're against this, aren't you?"

That hit him hard. "Why would I be against it if you're happy?" he wanted to know.

"Well, it kind of flies in the face of my entire life," she said slowly. "Plus there's the issue of your father."

"There is no issue of my father. I decided a long time ago that my parents' marriage was none of my business. I loved you both. That doesn't mean I expect you to spend the rest of your life alone because Dad died."

"It's such a relief to hear you say that," she declared, that relief obvious. "I was afraid...I feel like such a hypocrite. God, I can't believe I wasted so many years before I realized..."

"Hey, let it go. I'm happy for you."

"Thank you, darling. So tell me, who are you having your Thanksgiving with?"

"Just friends," he said vaguely, "And I'm late so—happy holidays, Mom. When you get around to it, I'd like to meet this guy."

"You will, Michael. You will just as soon as I can arrange it."

He hung up the receiver and stood there for a moment, trying to sort out the news that had rocked his world. Shocked, he had to fight hard to resist the urge to call her back and demand to know who she was and what she'd done with his *real* mother.

Except he thought he might like this imposter better, once he got used to her.

MICHAEL APPEARED in the kitchen doorway and Emily gave him a distracted smile. He said, "Miss Pauline let me in," and stepped aside to let that little lady precede him.

Miss Pauline gave him a friendly pat on the arm in passing. "I told him he's just in time," she reported. "Don't you think I should go ahead and serve that wonderful cheese ball you made, Emily?"

"Absolutely. And don't forget your marinated mushrooms." Emily finished basting the turkey and closed the oven door. Now she could give her guests her full attention.

There was something different about Michael, she saw at once. He looked almost distracted. Still handsome, but also distracted. She had to wonder why but decided against calling attention to it.

"We're glad you're here," she said formally.

"Please pull up a chair. We may as well have our appetizers in here, so I can keep an eye on things."

Miss Pauline nodded enthusiastically. "I love kitchens," she declared, "especially when holiday cooking is underway. The pumpkin pies, the turkey and stuffing..." She closed her eyes and breathed deeply. "Makes me think of home."

"Me, too." Emily took a cracker and sliced off a wedge of cheese, realizing that Michael hadn't moved. Her glance asked, *Are you all right?*

It seemed to shake him out of some kind of fog and he moved quickly to the table to set down the bottle of champagne he'd brought. "Everything smells great," he said, reaching for a cocktail pick and spearing a mushroom. "I'm starved."

"Help yourself, then, but don't eat too much," Miss Pauline warned. "Emily's preparing a wonderful repast. I wouldn't want you to spoil your appetite."

"Not a chance in the world." He popped the mushroom into his mouth and groaned with delight. "Fantastic. Shall I open the champagne now?"

Emily said, "Please," indicating the flutes already set out and waiting.

He seemed like himself again, but Emily found herself watching him open the bottle with more than the usual concern. Something was going on and she wanted to know what.

Strictly idle curiosity, of course.

EMILY TOOK a completely traditional approach to holidays, especially this one. In addition to roast turkey with dressing, she always served mashed potatoes and giblet gravy, candied sweet potatoes, green bean casserole, homemade cranberry sauce and yeast rolls, with a relish of fresh vegetables.

Dessert, of course, was homemade pumpkin pie with heavy cream she whipped and flavored herself. By the time they got to that final course, she was seriously in doubt that Michael would have room for anything more.

She'd never seen anyone eat the way he did. Should she be flattered, or was he simply starving?

She smiled at her own speculation.

He noticed and asked, "What's so funny, or shouldn't I ask?"

She plunged the knife into the golden brown pie. "I was wondering if you'd have room for pie—and whether you really liked my cooking that much or were simply famished."

He looked astonished. "You know I like your cooking. I've never eaten food this good in my entire life."

"Now you're putting me on." She lifted a wedge of pie onto a gold-banded dessert plate.

Michael exchanged an amazed glance with Miss Pauline. "Is she fishing for more compliments?" he wondered.

"I doubt it," Miss Pauline said seriously. "Emily isn't that kind of girl."

"I certainly am not." Emily extracted a double-sized wedge of pie on the second plate. "You're too extravagant in your praise, Michael. It makes me wonder."

"Well, don't. This was the best meal I've ever had and in the best company, too." His compliment included both women. "I've eaten here often enough to know you're a great cook, but this time you've really outdone yourself."

"You have, indeed," Miss Pauline agreed. She accepted the plate of pie mounded with whipped cream. "May I serve the coffee?"

"If you like."

Miss Pauline rose to fetch the carafe. Michael's gaze caught Emily's and he mouthed the words: *I mean every word.*

Embarrassed, she looked quickly away. She, too, had enjoyed the meal—not so much because of the food, although she was proud of her efforts, but because of her guests. Miss Pauline was a dear, and Michael...

Michael seemed newly vulnerable, for some reason, and therefore newly appealing. She could only hope she'd find out why before he left.

"OH, MY GOODNESS, that's enough!"

Emily paused, the serving spoon still in one hand and a paper plate in the other. "Are you sure? Let me give you just a few more sweet potatoes to take home. You seemed to enjoy those."

Miss Pauline shook her head. "I enjoyed everything, dear, but there's only one of me! That's plenty, really."

Emily smiled and set the plate on a large sheet of aluminum foil. "If you're sure." She began packaging the plate to go.

Michael watched the competent motions of her hands, conscious of the ridiculously contented smile on his lips. Not a crumb of pumpkin pie remained on his plate and he was enjoying his second cup of coffee. Emily might think his praise was effusive, but she was wrong.

With her share of the leftovers in a shopping bag, Miss Pauline bade him farewell. While Emily walked the little lady to the front door, Michael warmed the contents of his cup.

His mother was in love.

He shook his head, still having trouble believing the apparent change in her. It turned his entire world upside down. He remembered what she'd said: *God, I can't believe I wasted so many years before I realized…*

Realized what? That the sentimental people of the world were more to be envied than pitied? That love happened when you least expected it? That opposites really did attract?

Emily reentered the kitchen, her happy smile quickly replaced by a guarded expression. "May I offer you another piece of pie?" she asked.

He groaned. "I wish I could say yes, but I don't think I could stuff in another bite."

"I'll fix you a to-go plate, then."

Was she trying to get rid of him? That was a pretty broad hint. He rose. "I'd appreciate it. While you're doing that, I'll go check Dog's food and water."

"All right." But she wasn't looking at him. Instead she concentrated on dishing food onto a paper plate.

He let himself out into the backyard. Dog immediately rushed over to jump on him with muddy paws, then lick his hands, his shoes, his corduroy-covered knees.

The animal had no self-respect at all; he gave new meaning to the term *bootlicker*.

But Dog was happy. He had no idea that Emily daily teetered on the edge of calling the pound to pick him up and cart him away.

Squatting, Michael grabbed the squirming animal and pulled him close to look him in the eye.

"Dog, you've got to clean up your act," he said sternly. "Emily's just about at the end of her rope. Either you get on her good side or—" He drew a stiff forefinger across his throat with appropriate sound effects.

Dog just gave him that loopy grin and lunged forward with dripping tongue.

EMILY THOUGHT ABOUT IT all the time she was fixing Michael's plate.

Something was going on with him. He hadn't been himself, for sure. He'd been a little distracted, a little too effusive in his praise, a little too perplexed.

She'd ask him about it when he came back inside, she decided. Why not? Weren't they friends?

That word seemed to stick even in her thoughts. They *were* friends, which she'd never expected to happen. In fact, they were good enough friends that he'd seen her as most others never had: bitchy. Dog brought that out in her. Would the day never come when she'd get rid of him?

The door opened and Michael started inside, only

to be tripped up by Dog running between his legs to join the party.

"Hey!" Michael stumbled, grabbing the doorknob for support.

Patches, crossing the kitchen floor toward the food bowl, let out a howl and took off like a calico streak. Dog leaped forward, but Emily was too fast for him—practice, she supposed, grabbing his collar before he could work up a full head of steam.

"Dammit!" Michael untangled himself and reached for the animal. Picking him up bodily, the man heaved the wiggling mutt out the door and slammed it behind him. Turning, he glowered at Emily. "I hate it when a dumb animal makes a fool out of me."

She laughed. "Welcome to the club. That happens to me a dozen times a day."

"Yeah, I could tell you're experienced at heading 'em off at the pass. You're fast." He glanced toward the door. "I guess I should be going."

Emily took a deep breath. "Could you stay and talk a minute?"

His brows rose, and for a few seconds, he just looked at her. Then he nodded and sat down. "What's on your mind?"

"You."

"Yeah?" A smile quirked the corners of his strong mouth.

She felt herself flush. "Not the way you're thinking. I mean, is something wrong? You don't seem like yourself today."

He gave her a lopsided grimace. "I'd think that

would be an improvement, since you don't like the usual me.''

''I never said that, Michael. At least, I n-never said it in so many words.'' Uncomfortable, she had to steel herself to go on. ''I hope you haven't had bad news or anything.''

He seemed to consider. ''I did have news,'' he said at last. ''Very intuitive of you to pick up on it.''

''Is there anything I can do to help?''

''You already did.'' His glance took in the neatly cleared table, which had groaned with food only an hour ago. ''It's nothing, really.'' He looked embarrassed when he said it. ''My mother called just before I left.''

''Is she all right?''

''Better than all right, according to her. Apparently she's fallen in love.''

''Oh.'' Emily melted. ''That's wonderful.'' When he didn't respond, she added uncertainly, ''Isn't it?''

''I'm not sure.''

''Because it seems disloyal to your father?'' she guessed.

His smile was quick and sincere. ''No, nothing like that. It's…it's like she suddenly got religion, know what I mean? She never paid any attention to holidays, for example, but today she was all excited about Thanksgiving. She's apparently done a complete one-eighty and it makes me wonder.''

''Wonder what?'' It was the barest whisper.

''Wonder if I've been wrong all these years, too.''

"About?"

"Everything." He rose. "You."

"Me?" It was a squeak of alarm.

"Uh-huh. Emily, stand up, will you?"

Moving like a robot, she did. Once on her feet, she managed to utter only a single word: "Why?"

"Because," he said gently, "I want to thank you for everything."

And he swept her into his arms.

# 9

EMILY MELTED against him happily. Somehow this seemed like the perfect finale to a lovely holiday.

Unfortunately, the kiss ended almost before it began. Releasing her, he stepped back quickly.

She blinked in confusion. "What's the matter?"

"I'm not being fair to you," he said, looking astonished at himself for admitting such a thing. "I can't use you to try to figure out my life."

"Is that what you're doing? Using me?" Somehow she didn't think so.

He shrugged, apparently not entirely sure himself. "Maybe gratitude just got the best of me." He thrust his hands deep into his trouser pockets, as if to keep himself from grabbing her. "Look," he said abruptly, "I think I'm close to finding a new place to live."

The change of subject caught her flat-footed. "What are you talking about?"

"A new place where I can keep Dog. You'll be happy to hear you'll probably be rid of us both soon."

Her temper flared. "Please don't tell me what I'll be happy to hear."

"Okay, okay!" Holding up his hands, he backed away. "Forget I said anything and thanks for everything. I'll be going now."

"You do that, Michael." Temper simmering, she thrust the two paper plates of leftovers into his hands, then stalked behind him to the front door.

He stepped out onto the porch and turned back toward her, at which point she shut the door in his face.

She didn't know why but she felt downright insulted. Start to kiss her and then stop, would he!

He could just go find someplace else to eat Christmas dinner.

WELL, HELL.

He got scared, that's all. Scared of the way Emily made him feel, all soft and warm and fuzzy. Actually, that described most of the people he knew. Patsies. Dupes. The ones who need to be defended by sharp lawyers like Michael Forbes.

Only now he didn't feel all that sharp. He felt shaky and not at all sure he'd done the right thing. Actually, it didn't make a helluva lot of sense. If he felt like kissing her and she felt like kissing him back, why had he pulled away? Had he lost his mind or what?

Pulling into his parking lot, he killed the motor and sat there brooding.

Just because his mother had gone soft didn't mean he had to do the same, he finally decided. Emily was nothing to him except someone to look after his dog until he could do it himself.

Which had better be soon, since he'd lied to her and promised quick action on that front.

Damn.

He always knew there was a reason he didn't like holidays.

CHALK UP ONE MORE LOUSY NIGHT, thanks to Michael.

Sitting in the dark at the kitchen table in the wee small hours of the morning, Emily gritted her teeth and tried to calm herself. Somewhere she'd read that if you couldn't go to sleep within a reasonable period of time, you should just get up until you got sleepy again. Well, she'd been up for more than a half hour, and although she was plenty exhausted, sleep wasn't part of the equation.

She simply had to figure out how to handle this situation.

Number one, he was never going to get close enough to her again to even *think* about kissing her.

Number two, he was going to get his dog out of here by Christmas or she was calling the pound, period and end-quote.

Number three, she was never, ever, going to invite him to eat another morsel in her house, since the food was obviously a bigger draw than she was.

That hurt. That really hurt.

Rising, she headed back to the bedroom in the dark. Unfortunately, she stubbed her toe on the end of the bed and found herself hopping around and stifling swear words.

And thinking, *Just look what he's done to me!*

WHEN MICHAEL CAME BY Friday evening to play with Dog, Emily gave him the cold shoulder. *There!* she thought. *Let's see how he likes that.*

Apparently he liked it fine, or perhaps he was just so distant that he didn't notice anything amiss.

Which sure wasn't a boost for a girl's morale.

MICHAEL SAT ON A ROCK in the park, Dog before him with one ear pricked and tongue lolling out. They'd run all the way from Emily's house, the man giving out before the animal did.

"Good boy." Michael rubbed Dog's floppy ear. "At least you're always glad to see me."

Dog took a swipe at Michael's face with his tongue. Michael went on thoughtfully. "She's pissed, for sure. Do you suppose she knows I was lying to her?"

Dog's eyes widened as if he were seriously considering such a possibility. Michael continued rubbing the ear. "Which time?" he asked rhetorically. "When I said I was close to getting us a house or when I attributed that kiss to gratitude? Like anyone in her right mind would believe *that*."

Dog whined: he wanted to run some more. Michael rose and took a firmer grip on the leash. "I guess she's just fed up with me," he told Dog. "Who could blame her? I've really messed with her life."

Dragged down the street by his dog, he had to admit that she'd messed with his life, too. But no more. That was over.

Maybe.

MICHAEL RAN INTO LUKE outside the Dalton mansion where he'd gone for another interminable meeting with Sylvia and Four-Jay. The compromise with the Shangri-la aginners was still alive, but it was taking all Michael's negotiating skills to keep it that way.

Once he'd loved this kind of wheeling and dealing. Recently it had begun to bore him.

Luke waved and Michael altered his route. "What's up?" he asked.

"Not much." Luke's grin was almost sly. "What's up with you?"

Michael shrugged. "Not much. Your mom is pretty much keeping me busy."

"Yeah, I noticed. How's Emily?"

"Pissed."

"At you or that dog?"

"Both, I guess. We're kind of a team."

Luke laughed. "I hope Dog's more cheerful about that than you are. Are you sure you're feeling all right?"

"Now that you mention it, I haven't been feeling too good lately." Michael pressed a palm against his forehead. "Maybe I'm sick," he said, almost hoping it was true.

"Hell," Luke said, "you're not sick, you're in love."

"I'm in—what?"

"Love. *L-o-v-e,* love. You can tell by that sick feeling in the pit of your stomach, the one you keep trying to ignore because you're afraid—"

"I'm not afraid of a damned thing," Michael blustered. "If I was in love, I'd sure as hell be the first to know it."

"Famous last words. Ask me how I got so smart." Luke was openly amused now. He pounded a fist on the point of Michael's shoulder. "Just remember, you heard it here first." He strolled away to his car, parked next to Michael's.

In love.

Ridiculous.

If he was in love, would he have turned down Emily's invitation to dinner last night?

He wasn't in love, he was sick. Sick and tired of being a long-distant dog owner.

At that very moment, he vowed to find a house *quickly,* no matter what it took.

THALIA PLAYED with a French fry. Sitting across the booth in the local Burger Blast, Emily frowned.

Thalia had been leading up to something ever since they'd arrived to share a quick lunch. It looked as if she was about to come out with it at last.

She looked up suddenly and said, "About the wedding…"

Emily's heart sank. "There's no problem, I hope."

"No. Well, sort of." Thalia chewed on her lower lip and looked away. "The thing is, Luke's getting impatient."

"But Christmas Eve is only a few weeks away," Emily pointed out.

"That's the other thing. Whatever possessed me to pick Christmas Eve?"

"It's romantic?"

"Even so, for the rest of our lives our anniversary will be overshadowed by the holiday. Maybe we'd be better off to pick a nothing date that will be all our own.''

Emily's unease grew. ''Please tell me you're not planning an elopement. Please tell me that.''

''Oh, no, nothing like that.'' Thalia frowned. ''Well, actually, that's what Luke would like and what I need to talk to you about, Em. You've been working so hard on my dress.''

''Don't give that a single thought,'' Emily said, and meant it. ''You and Luke have to do what's best for you. Whatever happens, I've loved working on the dress. If you don't wear it, someone else can.''

''You, maybe?''

''Me?'' Flustered, Emily felt her cheeks warm. ''There's no one special in my life.''

''Come on,'' Thalia scoffed. ''What do you call Michael—an afterthought?''

''I call him an annoyance.''

Thalia laughed. ''I don't believe that for a minute. Wasn't Thanksgiving a success?''

''Mostly.'' Emily thought about Michael's distraction, about what he'd said concerning his mother's change of attitude, but somehow it didn't seem right to mention any of that.

The conversation turned to other topics, but Emily found it difficult to concentrate. Perhaps if she wasn't turning into a regular insomniac—she stifled a yawn.

''Not getting enough sleep?'' Thalia looked amused.

"I've been staying up too late," Emily lied. That darn dog!

That darn man!

MICHAEL DROPPED BY that evening after dinner to visit Dog. He didn't have any real conversation with Emily until after man and beast returned from their usual walk.

Once Dog was safely back in the formerly neat yard, which now looked like a cyclone had struck it, Michael knocked on the door to indicate his presence. Without waiting for an invitation, he walked inside.

Emily sat at the kitchen table, a teacup before her and a froth of pale pink fabric on her lap and trailing across the floor. He stopped short, struck by the beauty of the picture she made with her dark coloring surrounded by so much pastel.

But it wasn't that which most arrested him. It was the sparkle in her eyes and the glowing tint of her cheeks. She'd been humming under her breath when he entered, obviously happy with what she was doing.

"Oh," she said, the light fading from her eyes. "It's you."

"Who were you expecting?"

"You." She picked up her needle again.

He couldn't resist asking, "What is that you're working on?"

"Thalia's wedding gown."

She shook out the garment and held it before her, all bead-encrusted lace. He had no real idea what the dress actually looked like, since he was more interested in the person than the trimming, but he sensed how special and important this was to her.

"Beautiful," he said, talking more about her than the dress.

He was rewarded with a sparkling smile. "Thank you."

"Are they still getting married Christmas Eve?"

She nodded. "For a while there I was afraid—" She twisted the thread and broke it off. "But Thalia called just a half hour ago and said they'd stick to the original plan."

"That's good," he said, although he was completely indifferent to when Luke and Thalia got married. "Uh..."

She looked up curiously.

"I've found a house."

She recoiled as if he'd taken a swing at her. "You're kidding."

"I told you I would," he said defensively.

"That's right, you did. Weeks and weeks ago."

"Now it's happening. I'm on the verge of renting a house with a fenced yard on the north side of town—Tower Avenue?"

"I know where that is. It's nice over there."

"Yeah, I guess." What it was was big—way big. The house had four bedrooms and the family room was enormous. His furniture was going to rattle around in the place, but the house was available *now* and that was important.

It's not as if he'd be staying long, and speed was of the essence.

Emily's eyes narrowed. "You don't seem too enthusiastic."

"I am. Sure I am."

"Are you rushing your decision because I made such a fuss?"

"Yeah, well, I don't blame you for that."

Her mouth thinned out as if with the effort *not* to say what she was thinking. Her thank you was stiff.

"Once Dog's out of here, I'll send over a crew to fill in all the holes in your yard and replant the grass and take care of anything else he may have damaged or destroyed."

"Thank you."

"All you have to do is make a list."

"Thank you."

He glowered at her. "Will you stop saying thank you?"

"But I'm grateful." So cool, so collected.

The way he used to be. "It's all spelled out, chapter and verse, in our legal agreement," he reminded her.

"So?" Her brows rose.

"So don't say thank you! Say, *high time!* Say, *it can't happen soon enough to suit me.*"

"Which reminds me, when *will* it happen?"

"Can't wait to get rid of us, huh." Aware that his mouth had assumed a downward slant, he tried to correct it without success. "I'm shooting for December fifteenth. Okay? Is that soon enough for you? Just a little more than a week."

"That's soon enough for me." She stuck her needle in the little tomato-shaped pincushion on the table and stood up. Draping the gown across the chair, she gave him a quizzical glance. "Is there anything else?"

There was plenty, but he couldn't say it, not now, with her looking at him as if he was a perfect stranger.

"No," he growled, "there's nothing else. I'll keep to this same routine until the move."

"That will be fine." She led the way through the kitchen, across the living room to the front door, where she said calmly, "Good night, Michael."

"Good night, Emily."

And with that, he found himself standing on the front sidewalk wondering when he'd lost control of this relationship.

EMILY THOUGHT she couldn't sleep before?

Ha! Now she *really* wasn't sleeping. Worse—the dark circles beneath her eyes betrayed her plight to everyone she met.

She blamed it on Dog.

He'd started barking again, rousing the neighborhood almost every night. Michael insisted it was because wild animals were prowling around, but Emily doubted it. Yes, there was a lot of wildlife in the nearby forest, but that didn't mean—

Dog let out an awful howl and she sat bolt upright in bed. Silence followed and she lay back down again. This was driving her crazy! She couldn't wait for Michael and Dog to walk out of her life.

The next morning she stumbled out of bed, groggy and cross. Once in the kitchen, she could hear Dog whimpering outside and scratching on the door but tried to ignore the commotion. In fact, she was so fed up with the animal that once she was ready for work, she hesitated.

She should go out back and check Dog's food and water, but she was sure both dishes were full, since Michael took care of that every time he came by. The scratching of nails on the door made her grit her teeth. That would go on the list she made out for Michael: a new back door.

Oh, hell. She'd worry all day if she didn't do her duty. With quick annoyance, she threw open the door and looked down into a doggy face bristling with porcupine quills.

MICHAEL HADN'T EVEN HAD his first cup of coffee when the telephone rang. It was Emily.

"Come quick," she cried. "Dog's tangled with a porcupine and the porcupine won!"

"Ah, jeez." He tried to pull his wits together. "Is he all right?"

"He's got about twenty quills sticking out of his muzzle and he won't let me touch them. We'll have to take him to Luke, but Dog's too wild for me to handle alone."

"Okay, calm down. I'll be right there. Can you call Luke and tell him we're coming?"

"Of course. Hurry, Michael—please."

He hurried. In no more than fifteen minutes, he was standing in her backyard looking down at the sorriest critter he'd ever laid eyes on. Dog stood with head hanging and tail tucked between his legs. Quills a good two inches long protruded from his muzzle, reminding Michael of Emily's pincushion.

"Here, boy." He patted his thigh to call the dog to him, then snapped on the leash. "I'll carry him to the clinic," he told Emily. "I think that will be easier on both of us."

Emily nodded. "Whatever. Just hurry. Those things have got to hurt."

"Did you find the porcupine?"

"No. He made a clean getaway, as far as I can tell."

Michael couldn't help pushing it. "The barking lately must have been to keep the porcupine away. Dog was protecting his turf, Em."

She stiffened. "It's not *his* turf, it's mine. And I didn't need his help."

"He's only a dumb animal. As long as he's here, it's his." He turned toward the gate, and for once, Dog moved docilely by his side. "You don't need to hang around. Once Luke gets the quills out, Dog will be fine."

"I hope so."

At last he looked at her, really looked at her, noticing the pale cheeks and the strain around her mouth.

And realized she really was much more concerned about Dog than she cared to admit.

He whistled all the way to the veterinary clinic. He'd just discovered that Emily had a heart after all.

MICHAEL STOPPED BY Sew Bee It a couple of hours later to let Emily know what had transpired. When the front door bell alerted her to his arrival, she rushed across the room to him, leaving a customer waiting.

"Where's Dog?" she demanded. "Is he all right?"

He nodded. "Luke had to sedate him to get out the quills. I can pick him up at the clinic about three this afternoon. He'll probably be groggy, but there'll be no lasting damage." He grinned. "Except he may think twice before tangling with another porcupine."

She took a deep, relieved breath, which he noted. "In that case," she said as if it were of little import, "I have to go back to work. I've got a customer waiting."

"I noticed." Pure orneriness made him add, "I'll just help myself to a cup of coffee and wait until you have a few minutes."

Her shoulders stiffened, but she simply shrugged and went on about her business. He poured coffee and sat down on the wicker chair to wait.

She didn't seem in any hurry to return, which got his back up. He could outwait her, even though he knew work was piling up at his office. He'd finally had to turn off his cell phone to get some peace.

His secretary thought he was sick, regardless of Luke's opinion.

He settled down to wait.

IT EVENTUALLY DAWNED ON Emily that he wasn't going to leave no matter how long she tried to ignore him. If she was going to get rid of him, she'd have to see what it was he wanted.

Forty-five minutes after he'd entered, and ten

minutes after the last customer had been helped, she squared her shoulders and marched up to him.

"Sorry to take so long," she said untruthfully.

"I can see you are." He grinned. "Have a seat."

She did, then realized this was her store, not his, and glared at him. "What can I do for you?" she asked in a not-very-friendly tone.

"Nothing."

"Then why are you still here?" she demanded.

"To give you these." He held out a fist.

Automatically she extended her hand and he dropped three porcupine quills on her palm: vicious pointed things, white with black tips. She stared at the quills, then at him.

"I thought you'd like to see them," he said, ever so reasonably. "Can you imagine what damage a porcupine covered with those things could do to some unsuspecting little kid, say like your little neighbor, Davy? Dog did the entire neighborhood a favor by confronting that porcupine and sending him on his way. He'd have done the same if it had been a fox or—or even a bear."

She wrapped her fingers around the smooth barbs. The thought of Dog confronting a bear made her smile. "Whatever." She rose.

"Aren't you going to give him any kind of break at all?" he asked plaintively.

"There's no need," she reminded him. "Dog will be out of my backyard in just a few days and I'll never see him again. He can fight porcupines and bears in *your* backyard."

"That's cold, Emily." He dropped his empty cup

into the trash container beside the coffee service and rose.

"No, Michael, it's the truth. It's what's going to happen."

"Fine," he snapped, his expression almost angry. "Don't admit the obvious."

She watched him stalk toward the door, feeling vaguely unhappy with what had passed between them. Just as his hand touched the handle, she called after him.

"I'm glad Dog's okay."

Michael didn't even look back.

EMILY COULDN'T WAIT for December fifteenth.

Or maybe it would be more accurately stated that she couldn't wait for December sixteenth, when the fifteenth would already be past and her custody of Dog would have ended.

Naturally, Dog was on his best behavior.

As the date approached, she grew uncharacteristically anxious. Several times she found herself thinking that if Dog had been this good all along, it wouldn't have been such a trial to have him around.

Fortunately, she no sooner thought that than he dug his way out of the yard, ambushed a cat and ripped out another batch of flower bulbs. How foolish and sentimental she was to think kindly of him for a single moment! The animal simply had no redeeming social value.

Still, her anxiety remained, so she came up with a plan to make the whole thing easier. She'd invite

Miss Pauline to dinner and then wave a negligent hand at Michael when he said goodbye.

Certainly she would never shed a tear in front of that dear little old lady—not that she was afraid of losing her cool. Insurance, it was just insurance.

Miss Pauline accepted the invitation with alacrity.

"Will that nice Michael Forbes be there, too?" she inquired.

Emily shook her head. "He's busy moving into a new place," she explained. "He wouldn't have time. But you'll see him when he picks up Dog to take him to his new home."

"Emily, you're going to miss that animal," Miss Pauline predicted. "Now, admit it. You are."

"Sure, I'll admit it." Emily's grin felt forced. "I'll miss him like I miss a bad cold or an allergy attack. Really, this was the plan all along. I'll be delighted to have my yard back and so will my cats."

But in her heart of hearts, a few doubts had developed. Dog gone meant Michael gone, too. And as the song went, she'd grown accustomed to his face....

The fifteenth fell on a Thursday, so on Wednesday night Emily made advance preparations. When she went to work the next day, two freshly baked apple pies and two loaves of homemade bread rested on the kitchen counter. When she got home that night, she'd pop a large roasting chicken into the oven and peel potatoes and—

Drat! She stared around the shop unhappily. She was cooking enough food for a dozen little old ladies. Admit it, Emily Patton, you want to feed Michael Forbes one last time.

But she wouldn't. As distant as he'd been lately, he probably wouldn't stay if she invited him.

Prepared to face the day, she turned the Closed sign to Open and unlocked the door to the first customers. This should be—this *was* a glorious day, complete with gently falling snow. Everything in her life was returning to normal. Hell, it had even started to snow.

So why wasn't she jumping up and down? She should be shouting, "Hooray!?"

# 10

MISS PAULINE PATTED HER LIPS lightly with the hand-embroidered linen napkin. "My goodness," she declared, "you've outdone yourself, as usual."

"Thank you." Emily's stiff lips had trouble forming the words.

It was seven o'clock and Michael still hadn't come for Dog. Had something gone wrong?

She pulled herself back to the here and now. "Can I get you another piece of pie?"

"I couldn't hold another bite, even though it certainly is the best pie I've ever eaten."

"Thank you." And what am I going to do with one and three-quarters pies anyway? "You'll take some home with you, I hope."

Miss Pauline's smile sparkled with mischief. "If you insist, dear."

She sipped her coffee. "I was talking to Thalia the other day and she says you're making her wedding dress."

Emily nodded, the tight knot at the back of her neck loosening a bit. "I'm really pleased with the way it turned out. Would you like to see it?"

"Oh, may I?" Miss Pauline started to rise.

"Wait here and I'll get it." Emily was not eager to have anyone see how messy her sewing studio was, especially not this fastidious woman. "I finished it just last night."

Or this morning: When she couldn't sleep, as usual, she'd finally risen from her tangled bed at three o'clock to make the final stitches in the beautiful gown. Now all that was needed was the bride.

Gown draped over her arm, she reentered the kitchen. Spreading out the folds of the full skirt, she held her creation up for her guest's admiration.

Which was given unstintingly. "It's the most beautiful wedding gown I've ever seen," Miss Pauline breathed. "Emily, you're a wonder. I can't believe some smart man hasn't snapped you up already."

Emily's smile felt bittersweet. "Nobody wants an old-fashioned girl like me these days," she said lightly. "They want lawyers and doctors and career women."

"Then they're fools," Miss Pauline declared. "I'd think they'd be lining up for a woman who can cook and sew and clean and look beautiful while she's doing it."

Emily dropped a curtsy. "Thank you very much, but as you can see, there is no line. There's not even the *beginning* of a line."

At that very moment, the front doorbell rang. The two women, one young and one old, exchanged glances. Then Miss Pauline said softly, "Tell young Mr. Forbes that the line forms on the left."

And she winked.

MICHAEL HAD TOLD HIMSELF he couldn't wait to get his dog and retreat to his new home to nurse his wounded feelings, but it was a lie. He finally had to face that, after he'd frittered away three hours trying to think up reasons he should put off the dog transfer for another day.

Or week, or month.

Sure, he wanted Dog, but he didn't want to give up Emily to get him. What excuse would Michael have for visiting her nearly every day once Dog was removed?

It took considerable self-control to appear at her front door that night, but somehow he managed. Maybe she wouldn't be home. Maybe she had gotten tired of waiting for him and gone out. Maybe he'd have to come back another day, he thought, his spirits rising.

Maybe—she'd open the door and glare at him and say, "You're late!"

"Yeah, I'm sorry about that." He stepped inside. "Couldn't be helped."

"Well…"

Miss Pauline emerged from the kitchen just about then, pulling on her navy-blue coat with the fox collar. "Good evening, Michael."

He returned her greeting respectfully. "Don't leave on my account," he added.

"Dear me, no. That's not what I'm doing. This young lady has just fed me the most fantastic meal, but now it's time for me to go."

Emily looked alarmed. "At least let me fix a plate for you to take with you."

Miss Pauline waved that aside. "Give my share to this young man," she said with a smile. "He looks hungry. Emily, I must remind you that you left that beautiful wedding gown across a chair in the kitchen, which can't be doing it any good. On that note, I'll say good evening, children.''

Michael held the door for her and would have walked her to her car, but she shook her head.

"You two have business," she said. "I can find my way."

He turned to Emily. "Do we have business?"

"If you call Dog business, I guess we do."

"Oh," he said, disappointed. He'd thought Miss Pauline had meant something else—had hoped, actually. "Uh, you just want me to get him and go?"

"Do you see any reason to draw this out?"

He saw a million reasons, beginning and ending with fear—fear that he was falling in love with her. His eyes snapped wide at that possibility and he brushed past her, through the kitchen and out the back door.

Get the damned dog and get out.

Don't hang around and get yourself into any more trouble, he grumbled to himself. Emily isn't interested. She just wants you out of her life, and Dog, too. So your mom has done a one-eighty and everybody you know is getting married. So what?

Life was good before.

Would it ever be good again…without Emily?

EMILY STOOD at the kitchen sink, her back to the door through which Michael and Dog would soon appear. Then they'd walk out the front door and out of her life.

She was glad, dammit!

She'd never wanted anything to do with either

man or beast. So why was she holding her breath now? She should ignore the whole procedure.

The door opened, and despite her best efforts, she swung around to confront them. Dog grinned his loopy grin and banged his wagging tail against the door frame. Michael just looked at her, his expression somehow sad.

"Emily." He took a step toward her, the leash slipping from his hand. "I don't want to leave it like this between us."

"Like what, Michael?" She fought the growing tension.

"Like we don't give a hoot about each other when we do."

"Who says we do?" Because that was her biggest lie of all, she whirled and walked into the living room.

He caught up with her, his hands settling on her arms to halt her flight. "Emily, we've got to level with each other." Gently he turned her to face him.

"Michael, don't." She shook her head helplessly but didn't pull away.

He smiled, whispered her name and kissed her. Rising on tiptoe, she wrapped her arms around his neck and reveled in the moment. Maybe there'd never be another, but she'd take what she could get.

He lifted his head and stared down at her, his expression stunned. "Jeez," he said, "what's up with that? I feel like I've been hit by a freight train. You pack a real wallop, lady."

"I—"

The rest of whatever she might have said was lost in the horrible sound of shattering glass. For one dismayed instant they stared at each other, and then she said one word like a curse. *"Dog!"*

DOG SAT ON THE SKIRT of Thalia's wedding gown where the fabric draped off the chair and trailed on the floor. The glass coffee carafe lay in shards around him and deep brown liquid spread across the delicate pink satin.

Emily screamed. At the sound of it, Dog dropped onto his belly, his grin turning to a frightened whimper. Michael grabbed him by the collar and dragged him off the gown, but it was too little too late.

The gown sure as hell looked ruined to him, and Emily looked on the verge of homicidal mania. If she'd had a weapon, he had no doubt Dog would already be past tense.

"Emily." He held up one hand in a vain attempt to calm her. "I'll make it good, I swear."

"How? There's no way!"

"We'll find a way. It was my fault. I saw you. I got carried away and dropped his leash. If you want to blame someone—"

"There's plenty of blame to go a—"

The doorbell shrilled again and again. Even given the heightened emotions inside the kitchen, the sound clearly indicated considerable distress. Tight faced, she spun and advanced toward the door.

Karen Robinson stood on the porch, her face white and set and her voice betraying borderline hysteria. "Emily, is Davy here with you? Please tell me he is!"

Emily frowned. "I'm sorry, Karen, but I haven't seen Davy all day."

"All right. Thank you." The woman turned away, her shoulders slumping.

Emily caught Karen by the shoulders. "Wait a minute. What's the matter? Can't you find him?"

"N-no, and it's so dark." Karen's eyes glittered with tears. "An hour or so ago, he asked if he could come over here to play with Dog. I told him it was too late and he threw a temper tantrum. I sent him to his room but when I went back a little while ago to put him to bed, he wasn't there." She stopped, unable to go on.

Michael hauled a reluctant Dog out onto the porch. "I'm sure Davy's just hiding somewhere," he suggested.

"But I've looked and looked! Do you think I should call the police? I started to, but then if we find him hiding in a tree or something I'll feel so stupid."

"Call the police," Michael said, "just to be on the safe side. In the meantime, Dog and I will see if we can find him. Is that his jacket?"

She looked down as if she hadn't realized she held it. "Yes."

"Let Dog have a sniff of it. Maybe he's got some bloodhound in him."

Karen brightened. "Oh, I hope so! Davy just loves that dog so much."

Emily gritted her teeth. "Even when Dog keeps him awake all night?"

"Even then." Karen managed a shaky smile. "May I use your phone?"

"Of course."

Michael headed for the gate while Emily hurried to grab her coat off the rack just inside the door. "I'm going with Michael, Karen," she said. "Just close the door when you leave."

"All right."

Michael didn't slow his pace. A five-year-old boy was out there alone in the dark in that snowy landscape. There wasn't a minute to lose.

"Dammit, Dog, I want to look in the park!" Michael struggled to drag the protesting animal to the right, where streetlamps flooded the area with light.

Emily, bringing up the rear, stopped and looked around. "Michael, I think Dog wants to look in that ditch across the street."

"I don't think Davy would cross a street. I'm sure he's like every other little boy, myself included. It's beat into all of us not to cross streets by ourselves." He dragged Dog a few more steps, but the animal braced himself and refused to budge, even when the collar ended up around his ears.

"Let him go, Michael."

"Are you kidding? If we do, it'll take the U.S. Cavalry to catch him again."

"Maybe, but he's not the one I'm concerned about. He sees something, or smells something— whatever dogs do."

Michael hesitated, still holding the end of the leash. Hell, she could be right. Leaning down, he unhooked the lead.

"I sure hope you're right," he said grimly, "or

we'll be hunting for a missing dog as well as a missing boy.''

"If there's any justice, we'll find the boy and never lay eyes on the dog again,'' she snapped. "Look, he's heading right for those trees across the road. Come on!"

They sprinted after the galloping dog. Although there wasn't much traffic on the street at this time of the evening, an occasional vehicle did pass by. Jumping across the ditch, they hesitated. Michael swung the beam of the flashlight he'd grabbed from his car, sending thin rays of light to probe the darkness.

Dog had disappeared between those trees. Emily began to suspect Michael might be right about the park.

A shriek—not of fear but of glee—cut through the frosty air. Emily and Michael looked at each other and relieved smiles appeared simultaneously.

He grabbed her hand. "Dog found him,'' he said. "Is he great or what?"

"Or what,'' Emily said, but she went forward happily.

Dog cavorted around a cottonwood tree, jumping up against the trunk and uttering short, sharp barks. Michael pointed the flashlight up among the branches where Davy Robinson crouched, clinging with all his might to the rough trunk.

"Emily!'' the boy shrieked. "Get me down! Get me down!"

Michael craned his neck to look up. "Got yourself stuck in a tree, did you, partner?"

"Get me down!" Davy began to cry. Dog's barks changed to puzzled whines in response to the boy's misery.

Michael handed the flashlight to Emily before turning back to the tree, arms outstretched. "Come on, Davy. Slide off that limb. I'll catch you."

"I'm afraid!"

"A big boy like you? I don't think so. Come on. I'll catch you."

"You'll drop me!" The boy cried harder.

Emily stepped up beside Michael. "No, he won't, Davy," she promised. "You can trust Michael."

He gave her a surprised glance. "Yeah, you can trust me. Just slide off that branch and I'll catch you."

"Can I have your dog?" Davy bargained.

Michael chuckled. "No, but you can play with him."

Not easy, Emily thought, under the circumstances. Dog was moving clear across town. But this wasn't the time to apprise Davy of that fact.

The boy in the tree took a deep breath. "I'm coming!" he yelled, and shoved himself away from the branch. Emily gasped and automatically put out her own arms, but Michael was equal to the task. He caught the boy and then fell laughing into a snowbank. Dog jumped in and the three rolled around in the dark, screaming with laughter.

"Davy Robinson!" Karen charged into the little clearing, drawn by all the commotion. "You are in so much trouble, young man!"

Grabbing him into a bear hug, she hung on for dear life.

Davy struggled to get free. "I get to play with Dog," he protested. "Michael said!"

Michael rose, dusting off the snow. "Tomorrow, sport—if that's all right with your mother."

"It's fine with me," Karen said, her relief clear. "Now I'm taking this kid home. I hope the police have a sense of humor."

"The police!" Davy sounded impressed.

Karen stood her son on the ground and turned to Michael. "I can't thank you enough."

"It was Dog," Michael said modestly. "He found Davy. I'd still be scouring the park, myself."

Karen smiled at Emily. "You, too."

"I didn't do a thing." Which was true.

"We'll talk tomorrow," Karen said, moving back toward the street. "Thank you both." Dog trotted after them happily.

Emily fell in behind. "Thank God," she said.

"Yeah. That was a close one."

"Too close. Do you think—"

They stepped out of the trees just as car tires screamed against pavement, one of the most horrible sounds in the world. There was a shocking *thump,* then Davy screamed, *"Dog!"*

Michael and Emily leaped into the street in time to see a car speed off toward town. The reckless driver left behind the prone body of a mongrel dog and a hysterical boy sobbing at the animal's side.

"Dog pushed Davy out of the way," Karen cried. "I swear he did. Dog saved Davy's life. He's a hero. If he dies—"

"He won't die," Michael said roughly. Gently he scooped the limp dog into his arms. "I've got to get him to the vet hospital. Emily, will you call Luke and tell him we're coming?"

Tears obscured Emily's eyes and made speech difficult, but she managed to nod. "I'll—" She had to try again. "I'll meet you there as soon as I can."

"No need." Michael grunted, hanging on hard to the dead weight in his arms. "I know how you feel about this dog. I'll let you know how it comes out."

Speechless with offense, she stared after him as he strode beneath the streetlamps back to her house where his car was parked at the curb. How dare he dismiss her so easily! Did he think her heart was made of stone?

The anger strengthened her. "Karen," she said, "take Davy home. I'll let you know what happens."

"Do you think he'll make it?" She held her sobbing son close.

"Dog's going to be fine," Emily said, her voice only slightly unsteady. To herself she added, *He's got to.*

Back home, she called Luke's cell phone number and waited impatiently. His eventual greeting was testy.

"Luke! Thank God I caught you. Dog's been hit by a car."

"Dog? Is he alive?"

"Yes, but he's in bad shape. Michael's taking him to the clinic now. Please—"

"Doc's got emergency duty tonight, Em. I've got something else I have to—"

Thalia's laughing voice cut in. "Luke Dalton, you don't have a thing to do! You go take care of that animal. Tell Emily I'll meet her there."

The line went dead.

EMILY SLUMPED in a chair in the corner of the small waiting room at the pet hospital while Michael paced up and down, following a path already well-worn in the carpet. Luke had taken Dog into surgery more than an hour ago. After providing what comfort she could, Thalia had finally gone home.

Emily had only vaguely wondered why her friend was so dressed up in a winter-white suit and heels, but worry over Dog had pushed her curiosity aside.

Michael stopped in front of her. "I can't take much more of this," he exploded. "If Dog's not going to make it—"

From the doorway, Luke spoke. "He's going to make it, Michael. Calm down."

Michael whirled and Emily leaped from her chair. Luke looked tired but pleased. He came forward, his smile soothing.

"Dog's going to be as good as new inside a week," he said. "He'll need attention—"

"He'll get it," Emily said quickly, earning a startled glance from Michael.

Luke nodded. "Good. Fortunately, he's young and tough. He's got several broken bones and a slight concussion, but he's a fighter."

"Can I see him?" Michael asked.

"Sure. He's still pretty dopey, but it'll do him good to see a couple of familiar faces." Turning, Luke led the way into the interior of the hospital, down a hall and into a sparkling clean room where Dog lay swathed in bandages on a table.

"Oh!" Emily reached out a tentative hand. "He looks pale."

Michael's relief tinged his chuckle. "You could say that. Look—he's opening his eyes."

And wagging his tail, not with his usual enthusiasm, but in a kind of slow motion that broke Emily's heart. Tears filled her eyes and she blinked them back.

Dog whined, lifting his head as if it were almost too heavy. He licked Emily's hand and then, with a doggy sigh, settled back down. His eyes closed.

That did it. Tears streamed unrestrained down Emily's face by the time they reentered the waiting room. Michael turned to Luke.

"Hey, man, I can't thank you enough."

"Just doing my job," Luke said, but his words had a slightly cynical edge.

"Are we missing something here?" Emily patted her eyes and peered at him.

His brows rose. "Thalia didn't tell you?"

Emily shook her head.

"We were on our way out of town when Michael called."

"Oh, I'm sorry. Where were you going?"

"We were eloping."

"You were—"

Together Emily and Michael stared at Luke, then all three burst out laughing.

It was an appropriate end to the day's misadventures—if end it was.

MICHAEL BROODED over a cup of decaf in Emily's quiet kitchen. She sat across from him, apparently as deep in thought as he was.

Time to clear up a few issues, he reminded himself. "Okay," he said, his voice sounding harsh in the silence, "you've done your duty and then some. From now on, I'll take full responsibility for Dog."

Her head snapped back and she glared at him. "Over my dead body!" she declared. Taking a deep breath, she announced, "I've decided to keep him."

"You can't keep him!" He stared at her, horrified. "He's mine."

"Isn't possession nine-tenths of the law?"

He laughed incredulously. "Have you been watching TV again?"

"Don't make fun of me. I'm serious." She leaned forward and she *was* serious. "I just realized I'm kind of used to having Dog around. I like it."

"You? Dog-hater you?"

"Dog isn't your typical dog."

"That's true." He frowned. This could get sticky, but he couldn't back down. "What are you saying, exactly? Are we in for a custody battle?"

"If that's what it takes."

"I'm a very good lawyer," he warned, "and I wrote our contract. What chance do you think you'd have?"

"A very good one, Michael." She looked straight at him. "Do you want to know why? Because you're an honorable man who loves kids and dogs and you wouldn't take advantage of me."

He felt a warm glow at her words. "Still…"

"Michael," she said urgently, "don't you get it? Single-pawed, Dog has managed to drag me past all my fear and mistrust of canines. He's proved himself loyal and true. So what if he has a few little behavior problems? We'll get past that."

"You're saying you've learned to love him?"

She nodded decisively. "I have. I do. I realized it the instant I saw him lying there all bloody and broken."

"*I* loved him the minute we pulled him out of that Dumpster," he said indignantly. "Doesn't that count for something?"

"Not much. Look, I'm not unreasonable. You don't want that house you rented. Why not just keep visiting here whenever you want to, like you've done up to now."

"No good. I'm sick of being a long-distance pet almost-owner."

"Then we're at an impasse," she declared, her soft lips drawn into an uncharacteristically firm line.

That's when it hit him: the answer to this predicament. "Emily," he said, "I don't want to put Dog through the trauma of a custody battle. As far as I can see, there's only one fair way out of this mess."

"And that would be?"

"You'll have to marry me."

"Marry...*you?*" Her eyes were wide and astonished. "To avoid a custody fight?"

"No, because I love you. The custody dispute is just an excuse." Leaning forward, he caught her hands in his. "Say yes, Emily. It's better than playing plaintiff-defendant in a courtroom."

"Michael, I don't know what to say."

His chest tightened. "Say whatever you feel."

She licked her lips. "Okay. What I feel is love."

"For Dog."

"Yes, and for...you."

"Emily!"

"I'm not finished! I'm also feeling incredibly sleepy."

"I'm boring you?"

"No, you've been keeping me awake nights. Oh, Michael! I may never have another good night's sleep as long as I live...without you."

He leaped to his feet, drawing her with him. "Does that mean—?"

She nodded. "I'll marry you, Michael. I also promise we'll live happily ever after, just as soon as Dog learns to heel."

Taking her into his arms, he knew she was right.

# *Epilogue*

*The Shepherd's Pass Review, June 10—*

## Groundbreaking Ceremonies Bring Out Animal Passions

A ground-breaking ceremony for the multimillion-dollar Shangri-la number two housing development was held here Saturday, complete with speeches, ribbon cutting, stampeding sheep and renewal of an old feud.

As one observer remarked, "At least nobody fell asleep, like they usually do at these shindigs. That's progress, if you ask me."

The fugitive sheep are the pets of Reckless, a Border collie owned by Lorraine Myers, leader of the now defunct Shangri-la It Ain't movement. The sheep escaped while the dog was off duty and getting a checkup from Myers's son-in-law, Dr. Luke Dalton, D.V.M. Apparently frightened by all the people and activity just across the street from their pasture, they galloped right through the middle of the festivities, scattering dignitaries right and left and finally plunging into a decorative fountain.

Arriving on the scene moments later, Reckless rounded up his charges and headed them home, but not before they'd torn up the front lawn of Shangri-la number one resident Joyce Brown, who has promised a lawsuit.

The only injuries of the day were to the dignity of Mayor George Kelly, Shangri-la developer Joe John Jeff Jordan and landowner Sylvia Dalton. Myers at first shook off the incident, saying "It's all part of the rural country atmosphere" touted in sales materials for Shangri-la. "Animals have rights, too," she said. "I'm thinking of starting a local branch of People for the Ethical Treatment of Animals and see how they like that."

When the sheep were corralled and the program back on track, Jordan announced that the first homes in his new development will go to two prominent Shepherd's Pass couples: Dr. Dalton and his wife, the former Thalia Myers Mitchell, and Michael and Emily Patton Forbes, whose dog, Dog, was credited with saving a child's life last winter.

Lemonade and cookies followed the program, as did a brief tussle between Sylvia Dalton and Lorraine Myers, well-known locally for their decades-old feud, which was believed settled along with the Shangri-la dispute. Both women toppled into the pool lately vacated by the sheep.

As they emerged dripping, they were greeted by enthusiastic applause.

Photos, page seven.

*Harlequin truly does
make any time special. . . .
This year we are celebrating
weddings in style!*

To help us celebrate, we want you to tell us how wearing the Harlequin wedding gown will make your wedding day special. As the grand prize, Harlequin will offer one lucky bride the chance to **"Walk Down the Aisle"** in the Harlequin wedding gown!

### There's more...

For her honeymoon, she and her groom will spend five nights at the **Hyatt Regency Maui.** As part of this five-night honeymoon at the hotel renowned for its romantic attractions, the couple will enjoy a candlelit dinner for two in Swan Court, a sunset sail on the hotel's catamaran, and duet spa treatments.

A HYATT RESORT AND SPA

Maui • Molokai • Lanai

To enter, please write, in, 250 words or less, how wearing the Harlequin wedding gown will make your wedding day special. The entry will be judged based on its emotionally compelling nature, its originality and creativity, and its sincerity. This contest is open to Canadian and U.S. residents only and to those who are 18 years of age and older. There is no purchase necessary to enter. Void where prohibited. See further contest rules attached. Please send your entry to:

### Walk Down the Aisle Contest

| In Canada | In U.S.A. |
|---|---|
| P.O. Box 637 | P.O. Box 9076 |
| Fort Erie, Ontario | 3010 Walden Ave. |
| L2A 5X3 | Buffalo, NY 14269-9076 |

You can also enter by visiting www.eHarlequin.com
***Win the Harlequin wedding gown and the vacation of a lifetime!***
The deadline for entries is October 1, 2001.

*Makes any time special* ®

PHWDACONT1

HARLEQUIN WALK DOWN THE AISLE TO MAUI CONTEST 1197
OFFICIAL RULES
NO PURCHASE NECESSARY TO ENTER

1. To enter, follow directions published in the offer to which you are responding. Contest begins April 2, 2001, and ends on October 1, 2001. Method of entry may vary. Mailed entries must be postmarked by October 1, 2001, and received by October 8, 2001.

2. Contest entry may be, at times, presented via the Internet, but will be restricted solely to residents of certain geographic areas that are disclosed on the Web site. To enter via the Internet, if permissible, access the Harlequin Web site (www.eHarlequin.com) and follow the directions displayed online. Online entries must be received by 11:59 p.m. E.S.T. on October 1, 2001.

   In lieu of submitting an entry online, enter by mail by hand-printing (or typing) on an 8½" x 11" plain piece of paper, your name, address (including zip code), Contest number/name and in 250 words or fewer, why winning a Harlequin wedding dress would make your wedding day special. Mail via first-class mail to: Harlequin Walk Down the Aisle Contest 1197, (in the U.S.) P.O. Box 9076, 3010 Walden Avenue, Buffalo, NY 14269-9076, (in Canada) P.O. Box 637, Fort Erie, Ontario L2A 5X3, Canada.

   Limit one entry per person, household address and e-mail address. Online and/or mailed entries received from persons residing in geographic areas in which Internet entry is not permissible will be disqualified.

3. Contests will be judged by a panel of members of the Harlequin editorial, marketing and public relations staff based on the following criteria:

   • Originality and Creativity—50%
   • Emotionally Compelling—25%
   • Sincerity—25%

   In the event of a tie, duplicate prizes will be awarded. Decisions of the judges are final.

4. All entries become the property of Torstar Corp. and will not be returned. No responsibility is assumed for lost, late, illegible, incomplete, inaccurate, nondelivered or misdirected mail or misdirected e-mail, for technical, hardware or software failures of any kind, lost or unavailable network connections, or failed, incomplete, garbled or delayed computer transmission or any human error which may occur in the receipt or processing of the entries in this Contest.

5. Contest open only to residents of the U.S. (except Puerto Rico) and Canada, who are 18 years of age or older, and is void wherever prohibited by law; all applicable laws and regulations apply. Any litigation within the Province of Quebec respecting the conduct or organization of a publicity contest may be submitted to the Régie des alcools, des courses et des jeux for a ruling. Any litigation respecting the awarding of a prize may be submitted to the Régie des alcools, des courses et des jeux only for the purpose of helping the parties reach a settlement. Employees and immediate family members of Torstar Corp. and D. L. Blair, Inc., their affiliates, subsidiaries and all other agencies, entities and persons connected with the use, marketing or conduct of this Contest are not eligible to enter. Taxes on prizes are the sole responsibility of winners. Acceptance of any prize offered constitutes permission to use winner's name, photograph or other likeness for the purposes of advertising, trade and promotion on behalf of Torstar Corp., its affiliates and subsidiaries without further compensation to the winner, unless prohibited by law.

6. Winners will be determined no later than November 15, 2001, and will be notified by mail. Winners will be required to sign and return an Affidavit of Eligibility form within 15 days after winner notification. Noncompliance within that time period may result in disqualification and an alternative winner may be selected. Winners of trip must execute a Release of Liability prior to ticketing and must possess required travel documents (e.g. passport, photo ID) where applicable. Trip must be completed by November 2002. No substitution of prize permitted by winner. Torstar Corp. and D. L. Blair, Inc., their parents, affiliates, and subsidiaries are not responsible for errors in printing or electronic presentation of Contest, entries and/or game pieces. In the event of printing or other errors which may result in unintended prize values or duplication of prizes, all affected game pieces or entries shall be null and void. If for any reason the Internet portion of the Contest is not capable of running as planned, including infection by computer virus, bugs, tampering, unauthorized intervention, fraud, technical failures, or any other causes beyond the control of Torstar Corp. which corrupt or affect the administration, secrecy, fairness, integrity or proper conduct of the Contest, Torstar Corp. reserves the right, at its sole discretion, to disqualify any individual who tampers with the entry process and to cancel, terminate, modify or suspend the Contest or the Internet portion thereof. In the event of a dispute regarding an online entry, the entry will be deemed submitted by the authorized holder of the e-mail account submitted at the time of entry. Authorized account holder is defined as the natural person who is assigned to an e-mail address by an Internet access provider, online service provider or other organization that is responsible for arranging e-mail address for the domain associated with the submitted e-mail address. **Purchase or acceptance of a product offer does not improve your chances of winning.**

7. Prizes: (1) Grand Prize—A Harlequin wedding dress (approximate retail value: $3,500) and a 5-night/6-day honeymoon trip to Maui, HI, including round-trip air transportation provided by Maui Visitors Bureau from Los Angeles International Airport (winner is responsible for transportation to and from Los Angeles International Airport) and a Harlequin Romance Package, including hotel accommodations (double occupancy) at the Hyatt Regency Maui Resort and Spa, dinner for (2) two at Swan Court, a sunset sail on Kiele V and a spa treatment for the winner (approximate retail value: $4,000); (5) Five runner-up prizes of a $1000 gift certificate to selected retail outlets to be determined by Sponsor (retail value $1000 ea.). Prizes consist of only those items listed as part of the prize. Limit one prize per person. All prizes are valued in U.S. currency.

8. For a list of winners (available after December 17, 2001) send a self-addressed, stamped envelope to: Harlequin Walk Down the Aisle Contest 1197 Winners, P.O. Box 4200 Blair, NE 68009-4200 or you may access the www.eHarlequin.com Web site through January 15, 2002.

Contest sponsored by Torstar Corp., P.O. Box 9042, Buffalo, NY 14269-9042, U.S.A.

PHWDACONT2

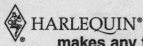

**USA *Today* bestselling author**

# STELLA CAMERON

and popular American Romance author

# MURIEL JENSEN

come together in a special
Harlequin 2-in-1 collection.

Look for

*Shadows* and *Daddy in Demand*

On sale June 2001

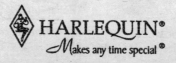

# HARLEQUIN®

*Makes any time special* ®